The Shaws are one of Britain's most influential, dynamic families, but one Shaw prefers to keep a low profile. Unfortunately, the limelight can shine behind-the-scenes ...

Lady Drusilla Shaw may be a bit introverted, yet she has the observant mind of a writer, capturing all of society's quirks and scandals. But when the novel she's been working on disappears from her room, that is just the beginning of her problems. Confident, magnetic Oliver, Duke of Mountsorrel, has taken an interest in Dru, and when he proposes, she is both thrilled and anxious. Her book depicts a ruinous family story that is uncannily similar to Oliver's real-life, not to mention libelous. The manuscript could surface at any moment—and eventually it does, in published form, for all to read ...

Oliver is bewildered by his new wife and her blasted book. Worst of all, how can he love a woman he no longer trusts? But when it becomes obvious that someone is taking their cues from the book in a series of attacks, he has no choice but to stick close to her. Their explosive connection in bed should take care of the heir-making, but for that to happen, Drusilla has to stay alive—and so does Oliver.

Visit us at www.kensingtonbooks.com

Books by Lynne Connolly

Emperors of London
Rogue In Red Velvet
Temptation Has Green Eyes
Danger Wears White
Reckless In Pink
Veiled In Blue
Wild Lavender

The Shaws
Fearless
Sinless
Dauntless

Published by Kensington Publishing Corporation

Dauntless

The Shaws

Lynne Connolly

LYRICAL PRESS
Kensington Publishing Corp.
www.kensingtonbooks.com

Lyrical Press books are published by
Kensington Publishing Corp. 119 West 40th Street New York, NY 10018

First Electronic Edition: June 2018
eISBN-13: 978-1-5161-0249-5
eISBN-10: 1-5161-0249-5

First Print Edition: June 2018
ISBN-13: 978-1-5161-0251-8
ISBN-10: 1-5161-0251-7

Printed in the United States of America

Chapter 1

Lady Drusilla Shaw bent over her work, growing ever more engrossed in the story she was telling. Her sense of time and place disappeared, as it always did when she was in her own world. Since childhood, she'd let her vivid imagination hold sway over reality, finding solace in the work. Being the middle child between two sets of twins had forced her to rely on her own company growing up. Now she preferred it.

She bit the end of the pen, wondering what to make her villain do next. He wasn't nearly evil enough for her liking. He had to do something really heinous, but she couldn't think of anything. That was partly because she was a member of an outrageous family. Indulged and cosseted by society, the Shaw children had to commit something really outstandingly shocking for society to turn its collective back.

With a stroke of her pen, Dru eliminated three uncles and their families, although she left the maiden aunt. Now the villain had one brother.

The nib snagged on the paper, leaving a blot behind. With a wordless exclamation of dismay, Dru reached for the pounce-box. She scattered sand over the offending mark, although in doing so she dragged her triple lace ruffles across the paper and made a worse mess. She had not donned the linen covers that protected her lace because she was due to go downstairs, and time was short. Now she was paying for that omission.

She grabbed her handkerchief, wrapped it around the lace, and squeezed hard. When she released it, the black had faded somewhat. Nobody would notice. Nobody except her mother. Since the lace was creamy white, it would bleach. Or something. Her maid could handle it. She'd managed enough ink stains before.

As if summoned, after a brief knock, Forde opened the door and stepped inside. "Forgive me, ma'am, but your lady mother is asking for you."

Dru glanced at the clock. "Damnation!"

As usual, Forde tut-tutted at Dru's profanity. Not for the first time, she felt a touch of annoyance at her maid's attitude. She had inherited Forde from her sister Claudia, when she had moved away on her marriage. Although Claudia's twin, Livia, was still at home, she graciously refused Forde's services and employed a new maid. Now Dru understood why.

But Forde could work miracles on ink stains, and she kept Dru's wardrobe in immaculate condition, so matters could have been worse. Forde was a London girl, though and through. She had the twang of the Londoner to prove it, although she did her best to cover it up.

Dru found the habit amusing and somewhat of a relief because Forde was perfect in every other way. Since she had no desire for her maid to see the ink stain, she concentrated on covering the mark, tucking the offending flounce up as if it were caught on something. Her mother would be very sad if she was late again, and the marchioness's sadness was something every member of the family avoided. Then her father would be disappointed, and that was even more unbearable.

On a vague smile, she left the room.

Outside, she nearly collided with her sister. Livia wore a gown in the latest style, a froth of lemon silk and pinked ruffles with the embroidery detail beautifully delineated. Her red-gold hair was drawn back to a glossy knot, with curls drooping on to her shoulders.

Livia drew back, studying Dru's appearance. "Your ruffles aren't properly arranged," she said, but a sudden smile flashed across her face. "They do call them ruffles, don't they? Maybe they should be, you know, ruffled. You look charming. Have I seen that gown before?"

Dru shook her head. "This is its first ball." She fluffed the skirt a little and smoothed the sky-blue silk over her panniers. Plunging a hand into her capacious pocket, she found her gloves. She concentrated on putting them on as she accompanied Livia to the drawing room, where the rest of the party would no doubt be waiting.

Balls were a waste of time. Nobody had shown particular interest in her this season, but she would go through the ritual of attending them. New, younger, more biddable girls entered society every year, outshining the veterans like Dru and Livia. She could not make herself too concerned. Her inheritance, a generous dowry plus an inheritance from a maiden aunt, meant Dru would never have to worry about money. Her status as the daughter of a marquess was assured.

Still, she had to admit that sometimes her potential to attract a spouse rankled. Only occasionally, because she kept busy enough.

Although Dru's mother didn't criticize, she did give Dru a long-suffering sigh. At least she hadn't reached the caustic remark or the terrible phrase, "You disappoint me, Drusilla." But she did say, brightly, "Ah, Drusilla and Livia. Are you quite ready to leave?"

"It is not fashionable to arrive too early," Livia remarked. A year younger than Dru, she was the leftover twin. Unlike Dru, her blond hair and blue eyes gave her an angelic appearance, one she rarely troubled to contradict, except when events called for it. Out of sight of their mother, she grinned at Dru.

As if to contradict her, the clock struck nine, its emphatic chime reminding everyone of the time. That was why the marchioness kept the ugly thing in the drawing room. It tacitly informed visitors tempted to linger that their time was up. The smirking cherubs dancing around the base told the same story, as if laughing at anyone who dared defy it.

They were laughing at Dru now. They laughed at her a lot.

Head down, she hurried after her parents and aunt. She concentrated on hiding the stain on her ruffle as Forde helped her into her hat and cape. Then outside, past the frozen footmen, and into the carriages. She didn't take much notice of the conversation as they drove the short distance to the mansion owned by her uncle, the Duke of Kirkburton.

"The spinsters traveling together," Livia remarked caustically. "Do men think they are so indispensable? Have you read the ancient texts?"

"*Lysistrata*," Dru murmured.

Her sister frowned, but Dru didn't explain herself. She would not discuss the old play, because she probably should not have read it in the first place. Her mother would undoubtedly not approve.

Dru shrugged. "I don't care." But she did. She poured all her dreams into her stories, even though nobody would ever read them, or even see them. She wrote them and then burned them. Writing was enough.

The carriage stopped with a jolt, right outside the Piccadilly mansion of the Duke of Kirkburton. Although she had known the place from childhood, the sight of the formidable house, more a palace really, still daunted Dru. Her cousin Julius, heir to the mansion, asserted he would have the place torn down when he became duke. Dru couldn't imagine Piccadilly without it. But many other great mansions had been sacrificed in the name of modernity and profit. The land they stood on provided the

West End with its elegant squares and gracious streets. A generation ago much of the area had been almost rural.

If she was of a philosophical turn of mind, Dru might have found something to ponder on. But apart from admiring the place anew, she did not remark on it. The circular drive before the house was packed with vehicles, people in staggeringly lovely and expensive clothes climbing out of them. Dru and her companions joined them.

Dru's father led the way and somehow found a way through to the shallow steps leading to the front door, which was flung wide open. Light glowed from the interior, blazing from every window on the first two floors, setting the night alight. Going inside, Dru felt the heat from the two flambeaux set in holders either side of the impressive stone portal.

Still, excitement simmered. Every time she attended a ball, or the theater, or any other society event, she had that expectation. Would she meet him tonight? The man who would make her world shine, the one she'd written about all her life? The fact that she'd met most of the eligible men in society, that there were no more left to meet, didn't stop that traitorous feeling of maybe this time, maybe tonight …

While a maid was helping her divest herself of her hat and cloak, an elbow dig from a nearby countess who did not even attempt an apology was enough to persuade her to take a step back.

Unfortunately, her heel caught in the ruffles of her petticoat, and she tumbled backward. Just what she needed—an undignified tumble. At least she wore enough layers to protect her. She'd probably take a few members of the peerage with her. Then the gossip writers would report on that and nothing else, and her aunt, the formidable Duchess of Kirkburton, would be severely displeased. And her mother would be disappointed.

She should have never come. She could have pleaded illness and stayed at home with her writing.

But none of her doom-laden prophesies happened. Instead, a pair of strong masculine arms caught her and drew her close to a wall of muscle. While the contact lasted barely a few seconds, its impact jolted her into total awareness. The dreamy cloud that surrounded her most times melted away. All she felt was a wall of muscle and being held in a secure grip. She would have given anything to subside into his arms, and for a moment she did just that. His arms closed around her, giving her a satisfying sense of security.

Dru forced herself to pull away. When she turned, she confronted a pair of startled gray eyes set in a face so ruthlessly masculine she wondered if a hard-bitten soldier had somehow forced his way into a society ball.

His unmistakable air of command easily dominated this hall full of the cream of society. Here, more titles and wealth abounded than anywhere else in the country. This man did not get his air of power from his wealth.

Recalling her manners, she dropped a curtsy. He responded, bowing slightly, but they hadn't been introduced, so they could do nothing more.

For all that, she knew him. Their paths had not crossed. The Duke of Mountsorrel attended few society events, but he could not elude them completely. However, he avoided single eligible ladies as if they bore the plague. His severe dress spoke of the Puritan, but he was no City merchant. If observers looked closely, they would see that his dark blue twilled silk coat and the matching waistcoat were the finest fabric and the best work money could buy.

He turned away, only to confront Livia, who stared at him blatantly. Her curtsy was even more perfunctory than the one a shaken Dru had given him. She received the same stiff bow before he turned around and left.

* * * *

A cupboard. Oliver found he'd entered an anteroom that was little more than a closet. So leaving it with dignity was out of the question. And he could find only one door. That damned woman had stumbled on purpose, he was sure of it, and her accomplice had been waiting for a chance to block him. Such snares would trap a boy barely out of petticoats, but Oliver should have known better.

He hated balls and social occasions with a passion he usually reserved for murderers and cabbage. Especially now, when one touch of warm female flesh had driven his body into hard, needy arousal. It didn't matter that the woman had been respectably clothed. He wanted her anyway.

Oliver took in the room with a comprehensive glance. That was all the place deserved. A hard chair and a table, and rough pegs on the wall. No doubt the unfortunate footman on duty spent hours here, but Oliver saw no trace of occupation. No book, no newspaper, not even a glass. He would have allowed the footman who occupied this room something to do. Even Charles's attendants had a more comfortable life, and God knew they had plenty to do.

Well, he'd tried. Even thinking of his brother had not caused his raging erection to subside. One touch, that was all it had taken. One accidental tumble. As if he'd never felt a woman's soft body in his arms before. Lady Drusilla Shaw did not even sport the abundant curves he preferred in his women. Her waist was impossibly slender. The notion of hoisting her up, his hands circling her waist, and driving into her took him by complete surprise. It sent a thrill of recognition all the way up his spine to the center of his mind. He would probably never rid himself of that vision now.

Yes, he knew who she was. One of the Emperors of London, hence her unusual name. They were all named after emperors and empresses of the past in a conceit invented by their parents. He'd seen the tribe working, watched the way they smoothly covered all parts of a ball. Many would be here tonight, since this was Emperor territory. They would watch him, he knew. Unmarried women abounded in the family, although their numbers had decreased of late.

He would not succumb to her ladyship's less than voluptuous charms. She had the appeal of a dainty, pretty woman, one who would break under his big body. No, she was not for him.

He couldn't even pace properly in this tiny space. So he put his self-control to work, leaned against the wall, and folded his arms.

Oliver waited until the murmur outside had changed to a dull roar and the influx of guests he'd arrived with had left.

Then he stepped out of the room, dusting off his waistcoat, and tried to slide into the maelstrom that surrounding him. To a great extent he succeeded. As he glanced up, he saw two women standing side by side, goggling over the banisters on the next floor. Lady Drusilla and her sister Lady Livia.

Those women should be hanged at dawn. Or banned from attending society events. Either would work for him. They had not the least idea of how to behave. Were it not for their fine clothing, he'd have assumed they were country girls up for the season.

With all the dignity he could muster, he ascended the stairs and greeted his hostess. The Duchess of Kirkburton, while diminutive in stature, towered over society as one of its best established and most influential hostesses.

Dressed in white satin with a plethora of ruffles, lace, and embroidery, her grace should have been swamped. However, her personality defeated any attempt to overwhelm her. Graciously she offered her hand. Gallantly, Oliver bowed over it, wishing he were anywhere but here.

He would put a bold face on his worries and concentrate on finding his life's partner.

"Your grace, I'm pleased to see you here. Welcome to my house."

Said the spider to the fly. Used to schooling his features, Oliver stretched his lips into a semblance of a smile. "It is entirely my honor, your grace."

Her bosom tightly constricted in stays that must have made breathing difficult, the duchess inclined her head. "It is a great pity you were not in town last year, sir. My daughter Helena would have been perfect for you. However, I do have another daughter, and she is dazzling the world. I would be honored to introduce you."

What an odd thing to say! Lady Helena had made an advantageous marriage recently. Why would her mother resent that? And she clearly did, from her frosty words as she skipped over one daughter and right to another.

The duchess's unmarried daughter was ten years younger than he, perhaps more since she had barely been out a year. While others might not balk at the age difference and some would welcome it, Oliver needed a mature female, someone of sense and gravity. Perhaps he should set his sights lower. A vicar's widow or a young woman of genteel family might prove a better duchess, if only because she was closer to the realities of life. She would have a lot of reality to manage. He had no intention of keeping secrets from his bride.

With a tug to set his waistcoat to rights, his invariable habit when making a decision, he bowed to his hostess and strode forward into the ballroom.

* * * *

"Just look at him," Livia murmured.

"Who?" Dru peered around the magnificent room.

"Mountsorrel."

"Mmm?" Not wanting to appear anxious and doing her best to forget the brief but memorable encounter, Dru shrugged. "Is he upsetting people?"

"No, he's dancing nonstop. Paying attention to all the young ladies. The unmarried ones, anyway."

Dru caught sight of the duke whirling a girl in pink around until she breathlessly laughed into his face. "She wants him to take her into supper. Or more likely, out into the garden for some air. Our sainted aunt ensures all parts of the garden are well lit. She'll have to work hard to find a dim spot."

Livia laughed. "But I'll wager *you* could discover one."

Dru shrugged. "I've visited this house many times. You could find a secluded spot too. Don't even pretend you could not."

She won another laugh for that. But Livia had drawn her attention to the one person she had wanted to ignore, and now she could not look away.

The vigorous country dance left the participants tousled and out of breath. All, that was, except the duke, who bowed calmly to his partner and took her back to her parents. After exchanging a few words with them, he moved on, leaving the girl staring after him wide-eyed. Until her mother delivered a sharp jab to her ribs. Now back with her parents, the girl seemed even younger than when she was on the floor. She was, Dru noted, possessed of a particularly fine bosom. Unlike herself. It took clever lacing to give her the cleavage she was sporting tonight. Another reason Dru tolerated Forde's behavior. The woman could tight-lace so well, she could force breasts up where there were none.

But on the one cavorting around the floor with yet another schoolroom miss? From their brief contact, she knew how little of his appearance owed to clever padding. His chest had not given way, not a bit of it. His arms, while clad in blue twilled silk, had revealed nothing but firm, well-exercised muscle.

She shivered. What could a man do with all that power? Men often made the mistaken assumption that women were innocent merely because they had little practical experience. Dru read a lot, and not all the books would have been approved by her mother. Had she known her daughter had read the full version of *Fanny Hill*, for example, she might have tried to regulate every book her daughter read. "Tried to" being the important words.

She knew what men and women did in the bedroom. She had even anticipated it with some eagerness, but these days, she'd stopped torturing herself and tried not to think about it. She cursed Mountsorrel for bringing that feeling back to her.

He appeared not to notice her at all. Once, when he was stripping the willow, separating from his partner to skip down the outside of the central column of dancers, he glanced up and caught her staring. Dru flipped her fan open and lifted it to cool her heated cheeks, lowering her eyelids in an expression of icy disdain.

He laughed.

She must stop looking at him. He danced with one young woman after another. He was hunting for a bride.

Dru curled her lip and turned away. The set was coming to a close. She had no desire to see another young woman make a fool of herself over this man. "When are they serving supper?" she asked Livia. "I swear I am famished." Flicking her fan before her face, she turned abruptly, with the aim of heading to the back of the room. Only to almost collide with her aunt, the hostess of this benighted ball.

Dru sank into her accustomed curtsy. She had of course made her obeisance on arrival, but her aunt enjoyed the attention, and it cost her nothing to give it again.

"Drusilla, is it not?" the duchess said.

Dru concentrated on lifting her head at exactly the perfect angle as she rose, but to no avail. Her stumble nearly overbalanced her completely. For standing next to the duchess was the duke. The Duke of Mountsorrel, not her aunt's husband. She regained her equilibrium, hopping from one foot to the other, making her hoops wobble, feeling like a complete beginner. Anyone meeting her would imagine she had been dragged up by careless servants, not nurtured by loving parents to become the best person she could be.

Perhaps that was as well. After all, she didn't wish to become further acquainted with his grace. Did she? She gave a tiny shake of her head. She should not indulge herself. He had no interest in any woman over twenty. That was for sure. If he danced with her, it would be a pity dance.

Heedless of anything but her own interests, the duchess plowed on, making the formal introduction. At least she could curtsy properly this time, but she did not make it as low. When she lifted her head she met his dark gaze directly. Let him be the first to look away.

He bowed over her hand. At his touch, skin to skin, she had to fight to repress her shudder. Only one word described the way she felt—recognition. Of what, she did not know. Nor did she care to find out.

Unfortunately, he stared back. A smile curved his lips. Had he noticed her reaction? He behaved as if he did, as if they shared a private joke. She refused to give in, absolutely refused to. "Lady Drusilla, I'm delighted to meet you...formally. May I request the honor of your company for the next dance?"

She could hardly say no. That would entail more touching, but she couldn't help that. At least she knew what contact with him meant. The sensation would wear off in time. She absolutely knew it. Gazing at him, she caught sight of a defect. A thin white scar cut across his lower jaw, leaving a clean line where the incipient stubble of his beard should be. Another smaller scar bisected his left eyebrow. Not noticeable at first, but once seen, never forgotten. The upper scar gave him a devilish look, as if he were perpetually quirking his brow. Her imagination went off on its own happy journey, as it often did.

When he led her on the dance floor, she was careful to keep her hand on his sleeve, needing all the armor she could find. The duchess had employed an eight-piece orchestra. They made an unholy amount of noise. That meant she did not have to converse. Except that he led her to the far end of the large room, away from the musicians. And to make matters worse, they were to dance a minuet. Partners did not change in this dance that required elegance and confidence for its effect. Neither of which she had right at this moment.

But she wasn't a marquess's daughter for nothing. Steeling her spine and schooling her face into immobility, she prepared for her ordeal. Unfortunately, immediately after she rose from her initial curtsy, she said, "You are very kind, spending time with the old maids."

He tilted his head to one side and offered his hand to help her up and display her as she paraded around him. "I have not seen any yet."

"Truly? Allow me to take you over to meet them."

"That, my lady, would not be proper. A single lady should not put herself forward, you know."

Was he goading her? Undoubtedly. Sadly, the slow simmer of annoyance burned her stomach and made itself known to her fevered mind. "I am sure my aunt would be delighted to introduce you. My sister and cousin are over there with the others. We have quite a society underway."

"Interesting. What do you talk about?" As she moved past him, her powdered hair grazed his mouth. "Eligible gentlemen? The latest fashions? Or patterns for knitted stockings?" He pointedly fixed his gaze on her sleeve. "Or how to get ink stains out of lace."

She pulled in a breath, trying very hard to control her outrage. She absolutely refused to rise to his bait. Except that she did. "The abolition of slavery and the utter ignorance of some menfolk."

His laugh told her she'd hit a mark. "Touché, Lady Drusilla. I stand corrected. Such women can change the world, can they not?"

"Indeed. And they are often possessors of the best family secrets. Together, we probably know every dirty little secret the highest in society are doing their best to conceal. We know how to keep secrets, too."

She danced a perfect round and lifted her chin.

His silence came as a surprise. Tension ratcheted up between them. Dru could hardly hear the music over the thudding of her heart. What had she said? "There is no obligation to share your secret with me, sir. I fear, however, that I will probably know it shortly. I can hardly help it. Let me speculate." She couldn't stop. Considering the angry stares he shot at her, she should be dead of shock and awe, but Dru had never given in. She decided on a few light sallies until he regained his temper. "Perhaps you have a secret sister, or your parents were never married officially. Or you keep a killer locked up in the attic of your remote house in Scotland." She didn't even know if he had a remote house in Scotland, but it sounded good. She had taken to reading Gothic romances recently, like the one written by Horace Walpole. Ridiculous things happened, enough to tickle her fancy and far removed from the world she lived in. Walpole poked fun at the stories while he dived in, and that appealed to Dru's sense of the ridiculous. She recalled the plot of the story she was working on. "Or maybe you are sheltering a secret heir, one who is so oppressed he dare not think for himself. He is kept hidden from society—"

Releasing her hand—positively throwing it at her—the Duke of Mountsorrel turned his back on her and strode away, leaving her stranded in the middle of the floor.

Rigid with shock, Dru stared after him. He didn't look back. Not that she expected him to, because she'd caught the expression on his face before he left. He was incandescent with fury. His eyes had flashed wide open before his mouth thinned into a hard line and the creases at the sides deepened. He'd spun on one heel, executing a perfect turn. She admired it even as she went hot and cold, the chill running down her spine turning her into ice.

And still the orchestra played the minuet.

She didn't imagine the lull in conversation or the way all eyes turned in her direction.

Then, as if by magic, her cousin Julius, the son of the house, slid into view. He held out his hand, his blue eyes telegraphing a message. She took his hand.

Julius resumed where Mountsorrel had left off, turning her once more before leading her forward. A polite smile touched his mouth. "We must do our best to ensure the riff-raff is denied entry in future."

Alarm touched Dru, together with a sense of justice. "No, please don't. I must have said something to upset him. I was trying to exchange conversation, but I hit on something that upset him, and he left."

Julius arched a slim brow. His immaculate attire and graceful demeanor were as typical of him as his appearing in exactly the right place. However, his icy formality had eased of late, ever since his shocking second marriage to a country governess. Because the woman had an excellent pedigree, society had reluctantly accepted her. If Eve had married into a different family, she might not have been so lucky, but Dru doubted she cared about that. She adored Julius and as far as Dru could tell, the feeling was entirely reciprocated. "What did you say, exactly?" He steered her into a curtsy.

"I don't know," Dru confessed, thinking back to before that abrupt exit had frozen her into a block of ice. "Just nonsense about a story I...read."

Julius didn't reply immediately. When they had traversed to the opposite side of the ballroom to the one where she'd suffered her worst humiliation, he said, "Which book?"

"I don't remember," she confessed, although she perfectly recalled passing on to her own less polished, but more scurrilous effort.

"He will repair his mistake," Julius said mildly, "Or he will pay. You do not have to concern yourself with keeping me informed. I will do that myself."

How could he possibly repair what he'd done? "I... I don't think there's any need."

"There is every need. You are an Emperor, and we are not treated with contempt. Ever." The glance Julius shot her told her he meant every word. If the Duke of Mountsorrel did not at least send her a letter of apology, he would find himself in trouble. The Emperors' reach spread past fashionable London to the City, the merchants and bankers there, and beyond. Duke or not, Mountsorrel would not find anything easy.

Dru would not help him. Although she suspected more lay behind the story than she knew, she did not care. He had better have left the building, or her cousins would waylay him, and she felt too vulnerable to face any consequences now. The man was insufferable, and one way or another, she would make him pay.

Her story needed a villain, a man who would torment and torture her heroine. Before tonight, she had not the faintest idea what he looked like or why he behaved as he did.

Now she knew.

Chapter 2

Dru almost tossed the offending ruffle at her maid when Forde helped her to divest herself of her finery. "See what you can do with this," she said, gaining some satisfaction when Forde's eyes opened wide in shock.

Every maid present tonight would have marked that. Forde would find herself the butt of jokes in the morning. Well, at least Dru would have company. She expected caricatures and gossip sheets to be full of the story and braced herself to ignore them gracefully. And to stay at home.

As Forde was helping her into her dressing robe, her mother appeared at her bedroom door. Lady Strenshall was similarly attired in a loose gown, more lace than pink silk, and an equally frivolous cap was tied over her curls. Waving impatiently, she dismissed the maid. "Lady Drusilla is not completely helpless. I'm sure she can finish her toilet for herself."

Forde's small "humph" was hardly audible.

Lady Strenshall let it go. Finding a chair, she dragged it up to sit by Dru, where she was staring at herself in the mirror. "I will not pretend that nobody noticed tonight's appalling incident," she said. "But I want to hear the event from your lips. What on earth happened, Drusilla?"

Dru put down the cloth she'd been using to wipe her cheeks and turned to face her mother, hands in her lap. She would have lowered her head, except she suspected her mother would know she was merely avoiding a difficult conversation. Then she would face a series of closer questions.

Best to confront this head-on. Marshaling her thoughts, she told her mother what she wanted to know. Mostly. "I admit I attempted to flirt with him, but in a crowded ballroom. He noticed a stain on my lace, but he did not seem too put out."

Lady Strenshall clicked her tongue. "Drusilla, how could you! Did you know your lace was stained before we set out?"

Never had she wished for a lecture, but she found herself doing it now. "Yes, Mama." With any luck, her confession would distract her mother enough for her to forget why she came here.

No such luck. "What was it stained with?"

Dru bit her lip. "Ink."

Her mother's mouth flattened and a double crease marked the skin between her brows. "I have told you to use the protectors. Better still, do not go near your desk when you are in full dress. Your pastime is becoming difficult to manage."

Dru would have lied, claimed an accident, but her mother would know. "I regret what I did. But nobody else noticed."

A slim brow rose. "Do you truly believe that? I would wager most people who attended that ball saw the mark. They miss nothing. And then to make a spectacle of yourself on the dance floor..." She lifted her hands in a gesture of despair. "Drusilla, I hate to remind you my dear, but you are twenty-six and unwed."

"I am aware of that, Mama."

"You girls begged for the privilege of making your own arrangements. We are fortunate. As Shaws, and as Emperors, we hold a position in society that is close to unassailable. We have enough resources to ensure you will never starve. However, you can destroy it. Your father and I want to see you happy, my dear."

Dru would have done anything to avoid this moment. Her mother was about to express her disappointment.

Her tone had softened, dropped into a gentle sweetness. "A single woman is at a considerable disadvantage. As a spinster, she is one level below the married ones. Her social status is deeply compromised, and she does not have the freedom a married woman can command."

When Dru opened her mouth to object, her mother plowed on.

"You know that is the truth. Respect, command, and a good family can be the best a woman can have. It breaks my heart when I think you and Livia will never know that."

Oh, dear. Dru had no ambition to become a great lady, a society hostess, political or otherwise. And a husband would be an inconvenience. He would most likely ban her from her favorite occupations. Insist she paid him attention. Maybe she would find a husband content to leave her in the country. Many couples held separate lives, only coming together to make heirs. Dru knew of at least two cases where the heir was produced when the husband was elsewhere, but he had not demurred and accepted the child as his. Nothing short of Immaculate Conception.

Even as she recalled those arrangements, she repudiated them. She did not want to be a symbol, a cog in the clockwork of a family timepiece. She picked up the hairbrush and passed it through her wet locks. She hated going to bed in hair powder.

When she remained silent, her mother laid her hand gently over Dru's. "I was nineteen years old when I met your father. I liked him, but I thought no more of it until my mother informed me that I was to marry him. Then and there I promised myself I would not put my children through the same ordeal."

Dru gaped. She had always thought her parents devoted to each other. They worked together and sought each other's company. Could they have hidden a dislike all these years?

She gave her mother her full attention. "You did not like my father?"

"I didn't say that. I did not know him. After my parents informed me of the betrothal, they allowed us to spend time together. Over the first two years of our marriage we came to know each other, and eventually we found love together. You will do the same. I am certain of it."

Dru swallowed. She had not expected anything but a reprimand from her mother. But the words made her think. Was it such a bad thing to marry for practical reasons? Should she not at least consider it? Carefully, she laid the hairbrush down. "Mama, are you saying that you will arrange a marriage for me?"

"We consider it in your best interests. My dear, you do not want to become a spinster. You will have enough to ensure you never starve, but you will have no freedom. You could live independently, but that would mean a small house with a companion for propriety. Nobody will consider you of any importance. That is the way of the world, my dear."

"You want me married?"

Her mother grimaced but didn't answer her question. Instead, she said, "We have had some interesting enquiries recently, my dear."

"Oh." What was she supposed to think about that? As if she were a house for sale? For sale. Someone wanted her, but because of her influential family and her generous dowry. Not for herself. She was not special, didn't have any particular talent, or none that society would value. She always thought of clever, witty remarks an hour after they would have been useful. She smiled pleasantly, danced adequately and conversed with a certain amount of intelligence but not brilliance. Unfortunately, her appearance could be described as pleasant, also. In fact, apart from being a Shaw, she didn't stand out at all. "So who are they?" Perhaps someone had been holding a desperate, passionate desire for her.

She listened to the achingly short list. A widower with three children, all girls, no doubt looking for a mother for his children and an heir. Fifteen years older than she was, which would not matter if he were not a pompous fool. But an earl, and a suitable match. And a man two years older than she, a younger son, which she would not object to. Except that she and most of society happened to know that he was not interested in the fair sex. He would want a comfortable wife who would lend him respectability. Lastly, a rake, and gambler.

"Why him?" she asked.

"Because his parents have found a way to put most of his inheritance out of his hands." Her mother's eyes danced. "They would like a wife to steady him. She would control the finances through a trust. It would be a challenge. You cannot deny that."

"It would," she said doubtfully.

The man was handsome, personally charming, but she had avoided him for a very long time, and she would continue to do so. Interesting that his family considered her a steadying influence. Rather sad, too. While Dru had always been aware she was not one of the most prominent members of her flamboyant family, she had not considered herself an antidote before.

Her mother went on to list two more gentlemen Dru had barely noticed. An earl and a baron. One she suspected of having a tendre elsewhere to a woman society would never accept. That sounded like a complete disaster to her. The other was wealthy, but from trade. Not that it bothered her. Heavens, her own cousin had resorted to getting his hands dirty in order to restore his family's fortunes. She only liked him the better for it. But she would prefer a husband who did not measure the same around his body as he did top to bottom, and his lordship was not particularly short. Heavens, had he really expressed a serious interest in her?

And that was that. "No more?" she asked, but not with any expectation.

"The season has only just begun." Did her mother truly think anyone else would come forward?

"And you would allow me to make my choice?"

"Within reason."

Of course. Reason had to prevail, even in matters of love. Except Dru wished it did not have to. A romance, something torrid and passionate, a man totally devoted to her—that was what her heart yearned for. All her family had found the people they loved, their other halves. But not her, and with a heavy heart she had to admit that she probably would not. The best candidate was the widower, the most challenging the rake, but she was attracted to neither. The others were hopeless.

Her mother got to her feet in a swirl of silken skirts. "I would have your answer by the end of the month. Mark me, child, if you turn down all of these suitors, I will choose one for you. Do not hold out for love. That is usually something that comes with effort."

"But my brothers and sisters married for love."

"It did not come immediately, nor did it come without effort."

After kissing her daughter goodnight, Lady Strenshall left.

This was usually Dru's favorite part of the day. When the candles glowed, the curtains were closed and silence closed in on her. Blessed and welcome. Except that in London, the night was never completely silent. Even at this hour, people moved around outside. Vague murmurs and the occasional shout reached her ears, as well as the sound of iron rims against cobbles as a carriage swept past. But it had a muffled air, as if the atmosphere itself conspired to move slower and transport sounds with a softer edge. The crisp, sharp morning sounds did not suit Dru half so well.

Tonight, she barely took notice of the night. Her mind was too disturbed to enjoy it.

Carefully folding back the long sleeves of her robe, Dru walked slowly to her little desk by the window and found the key that opened the drawer. She could spend an hour or two dreaming in her own world, visiting the people who were wholly hers. She picked up the spectacles that prevented her getting eyestrain from working too long, propped them on her nose, and took her seat. Then she reverently drew out the ever-thickening sheaf of paper. In the place of a journal, she preferred to make fantasy real and draw on the people she loved and the ones she disliked to create something totally impossible but as scurrilous and amusing as she could make it.

And now she had the character of the villain. A totally selfish and ignorant man whose only interests were the ones he designated as his and who used and abused everyone around him. Dru recalled Mountsorrel's slightly crooked nose and the way one brow lifted marginally higher than the other. She thought of the full lips, too soft for his face, and the thin white scar on his jaw, no doubt the remains of some long-ago minor accident. And his hands, so elegant, but with a strength that could overwhelm in an instant. She imagined them around her throat. They would go around easily. He might be able to encompass her neck with one hand. And he would press there, until the breath left her body. Of course nobody would be able to see his wickedness except for the heroine. He would be charming to most people, his first mode of attack when he wanted to achieve something particularly dastardly.

What would be the act that set him on his evil path?

Ah, yes, she had it. Why should he not kill his father and his brother? Nobody would stand in his way. Oh, she would make a memorable villain out of the Duke of Mountsorrel.

* * * *

A tap came on the door while Dru was dressing the next morning. "There's a gentleman downstairs to see you, my lady. Your lady mother is sitting with him."

Dru glanced at Forde, who was adding the final touches to her hair. "Just pin on the cap. It looks fine." Annoyed, she pulled off her spectacles and shoved them down the front of her bodice, her habit when she wanted to locate them. Once she had done her duty she intended to lose herself in her story for a few hours. She had been looking forward to those hours. Now they were cut short by a gentleman caller.

Of course. Her mother would be starting her campaign. No doubt one of the men on the list was making his first approach.

Forde made a tutting sound under her breath, but did as she was asked, pinning the scrap of lace on top of the coil of shining, dark hair that she had just created. Lappets fell down but they did little other than add to Dru's adornments.

She wore yellow today, with a string of pearls around her neck. As usual, she had declined hair powder, but that had not stopped Forde's mouth tightening in unspoken disapproval. But the maid did have a gift for making Dru look her best.

Dru braced herself to greet whomever it was with her finest society manners and a smile. She still felt as if she were being interviewed for a position in someone else's household as she went downstairs to the green drawing room. A footman opened the door for her. The Strenshalls didn't always insist on a servant in full livery opening all the doors, but he would have snapped to attention for a visitor. She smiled at him, and he relaxed his expression enough to nearly smile back.

She halted abruptly. The man who rose to greet her was not anyone she had expected to see.

The Duke of Mountsorrel bowed.

Hastily recalling her manners, Dru dropped a slight curtsy. "Your grace," she greeted him, not knowing what else to say.

"Lady Drusilla."

As she swept around the sofa to greet her mother, Lady Strenshall gave her a meaningful glance, but Dru was not sure what to infer. If her mother was receiving his lordship, she should listen. Maybe it was that.

He didn't give her a chance to sit but began speaking. "Lady Drusilla, I have an apology to make. Indeed, I am deeply sorry for my behavior last night. Nothing excuses that."

Startled, she blinked up at him. "My lord, it is kind of you to call. I accept your apology." His surprising apology. Perhaps Julius had spoken to him after all.

He nodded. "Thank you, although it is more than I deserve." He grimaced. "However, my apology is not enough to stop tongues wagging."

"I fear that is true," her mother broke in. "I have heard several reports of discussions in drawing rooms." She tapped a newssheet lying on the sofa by her side. "It has reached the papers. We can only mend what happened."

"Mend?" Dru asked cautiously. "What are they saying?"

Lady Strenshall heaved a sigh. "Unfortunately, they have chosen you to be the butt of their comments. Lord Mountsorrel is society's darling at present."

The marquess groaned. "Sadly, that is true. They have decided we quarreled on the dance floor and you passed a few unforgivable remarks. Fortunately, nobody overheard us, but that is not stopping the gossip."

What could she have said? Dru still had no idea why he'd walked away. "I didn't realize the story had spread so fast." With an effort, she stifled a yawn. She had been up late last night.

"Then you should have," her mother said sharply. "You have been on the town long enough to realize that. Have you any plans to counter the gossip?"

Dru hung her head. "No, Mama."

"Then listen. Mountsorrel has proposed that he take you for a drive in the Park."

"Now?"

"Now."

Lifting her head, she met the duke's amused gaze. He'd seen her shock. She flicked at her skirt. "I cannot ride in this gown. It is too—"

"Nonsense!" her mother declared roundly. "The weather is fine, and you look charming. Moreover, you will draw the eye. Do you not agree, Mountsorrel?"

"I…ah…indeed, Lady Drusilla looks delightful," the hapless duke replied. When Lady Strenshall was determined to achieve her objective, nothing stood in her way.

Knowing this, Dru accepted her fate. "If you will allow me a few moments to find my hat and gloves, I'll be ready directly." And change her satin slippers for something more practical, although she did not mention that part to her mother. When the marchioness graciously agreed to her request, Dru lifted her skirts and scampered upstairs.

* * * *

Oliver suppressed a sigh. How long did it take to find a pair of gloves and a hat?

As Lady Strenshall finished her second dish of tea, she broached the subject of Drusilla again. "We cannot put up with Drusilla becoming the center of attention. It would distress the poor girl, and she does not deserve it. If she said something particularly egregious, she must of course apologize, but she needs to look about her. Lord Strenshall has received several flattering offers for her hand recently, and we are seriously considering them. I'm sure I can trust you to keep my confidence."

And if he did not, she would know who was to blame. "Naturally, Lady Strenshall. I am delighted to hear the news." So they wouldn't want any gossip where Lady Drusilla was concerned. He understood. "I had thought of letting it be known that I was taken suddenly ill. Lady Drusilla of course knew this and allowed me to leave her."

Her ladyship nodded. "That will serve our purpose excellently. I'll inform my daughter. And her cousin Lord Winterton."

Oh, good lord, had he become involved? Of course he had. Clever, dangerous Winterton would not let a slight to his family stand. He was more formidable than his mother, and that was saying something.

"He took over the dance you abandoned," her ladyship calmly informed him. "We will let him know." She paused, and adjusted the sugar tongs once more. "If today's excursion is a success. I cannot allow my daughter to become a laughing stock, especially at this important part of her life."

Oliver felt two inches high under her mild comment. He would ensure that it was. If she said she hated the sun, he'd agree with her. If Lady Drusilla claimed she was dressed in purple instead of that charming primrose, he would smile mildly and tell her purple became her vastly.

He did not want gossip spreading any more than she did. He had a great deal at stake, if she only knew it. However, he would not let that small detail fall. He was an old hand at keeping secrets. He prided himself that he had never allowed an unconsidered word to drop from his lips. Even last night—but last night he had acted rashly, as his own mother was only too eager to remind him this morning.

Damn. If Lady Drusilla had seen the vicious gossip in the papers, she was bearing up well. Either that or she was used to it spreading its vile wings over her family. But not directed at her. She did not deserve it any more than she had merited his behavior at the ball. She had hit a sore spot, one she would never understand, but that was not her fault.

Lady Drusilla reappeared. Her hat, while plain, had a bunch of silk primroses pinned to one side and became her, giving her a flirtatious air she had not displayed before. Her smile charmed him, and she carried a frivolous parasol that was totally unnecessary, but he enjoyed the way she deployed it as they left the house.

Although the sun had made an appearance that morning, it seemed to have retired for the day, and a sheet of white clouds masked the sky.

"Oh dear," she said, glancing up. "Do you think it will rain?"

"I doubt it," he answered as he gallantly offered his arm. "The clouds are too high up for that. They will probably give their all to Yorkshire later on today."

"My brother is in North Derbyshire," she said absently, still staring up as if afraid to meet his gaze, "he will probably be glad of the benefit. Crops and such. He seems terribly rural these days." She returned her attention to him, or more precisely, the shallow steps she needed to negotiate to leave the house. This being a fashionable part of London, they had a stretch of paving stones to cross before reaching the carriage. She took them carefully, as if afraid she would stumble.

He had not thought her particularly clumsy. Had she somehow hurt herself?

She flicked a glance up at him and smiled, the expression cautious. He stopped and turned to face her, alarming a pair of chairmen who had to swerve to carry their burden past them. Chairmen had a good command of the English language, particularly in evidence when they passed by.

Lady Drusilla suppressed a snort, and her eyes crinkled, as if she were about to smile. Strain marks appeared at the corners of her mouth. If he had not been so close, he would have missed the slight fleeting marks. He smiled in return. "Would you like me to pursue them and strike them down?"

"Not at all. They have a living to make. It cannot be easy, carrying that great sedan chair around all day."

He glanced after the pair trotting along the street. The chair held a slender woman in full regalia, he'd noticed absently. They would have more taxing burdens that day. "You are quite right. We should all thank the heavens for the fact that we were not born chairmen."

"Indeed." Her voice held barely restrained mirth. "But I have learned several new words today. Their use is most inventive."

He glanced back at her, not sure how to take that. Her reputation as a gently nurtured lady did not follow her. He would love to teach her some more words if they made her smile in such a winsome way.

No, he would be good. He would be as mild as a sleeping baby. Except he needed to keep his attention on his frisky horses. He probably should have sent his groom to tool them around the streets while he waited for her ladyship. They were snorting, and one stamped impatiently.

He was pleased to see that Lady Drusilla stepped firmly toward them, showing no trepidation. He had thought her a mild miss until she had startled him with her observations last night. She had never stood out in company. When he'd made discreet enquiries he'd received only moderate responses, and until this morning she had never featured in the more notorious gossip sheets. He feared her new appearance was entirely down to him. He had not needed his brother to point out that he had to make amends. In fact, Charles had not done so, although Oliver had expected him to.

Now he had her to himself he became aware of her less obvious charms. She smelled of something sweet and sharp—a flower, not as overpoweringly sweet as a violet, more like the light scent of the primroses she wore in her hat. Aware the flowers were silk, he could only come to the conclusion that it was her.

Desire swept over him, sudden and unexpected. He had felt something similar last night, but their quarrel had put his initial response to her out of his mind. Now he recalled it.

Turning hurriedly, he extended his gloved hand to help her into his carriage. He had brought the curricle. Light and two-wheeled, it was considered a sporting vehicle, rather fast, and with his pair of grays, would take some skill to drive. To do her justice, Lady Drusilla mounted the small step confidently and settled herself without checking for the position of the hand-holds.

As he stepped back, he caught sight of something glittering on the gray pavement. Bending, he retrieved a small pair of gold-rimmed spectacles, the kind lawyers perched on their noses when they wanted to make a point or read particularly fine print.

"Oh! May I have those, please?"

Oliver placed them into her imperious outstretched hand. "They are yours?" Looking up into her face, he noted her anxious expression, her frown. He might have taken it as displeasure, were it not for the way her throat moved when she swallowed.

"Yes, indeed. I only use them when my eyes become tired. I am perfectly fine usually."

That accounted for the occasional blank look he'd noticed last night. Was the way she had fixed her gaze on him a symptom, too? He would prefer if it were not. He'd rather she stared at him because she wanted to. That was the one part of last night he had enjoyed. She'd gazed at him as if he were a hero. Very few people looked at him like that. "What do you do to tire your eyes so much?"

He had intended the remark as a light sally to give him time to walk around to the driver's place, where his groom was holding the reins ready for him. However, the cloud that passed over her face was not due to the overcast day.

As he leaped up to his place and gathered the reins, he had little time to look at her, but he puzzled over the conundrum on the way.

The gilded iron gates lay fully open, and Oliver did not hesitate driving through.

"I want to apologize again for last night, but this time less formally," he said. "I am truly sorry for upsetting you in that way." The groom behind them was too far away to hear what they said, so long as they kept their voices to a moderate conversational level.

"Upsetting me?" Her light tone held laughter, but not the spontaneous expression of shortly before. This was undoubtedly her society voice. "I assure you, sir, I merely exchanged one partner for another. My cousin Julius proved a more than superior substitute."

A subtle insult Oliver could not but admire, even though she had aimed it at him. Now settled in the procession of the great and the good who made Rotten Row their own at this hour, he spared her a glance. "I am delighted to hear it. However, the journals were not so kind, but I am sure this public appearance will assuage their curiosity. We'll put it about that I was taken suddenly ill last night. I care not how they traduce me. They may say I was drunk or that I have the manners of a yokel, so long as you are left unblemished."

"Did Julius speak to you?" Her question sounded genuine, although he was still finding his way around this enigma of a woman.

"Not yet. I have that felicity later today."

"Ah. So he didn't tell you to say that?"

This time he fully turned his head to meet her gaze directly. "No, he did not." Did she think he was so lily-livered as to respond to a threat, however carefully worded?

She hunched a shoulder, inadvertently drawing his attention to her linen-covered bosom. "It sounds like something he'd have drawn up, that's all."

Her skin glowed through the fine lawn, and he felt a jolt of something he should not be experiencing for a single lady—physical desire. He longed to draw that fabric aside, to touch the soft flesh underneath. "Maybe we think in the same way."

"Nobody can match Julius."

What was he, some kind of god? Oliver considered Lord Winterton a pleasant, though somewhat finicky, fellow. His lean figure and elaborate clothes belied a man of whipcord strength, as Oliver had witnessed recently in a fencing studio. He would not like Winterton as an adversary, although he had to admit, the encounter would be interesting. If he needed to, he'd take the Earl of Winterton in any contest he chose. He anticipated the encounter with some eagerness.

"So you're being a gentleman now?" She flicked out her fan, not plying it, but examining the flowers and portraits painted on the delicate surface. "Truly, sir, I do not know what to make of you."

"You mean after my churlish behavior of yesterday, I take it?" What did she want, blood? He would not abase himself.

A woman he vaguely knew smiled at him from an elegant landau moving in the opposite direction. He nodded back and touched his hat with his whip. But her image faded from his mind as soon as she had passed.

"You are an enigma, sir. I thought I knew most members of society tolerably well, but you do not spend a great deal of time in London. Our paths outside the city have not crossed."

His mouth tightened. "I prefer country pleasures. London is crowded and dirty."

"And invigorating." She snapped her fan closed. "I enjoy the crowds and the excitement. There is not another city like it in all the world."

He sent her a smile. "True enough. So we had better show these crowds how friendly we are."

She smiled back.

Oliver forgot where they were and what he was supposed to be doing. Her smile dazzled him, as if the sun had come out from the bank of clouds and decided to surprise everyone. In a flash of insight he recognized a fellow traveler, someone on the same road he was trudging along. Only

Drusilla made it a joy instead of a duty. She saw the flowers where he only saw tangled weeds.

He would fight for an outlook like that. But would he fight for her?

Yes, he would. With a suddenness that was most unlike his usual decision-making process, he put himself on the side of the angels. "One ride in the park won't convince our critics," he said, before he could change his mind.

"They will have forgotten us in a few days. Scandals happen all the time. Kitchen maids will be using the papers to light the fire with next week." She dusted an imaginary speck off her gown, avoiding his gaze. So she was not unaffected by him. Triumph soared through him, as if he'd won a great victory.

"We need to prove our cordiality, if nothing warmer. And I owe you at least one minuet."

"Pooh, you owe me nothing." She made a delightful scoffing sound at the back of her throat. "You have paid your debt, sir."

"Your generosity does you credit, but I fear we cannot abandon one another so precipitately. In short, Lady Drusilla—"

Of course the sparkiest gray had to choose that moment to stumble.

The delicate carriage lurched, its wheels creaking ominously, and then something below them snapped, the sharp sound shocking him into taking action. This vehicle was high off the ground, the black wheels large and showy. Cursing, Oliver tightened his hold on the reins, but the horse that had stumbled was already on its knees, jolting the curricle off-balance.

Gravity did the rest. Oliver cast any attempt at control aside. Grabbing her around the waist, he went forward as the carriage lurched sickeningly to one side, rolling as he pushed away from the vehicle. He had no choice but to go in the same direction as the carriage. However, he could at least ensure they fell clear of it.

They hit the ground with a sickening thump. Oliver turned them midair so he was beneath her, his body taking the brunt of the crash, the impact knocking all the breath from him. She fell over him with what should have been a delightful mess of silk and perfumed body. Oliver had no time to do anything but cushion her fall.

Cries came from all around them, together with the sound of wheels and horses, the orderly procession disrupted by their catastrophe. Fortunately they must have had some notable whips following, as they did not find themselves under any carriages or hooves.

After one sharp cry, Lady Drusilla fell silent, but the heaving of her breasts over his chest told her she was still alive.

With a supreme effort of will, Oliver dragged breath back into his body and lay still, as people surrounded them, chattering and exclaiming. Curls tickled his mouth. "Are you awake?"

"What?" came her delightfully acidic response. "You expected me to fall asleep midair?"

Chapter 3

The abrupt nature of the accident shocked Dru into making the kind of tart remark her mother would not have approved of. She was alive and relatively unhurt, although shocked and sprawled over the duke. As it was, she had become the center of attention again, and all because of this man.

He'd fallen on his back and pulled her over him. Lord, how badly must he be hurt?

Her second thought was for her modesty, but glory be, the light cane of her hooped petticoat had snapped on impact. Although she lay in a tangle of yards and yards of silk, her lower body remained covered. If the journalists were about, at least they couldn't report that everyone had seen what Lady Drusilla Shaw had to offer a man.

The duke was as tangled up as she, so rising to her feet and making a graceful exit was an impossibility. Not that she had any inclination to do so.

"I suppose you know this means we have to meet again?" he asked, his voice breathless. Not surprisingly since she'd landed fully on top of him.

The close contact as much as the fall undid her. She had not been this near to anyone for a long time, and the physical proximity drove any common sense she had left far away. Her first instinct, as always, was to throw up her shields. "I know nothing of the kind."

"Lady Drusilla, you are a complete and unexpected delight."

Then he kissed her. He kissed her! Not lingering, but he pressed his lips to hers in the briefest of caresses. Her senses swam, more than when she'd flown into the sweet air and felt him reach for her.

"Sir!" She tried to sound indignant, but she couldn't manage it. For two pins she'd continue to sprawl over him and claim a kiss of her own. More, she wanted more.

He gasped, drawing more air into that large body. Shocking and instant, her attraction to him had increased threefold. But she could not let him know. He could not feel the same way. He had stolen the kiss out of sheer devilment. His senses weren't overset. He hadn't felt that instant arousal. Why would he?

She should probably roll away from his chest, but his solid masculinity—and the way his body warmed hers through the layers of fabric—fascinated her. They were intimately twined together by her skirts, as if in bed and tangled in sheets.

Where had that thought come from?

People chattered around them, offers of help appearing from all directions. Dru pushed her hat back, feeling the broken straw. She must look more like a scarecrow than a lady of fashion.

He stroked her, roaming his hands over her. Dru was too far gone to complain, although her mother would have her guts for allowing a man such intimacies. She liked it.

"Can you get to your feet?" he asked softly, but while he said that, he still held her close.

Disappointment washed through her when she understood why he was stroking her. He was checking for broken bones. She was letting her imagination run wild, as usual. "I believe so, although my skirts are somewhat in the way."

His responding chuckle struck her as deeply inappropriate, and a little off-key. "I will endeavor to remain completely still while you disentangle yourself. If you ask me for help, I will render it, but I think if we both move at the same time, we will merely make matters worse."

"Your grace!" That was the groom.

"Tell me." He sounded resigned.

"One 'orse limping, but I don't think he's hurt bad. I've got t'other tethered close by. The curricle's a wreck."

Trust a groom to care more about the animals than the passengers. Dru caught her response before it left her lips. Lifting her head she discovered she was nose to nose with the duke. Delight hit her before she could repress it, and her smile reflected it. "We will be the talk of the town," she murmured, so only he could hear.

"The talk of the country. They will say I did it deliberately, and I fear, had I known the delights in store, I might well have."

"Nonsense!" By dint of tugging hard and ignoring the rips as the delicate lace at her elbows gave way, Dru managed to lift her arms and prop them on his chest. He groaned as she levered herself up. Served him right, she thought with a vicious smile she immediately regretted. After all, he had tried his hardest to shield her fall. "You aren't the best whipster I've ever driven with."

His eyebrows came together in a pained frown. "Had the others known what felicity they could have, they might also have done the same." But that answer set something between them.

Honestly, would nothing suppress the man? His hands came to rest on her back, gently, as if holding something precious. As they stilled, she realized he was shaking, a fine tremor racking his body.

They exchanged a look of pure honesty. "You were worried."

"Of course I was." His irritability did not hide the fear in his eyes. Even now, when they were obviously both little the worse for the tumble, he had concerns. About her? "In case you've forgotten, Lady Drusilla, your mother gave you into my care. Of course I am concerned." He firmed his grip on her, and the fine trembling stopped. Only because he was holding her too tightly to let it show. "You should take care when you distract me from driving."

As if any of this was her fault! Dru bit back her acid response. He really was worried and trying to cover it up. His sharp response did not fool her for one moment.

But she had too much humanity to deliver the jab he deserved as she scrambled up. A gentleman gave her his hand as she stood. After thanking him in a perfunctory way, she took no notice of the avid crowd that stood watching her disgrace. The brim of her broken hat fell over one eye, and she pushed it up as Mountsorrel sprang to his feet.

He shook his coat into place. Apart from a few smears of mud, he looked fine. She was a wreck. His groom handed him his hat, and he propped it over his bare head. His wig must be lying in the mud.

Dru preferred him without it, anyway. Under the fashionable wig he had short-cropped dark hair, so thick she wanted to test it with her fingers to discover its softness for herself.

She was a complete mess. The people crowding around them did not have to tell her so. One side of her hooped skirt had completely collapsed, crushed and broken in the fall, but the other side annoyingly remained, giving her a lopsided appearance. Her bodice was twisted and filthy with mud, and the linen fichu that was supposed to cover her bosom modestly had been mostly pulled away. If she tucked it back in she would only draw more attention, so she left it be and concentrated on ridding herself of her ruined and useless hat. The parasol had disappeared, probably under the remains of the carriage, which lay on its side a short distance away. The back wheel rotated uselessly, and shards of wood lay on the grass.

"A back wheel broke," the groom said, pointing out the obvious.

"I say, that was excellent control," someone said.

Her cousin Ivan stepped out of the melee of fashionable oglers. He whipped off his coat and slung it around Dru's shoulders. She subsided gratefully into its warmth.

"The whole business could have been much worse," he added, holding out his hand to Mountsorrel, who took it in what looked like automatic response.

"If I had been paying more attention I could have done better. I felt the unevenness of the ride, but I assumed the skittish horses were responsible. The wheel must have been giving way since we entered the Park." Mountsorrel took a decisive step toward her, taking her hands in his and turning them over. His were clean, because he'd stripped off his gloves, but she still wore hers, and they were covered in mud. "Are you sure you are unhurt?" He spoke to her as if she were the only person there. The only person who mattered.

Her ears still rang with the sickening crash when the wheel had split, but she was not, she realized with surprise, seriously injured. "I daresay I have a few bruises, but I am perfectly well. How about you? I fell on top of you."

He tried not to wince when he shrugged, but she saw the slight hesitation and knew what it meant. He was more hurt than he wanted to admit. "I am, as you see, hale and hearty. But you? I will take you home, and you will have a physician to look over you." He scanned her visually, a frown between his brows.

Although shaken, she was far from badly affected. "I don't need a physician," she protested. "I don't have any broken bones, and I am certain I have no other serious injuries. A hot bath will probably put me to rights better than having a strange man poking and prodding me."

Gray eyes opened wider, and she knew she didn't imagine the heat that flashed across them. Too late she realized what she had said could have more than one meaning. Poking and prodding of a different kind shot into her mind and she turned away hastily. Only to see her cousin suppress a grin.

"While I appreciate your help, cousin, I do not think I need trouble you any longer."

When she tried to remove his coat, Ivan held it in place. "On the contrary, your lady mother would string me up if I left you alone now. I will take you to her, if you will permit it. I have my carriage just down the way. I was taking Lady Branwell for a drive, but I am sure she will not mind shifting over a little in the circumstances."

"I wouldn't dream of discommoding you," Dru said stiffly. She had no desire to prolong what was turning out to be an embarrassing display. Ivan leaned closer. "Don't be awkward, Dru. For heaven's sake, come away." He spoke so quietly she could barely hear him, but his words had the desired effect.

"If Lady Branwell is sure. I am very muddy."

"If it weren't for the rain we had yesterday, the ground would have been much harder," someone from the crowd commented. "It's the hardness of the ground that matters, eh, Mountsorrel?"

Dru was turning, but she caught the duke's features as they stiffened into a haughty mask. By now, she knew him well enough to tell that something had struck him hard, and it wasn't the muddy ground.

Lady Branwell actually elected to take shelter with her husband, who was riding alone. The crowd watched, amused, as she made him alight and lead his horse. "She must be desperate to actually talk to him," Dru remarked acidly. The Branwells were not on the best of terms.

"Have you seen the back of your gown?" Ivan answered her. "I shall need to reupholster my carriage seat after I have taken you home." When she tried to pull away from him, he growled and tugged her closer. "Oh, no, you don't. I will perform my duty, or your father will have my head. So will mine, come to that," he added ruefully. "Let them gossip. You don't have to listen to it."

Tears threatened to overwhelm her as her reaction set in. She recognized it for what it was—shock—but she could not control it.

Briskly, Ivan helped her into the seat of his own vehicle. Someone had the foresight to lay a blanket over the part of the seat that she now occupied. At least she did not have to blame herself for ruining his upholstery.

Ivan deftly turned his horses and set out for the entrance to the Park. Dru sat stiffly beside him, hands folded in her lap, ignoring the stares of the people they passed. By morning they'd be the primary topic of conversation—again. "We meant to put the rumors to bed with this drive," she remarked, careful to keep the tremor from her voice. She did not want him to know how shaken she was. Not only for her own sake, but because she'd discerned something disturbing in him. He had worked hard to hide his own distress, but she had seen it, sensed it. Instinctively she knew she needed to keep the duke's secret. She would not talk to anyone about his reaction. "We planned to drive in the Park, so people could see we were perfectly friendly, and last night meant nothing."

"Instead, you've increased the problems tenfold," Ivan said dryly. "Such a pity, but this incident will most surely resurrect the old stories."

"What old stories?" She could not think of anything that fitted.

Ivan spared her a glance as he took the corner out of the Park. "You don't know?"

"Know what?" After the events of the morning, she was close to snapping.

"Goodness me," Ivan said mildly. After negotiating a particularly busy corner, in which he deftly maneuvered his way around two carriages trying to take up the whole street, he spoke again. "He has a brother. Did you know that?"

Dru was forced to admit that she knew little about him, except he was wealthy, a duke, and annoying and appealing in almost equal measure.

"Ah." Ivan glanced at her. "I can't believe that your mother didn't tell you."

"I only met him last night, and we didn't expect him to call today. He doesn't come to London often. I knew of his existence, but that was all." Guiltily she repressed memories of her story and how hard she'd worked on it. The crossings-out would have to be carefully rewritten to clean copy. But not now. She forced herself to stop her mind going to the place where it was safe and happiest.

"I see. Did you notice his scars?"

What was this, a guessing game? Dru grimaced. "Yes, I noticed them. Clean, as if glass had cut him." Or a knife. She'd made it a knife in her story. She'd used those scars mercilessly, and given them a sinister history.

"Exactly. He got them in an accident when he was sixteen. He overturned a carriage, just like today, except without such a happy outcome." He grinned at her, a sudden flash of amusement. "You know it was, coz. You got away lightly."

Dru wasn't about to disagree with him.

"He was driving, and his younger brother sat beside him. Charles."

"Charles and Oliver?" she questioned.

"Yes. Their parents came from families who took opposite sides in the Civil War. The names were a symbol of compromise. Or a grand joke, nobody is sure which." He took another corner.

Gratefully, Dru recognized her cousin's sedate speed compared with his usual neck-or-nothing driving style.

"The horses dragged them away. Charles managed to cut them loose with a knife he had in his pocket, but the carriage overturned and collapsed. Oliver sustained a few cuts and bruises, but Charles was not so lucky."

"Is he alive?" she said, hardly daring to breathe.

"Yes, but to this day he lives as a recluse. He was badly injured. Nobody except his family knows how much. Most people believe he went mad or imbecilic in the fall."

"Oh, no!" Her hand flew to her mouth. How could she have known? She would rewrite the story tonight and eliminate the brother she'd locked in a dungeon. In her story the villain had hidden the brother nobody knew about away in a dark place, where no one would ever see him again. But the plucky heroine rescued him. She fell in love with him, and together, the imprisoned brother and the heroine won the day.

She would have to change it completely. She couldn't allow that story another minute's breathing space. She would rewrite it this instant. The brother would go, and she'd put another character in his place. The scars would have to go, too.

How could she have allowed her characters to do that?

Numbly she let Ivan to chatter on, about the rumors swirling around the Duke of Mountsorrel and his family. Apparently the gossip had barely died down. That was why he did not come to London often and why he preferred to stay in the country.

He had caused his brother's injuries. Oh, what a mess.

* * * *

A surge of relief hit Oliver the moment he stepped through the door of his family's London home. They had a neat house close to Grosvenor Square, modern, filled with furniture that his mother had bought new. Only a few family portraits remained to haunt him. He liked it, but not so much it gave him a feeling of coming home. He liked that, too. His ancestral seat had too many bitter memories and reminders.

One kiss and his world had rocked on its axis. At the first touch of her lips his good intentions so nearly disappeared into thin air. He'd seen those lovely, soft pink lips, gazed into her eyes and seen the same attraction in them that was sending his body into instant alert. The pain of landing on the ground melted away, and only claiming that kiss had mattered.

"We are so glad to see you well, your grace," the butler said. London servants would not have dared to make such a personal remark, but because Charles preferred familiarity, he had brought his servants up from the country. "We heard of the accident in the park."

"That didn't take long." His mouth flattened in distaste. "Of all things I dislike gossip."

"The groom who brought the horses back regaled us with the news."

Oliver had remained at the scene until the remnants of the curricle had been removed. He had sent the horses back as soon as he had assured himself they were not injured, merely shaken. They needed familiar routines and people around them. They had been too fresh and skittish that morning.

He had worked so hard at his driving, but the old adage about pride going before a fall was true. And he'd fallen hard.

"Your brother has sent for news. He is deeply concerned."

"I'll visit him immediately." Charles must be profoundly perturbed.

As he climbed the stairs to Charles's apartments, he winced, his bruises making their presence felt for the first time.

At the top of the stairs, his valet waited. He didn't prevent Oliver from ascending the second set of stairs, but did murmur, "I have ordered hot water, sir, and a bath to be sent up."

"Thank you." Oliver heard the news with relief. Of all things, a hot bath would put him to rights.

He handed Robinson his ruined coat, but had no time to do anything except grab the proffered banyan from his valet's hand. He didn't want Charles to see the state of his clothes. Their condition might remind him, as it had Oliver, of that previous accident. The one they rarely talked about, because of the distress it caused everyone.

Shrugging on the light robe of dark blue silk, he went up the stairs.

Charles's rooms lay at the end of the hallway, close to the backstairs. He preferred solitude. Indeed, Oliver had some trouble persuading him to accompany them to London, but he couldn't bear the thought of his brother alone and neglected in the country. For Charles refused all visitors. And how could he get to know anyone if he had them all turned away? Perhaps this time, he'd venture out.

As always, Oliver braced himself before he entered the room, steeling his resolve. Every time he visited his brother, guilt slapped him hard, pouring through him. But that was his cross to bear. He would not add to his brother's troubles. He twisted the doorknob and went in.

Charles sat in his chair, a small table by his side, which held his bell and a decanter. He lifted his hand in greeting, the elegant fingers wafting in the air, dark against the light streaming in through the wide windows. "I heard what happened. I was worried," he said simply.

Oliver shook his head. "I am well. A few bruises, that's all." Damned painful ones. His arse would be black and blue in a few days. But Charles didn't need to know that.

"Thank God." The edges of Charles's mouth turned up, and his eyes crinkled at the corners. At times like these, Oliver was struck by their similarities, not differences. In their childhood they'd been inseparable. But the memories of the way they'd run and laughed over every inch of their ancestral home only pained him these days. He would give his title, his fortune, everything to have those times back.

Since Charles seemed in good spirits, Oliver ventured to make a joke. "I should probably give up driving. Be tooled around the Park in a landau."

Charles shook his head. "It was not your fault. I am sure of it. Any more than our accident was." He held up a hand when Oliver would have spoken. "No, I will not have it, and I have told you so. I saw the rabbit seconds before it disappeared under the horses' hooves. If anyone's fault, it was that rabbit's, and he paid for his mistake dearly."

As Charles had paid for Oliver's error. Oliver had lived that moment over and over again, but he could never recall a rabbit. But since the subsequent moments had been filled with screams and the sounds of crunching wood and bone, he could not be sure he remembered anything properly. The haze of the accident had at first infuriated him and then dismayed him. But when his memory had returned, he wished it had not. These days he had learned to push what memory he had away. His most vivid recollection was of the sounds. They had returned to him in a nightmare, about a week later. Garbled shouts of alarms and screams—his—accompanied the horrible, sickening silence that foretold the unfolding disaster.

Today he had kept his wits. He'd saved them both.

But not the man sitting before him. Charles could only lift himself out of his chair by a supreme effort. He continued to try, but his legs would not hold him. He had lost the feeling there, and his bones had knitted badly after the carriage wheel had shattered them.

At least Charles was himself today, his smile and the glint in his eyes the true Charles, not the one of the uncontrollable tempers and the even more terrifying fits.

"Come and sit, old fellow. I'm sure you could do with a little brandy." Charles lifted the decanter, and before Oliver could say anything, had poured two tumblers of the stuff.

Oliver had never taken to brandy. He would ask for Madeira or port, or even unfortified wine after dinner. The smell of the spirits made him feel mildly nauseated. They'd given it to him after the accident, and even a sniff of it had made him vomit for some time afterwards. By sheer willpower he had forced himself to tolerate the stuff. Now he forced back his instinctive reaction and sipped the drink, holding his breath.

Charles gulped his own portion and poured another. His intake worried Oliver sometimes, but he could do little about it. As Charles had said, didn't he deserve some compensation for spending his days in a chair?

"You were interested in the young lady last night. What was her name?"

Charles kept in touch with all the gossip. His three assistants gathered it for him, assiduously bringing him up to date. Sometimes his avidity concerned Oliver, but if he could use it to draw his brother back into society, then so much the good.

"Lady Drusilla Shaw. Oldest daughter of the Marquess of Strenshall," Oliver said briefly. "I want to put the speculation about us to rest."

Charles's lips curved in a smile. "I thought you came to London to marry. Lady Dru is single and from a great family."

"But if I court her, I don't want it to happen as the result of a scandal."

"You do not want to marry, do you, Oliver?" Charles asked softly. "You have your mistress and a comfortable life. You have heirs."

Oliver bit his lip and picked up his brandy, more for something to do rather than because he wanted it. "You are my immediate heir. The heir presumptive." And if he remained unmarried, the next Duke of Mountsorrel.

"My dear boy, I am convinced I will die well before you. Don't concern yourself. And we have cousins who are perfectly acceptable."

If something happened to him, Charles couldn't sustain the weight of responsibility he would have to undertake. With the business of his title, and now the necessity of finding a bride, Oliver had less time for Charles—something he bitterly regretted when he entered his brother's room and received his smiling welcome.

Charles would not easily sustain that burden. So Oliver must find himself a bride and set up his nursery. The alternative was to appoint reliable trustees, but Charles had a strong sense of duty. He would not shirk the expectations made of him as duke.

"Wait until you find a woman who pleases you," Charles said, his melodic voice filling the air with persuasion. "Marry her then."

Still nursing the tumbler of brandy, Oliver lifted it to his mouth and let the fiery liquid bathe his lips. He repressed his shudder. "Nevertheless, I have promised to take a bride. I'll not take a petulant miss who thinks only of herself. I will choose carefully." He put down the glass. "You could help. Come with me. Advise me. I might choose someone you cannot bear."

To his disappointment, Charles shook his head. "Of all things, I detest the thought of people staring at me with pity. They would, you know."

Yes, they probably would. "But an appearance would allay some of the wildest rumors."

"Perhaps." Charles shrugged. "Let me think about it."

Although society knew of his existence, some refused to accept it, saying Charles had died in the accident, or that he was simple, his mind irretrievably damaged. The more imaginative stories spoke of him being a prisoner, kept under lock and key because of some whim of Oliver's, that Charles was the true heir and Oliver was keeping him prisoner. He ignored all the rumors and answered politely when people asked after Charles. At his brother's request, he only discussed him in the vaguest of terms. No servant entered this room when Charles was in here, apart from his three assistants, Oliver, and their mother, when she was in residence. Their mother did not see her sons often. She lived in Oxfordshire with her second husband, Lord Bixby, and they preferred the country life to town.

Charles suppressed a yawn behind his hand.

"I'll go," Oliver said, making to stand.

"No, please don't. I promise to sleep when you are gone," Charles's voice coarsened and grew considerably quieter.

Oliver leaned forward, the better to hear him.

"What is Lady Drusilla like?"

"Pretty," he found himself saying but then halted. Yes, she was pretty, although he had never considered the matter before. Her soft golden brown hair would feel silky, he was sure, and her smile, especially when she was taken unawares, made her eyes sparkle. "Her figure is neat." By no means voluptuous, although under her fichu her bosom gave promises of soft skin and enjoyable heat. "She is a trifle under average height. She has the kind of wit that passes you by unless you are paying attention." That helped to explain why she had so far been overlooked. "She…has small hands." He could still feel the imprint of that small hand in his as he helped her into the carriage.

Charles's mouth quirked in his typical smile. "You do not sound like a passionate lover. If your feelings for her are so mild, you are probably best avoiding her. She seems to be a bad luck token."

He was attracted to her. Yes he was, although he had not fully realized it until now. "Do you believe in such things?"

Charles didn't answer before he had poured himself a third brandy, a considerably more generous portion than before. He lifted the glass to his lips using both hands, as he sometimes did when he was tired and afraid he would lose his grip. After he had put the half-empty glass down, he spoke. "Not really, but the events are there. Why did you abandon her at the ball?"

Oliver thought before he spoke, not wanting his brother to know the real reason, but not wanting to lie to him either. "We have agreed to say that I felt suddenly ill. Otherwise, the Emperors would probably come for their revenge."

He spoke lightly, but he did not miss the wide-eyed alarm that crossed his brother's face. "Then you had better avoid her. Oliver, you do not need to rush this decision. Find a duchess you can enjoy, not one you merely tolerate."

Oliver sighed and leaned back, crossing a knee over the other. "You are probably right. I will not seek her out. Today has taught me that, at least."

Charles nodded. "Good." His voice almost disappeared.

Getting to his feet, Oliver picked up the hand bell by Charles's side and shook it sharply.

At once, his primary caregiver, Burnett, a burly man with a gentle disposition, entered, took one look at his master and nodded to Oliver. "Your grace, I will take care of him now."

"Of course."

Charles left to get into his cold bath and try to ease his bruised and aching body.

He did not succeed very well.

Chapter 4

A few days later, Oliver arrived home after a morning ride. Finally, his bruises had subsided enough for him to enjoy the crisp air. To his disappointment he did not see Lady Drusilla. He'd written to her, and received a polite reply, so he knew she was recovering and staying at home for a few days. But he'd hinted he'd be in the Park today. A shame she hadn't taken the bait. Perhaps she didn't want to.

She was probably right. That kiss, however brief, had shaken him far more than he liked. He'd come to town to find a sensible, amenable partner. One who would provide heirs for his nursery and share some of his duties, as well as help him with Charles and his moods. For that he did not need a woman of the imagination and family of Lady Drusilla Shaw. However much he might be attracted to her.

She had probably made a similar decision. Bad luck, if one believed in it, seemed to trail after them. They'd appeared cordial enough, and nobody had seen the kiss he'd claimed. They had mended the incident at the ball.

But the thought of someone else kissing her, claiming her, still ate at him. He liked her, damn it, and his body had responded to her in a shocking, not to say startling, way. He couldn't allow any woman to have that kind of effect on him. He had to keep his head.

Riding around to the mews at the back of the house, he dismounted and handed the reins to the groom. "The new horse is behaving well." He'd purchased the sweet-tempered mare for his mother, who had asked him to look about him for a new mount. He'd send the gray into the country with his compliments.

The overpowering smell of horse manure and hay reached his nostrils. He drew a deep breath. Learning to become an excellent whip and rider had taken many long hours. Understanding his horses, taking care of them, so the scent reminded him of his years spent with his grooms.

Smiling, he strolled into the building. It stood in the mews behind the house, so he could walk through the gardens to go inside. His staff greeted him—the two other grooms he kept in town and the stableboy—all pausing to touch their foreheads before getting on with their work. As well as the carriage horses, he kept two mounts in town.

Stepping inside Blaze's stall, he slapped the chestnut's rump. The horse snorted.

"I'll take you out tomorrow, boy," Oliver told him and turned to inform the head groom. "I've been neglecting him lately. Can you have him ready early?" He would of course check the tack himself, even though he had complete confidence in Halford. The groom had been with him since a year after the carriage accident and Oliver would trust him with his life.

Halford nodded. "I'll make sure he's ready for you, sir." Snatching off his cap, he scratched the back of his neck.

Oliver paid attention. The gesture meant Halford wanted to talk to him. "Was there something else?"

"Yes, your grace." Oh, dear. Halford only used Oliver's full honorific when broaching an awkward subject. He straightened, meeting Oliver's eyes. Even though the groom stood half a foot shorter than Oliver, nobody ignored him. He ruled Oliver's stables with the control of an absolute monarch. Knowing a good man when he saw him, Oliver always listened to his concerns. "I took a look at the old curricle, sir."

"I told you to get rid of it. I never want to see the thing again." He would attend the sale rooms tomorrow and purchase a new vehicle and team. He wouldn't be driving the grays again.

"And that has been done. I sent the chassis away, but I've kept the wheels. I thought one could come in useful and the other could go for firewood. The axle is fine, sir. But the wheel is not."

He would have sold the chassis. Oliver had given the whole thing to Halford as a perquisite. He didn't want it near him again, so Halford's news was not welcome.

"Yes, you said that had given way." What was the man getting at? Irritation scratched at his voice.

"The thing is, sir, although the wheel's in a bad shape, I think—" He moved closer and lowered his voice. "I think it might not have been entirely an accident."

Shock sharpened Oliver's senses, sending him into full alert. "What do you mean, man? Explain."

"The wheel was deliberately weakened. The place where the loose spoke met the outer rim was shaved away. Very carefully, so most people wouldn't have noticed."

"But you did."

"I did, sir."

Keeping an eye on his horse, Oliver leaned against the side of the stall, uncaring whether the rough slats caught the fine fabric of his coat. He believed his head groom. Halford had been alive nearly twice as long as he and had been working with horses for longer. What Halford didn't know about horses wasn't worth knowing, and he'd extended his expertise to vehicles too.

"Who would do that?" He kept himself in control, but anger was simmering under the surface. Some men would take an ill mood out on their staff, but Oliver had never been one of those.

"Not our people, sir, I'm sure. We don't have London staff in the mews." Some families employed servants when they came up to town, but because of their situation and his brother's insistence on discretion, Oliver did not. He transported the people he needed from home when they paid their rare visits to the city.

"Then who?"

Halford shook his head regretfully. "I don't rightly know, sir. We get deliveries, hay, feed, tack, leather soap, knives, you name it, and they don't come from the same place. The house servants sometimes nip in here, too. I'll look over the books. That's for sure." He heaved a sigh that came from the depths of his being. "The door's open most of the day. To be honest, anybody could have slipped in here."

Oliver rubbed his chin, deep in thought. Whoever had done this had put Lady Drusilla in danger, and when he considered that his anger tripled. Forcing himself to think analytically was much harder than usual. Accustomed to controlling his moods, Oliver didn't like the way his temper threatened to rip out of control. That did not happen. Did. Not. Happen.

"Somebody came in here and weakened the wheel. They wanted to kill me." His voice shook. "And anyone who might be with me." The carelessness of the act appalled him as much as it angered him. Did they know he would be with Drusilla? He had made no secret of his intention, but who would have thought it worthwhile to use that?

Halford shrugged, his taut body rippling with well-used muscle. His stature fooled many people, but Oliver had seen enough examples of his strength never to take the man for granted. Neither did any of his staff. "I don't think so, sir. More people are injured from carriage accidents than are killed. They might have wanted to hurt you, but if they wanted to kill you there are better ways of doing it without raising the alarm."

That was true. Oliver nodded. Blaze shifted, drawing Oliver's attention. He moved to pat the horse's neck, taking comfort from the animal's sleek solidity. "So probably a visitor, maybe a delivery man, or a paid agent. And somebody who wanted to hurt me. Deliver a warning?" He shook his head. "I've done nothing to deserve that. Not to my knowledge, at any rate." A suspicion curled in his brain. Did someone want to hurt Lady Drusilla?

He could not dismiss the possibility. The Shaws were a rackety lot, and they'd made enemies in their brilliant careers. That would widen the possibilities to an appalling degree.

"Maybe somebody wanted to hurt her ladyship, sir," the groom ventured.

"If that were so, it would have to be after I'd declared my intention to take her driving." The time scale worked in his favor. "Only the household knew that, until I took the vehicle and tooled it around to Grosvenor Square. And the groom never left the carriage alone."

"I made sure of that, sir. No, it was done here, or somewhere quiet, where they had the chance to get the job done."

If someone had tried to hurt her, they would find they had taken on the wrong person. Oliver wasn't easily scared off. On the contrary, he took such acts as a personal challenge. He was going nowhere.

The scent of the stables soothed him, and petting Blaze gave him something to do while he pondered the problem. He would cleave a bit closer to Lady Drusilla. He'd already asked her for permission to become better acquainted. That would turn into courting, while he watched and assessed. He would keep this to himself for the time being, but he'd certainly be more alert.

"Do not change any of your routines," he said. "But find an excuse to watch. I don't want to alert whoever is doing this and drive them away."

"You think they might try again?"

"I don't know. Making me crash the curricle in the park might have been the extent of their plans." It had, after all, brought society's attention back to what had happened to Charles and Oliver all those years before. But why would someone want to do that? To discredit him? Perhaps so. He needed more information.

He had a few business matters to attend to while he was in town, but none were out of the ordinary. A border dispute with a neighbor, the re-roofing of a minor house on the estate, a few other routine matters. There was, of course, the experimental sinking of a shaft at the corner of his land, where he strongly suspected a good seam of coal lay. That was his only new venture. But would anybody bother to come to London and attack him? That was stretching credibility too far for his liking.

The crash could dent his reputation for dependability. The City relied on scandal and gossip.

More likely, whoever did this wanted either him or Lady Drusilla to be hurt or distressed. And because he would not allow her to be hurt, that meant he would cleave closer to her.

Wherever she planned to go next, he would be there.

Why did that decision feel so good?

Chapter 5

Dru flicked open her fan and held it in front of her mouth. "If that soprano screams once more, I'll scream right along with her."

Livia drew a sharp breath. To assuage some of the tedium of this event, Dru had been trying to make her sister laugh for the last half-hour. But that was the nearest she'd come to it. This music recital had to be the worst she'd ever attended. And that was saying something.

With the season in full swing, Lady Comyn had declared her patronage of the new soprano from Italy. This evening was to launch of the latest sensation on society. She'd invited the great and the good to attend, and a hundred of society's finest had accepted. They sat and watched this disaster.

And it had started so well, with a few arias from a moderately good tenor currently appearing at Ranelagh Gardens and a bass baritone who amused them with folk songs. But the star, the soprano, had turned everything bad. They had to sit there for at least another hour before they could applaud politely and go home.

Livia expelled the breath. The soprano chose that moment to screech a top note that put Dru's teeth on edge.

Livia dissolved into giggles.

The people in the row before them growled. Some turned, fingers to lips. When Livia reddened, Dru took pity on her. She coughed, and then coughed again, pulling out her handkerchief. Taking the hint, Livia followed suit, continuing until the signs for hush turned to tuts. Their excuse manufactured, Livia and Dru worked their way past their parents to the end of the row and out of the room. Not a few longing glances followed them, but everybody present could hardly use the same excuse. However, a few coughs did chase them out.

Hurrying upstairs, they found the room put aside for the ladies. The three maids waiting inside got to their feet hurriedly, dropping newspapers and assuming the calm expressions expected of every good maid. Dru waved them aside, while Livia shook with uncontrollable laughter.

Her explosion came barely in time, and with the bewildered maids looking on, Livia alternately howled and cursed at her sister. "This is your fault!"

Dru executed a perfect curtsy. "*Mea culpa.* I'll take any punishment you care to inflict. It was worth it, every bit." She was not immune to the effects the soprano had on her listeners. "I swear, the whole of the audience wanted to do that. What on earth got into Lady Comyn, to inflict that horror on us?"

"She said the woman was the best voice in a generation. She has tin ears if you ask me."

Livia wiped her eyes with her handkerchief. "I will never forgive you. Oh, wait. You saved me an hour of that dreadful woman. I will forgive you." Lifting a hand, she summoned a maid. "Can you find us a glass of wine?"

The servant left the room but came back almost immediately. She bobbed a curtsy and addressed Dru. "Your ladyship, there's a gentleman outside asking after you."

"Really?" One of her cousins, no doubt. Two of her brothers were in town, but neither had accepted Lady Comyn's gracious invitation. However, she'd spotted Ivan stoically suffering, and Max was sitting there with Sophia, his lovely wife. He'd exchanged a totally blank look with her, by which she'd inferred that he was bored rigid and would rather be anywhere else.

"They used us as an excuse," Dru said to her sister. Anything to get out of that torture chamber.

She went outside the room and closed the door quietly behind her.

Lord Trelawny bowed. "I was concerned for your welfare," he murmured. "You seemed quite overset."

"Thank you."

Lord Trelawny was the most promising of the men who had prosaically applied to her father for permission to court her. Despite his age, Trelawny appeared a well-set-up man. His tall, ascetic figure and hook-like nose gave him a superior air. However, she knew he was considerate. She could not imagine such a man getting on the floor and romping with his small children, as her father used to. However, Lord Trelawny was in his late forties. He had many years of vitality left to him, and she was not straight out of the schoolroom. The more unkind in society had suggested he could look in the stables to find his perfect match.

"I wanted to visit you, my lady, as your mother may have mentioned to you, but your unfortunate incident in the park overset my plans."

He talked to her with a pomposity she could not like. Perhaps, though, he didn't know how to approach females. He'd been married for twenty years, and he must have considered himself settled. Nevertheless, she responded tartly. "I regret upsetting your plans, my lord."

He favored her with a kindly smile. "It was hardly your intention, Lady Drusilla. But I trust you will not go driving with the Duke of Mountsorrel again."

"Oh, I have complete confidence in his grace."

"You do?" Lord Trelawny managed the note of doubt without emphasizing it. He did not need to. The implication was enough to express his displeasure. "Did he not tip you out and nearly cause you serious injury less than a week ago? Is that not enough?"

"Sir, he hardly tipped me out on purpose."

"I only tell you what many are saying behind your back. I do not wish to encourage gossip. I prefer to address the matter directly. My late wife always admired that in me. 'Trelawny,' she would say, 'You are the most straightforward of men, and I thank you for it.'"

He was wooing her by referring to his last wife? Dru flicked her fan open. "You must miss her terribly."

His lordship raised a sigh. "Some days, for sure. But we cannot forever dwell in the past. My poor children need a mother and I need a wife."

"I hate to interrupt your tête-a-tête," came a familiar, deep voice from behind her. "I only meant to ensure you were well."

Dru spun around far too quickly, setting her panniers bouncing in a way her mother would not approve of. She took a sharp breath. "I didn't see you inside," she said to the Duke of Mountsorrel.

He gave her a smile that completely melted her. All he had to do was stand there, and he had her in the palm of his hand. "I arrived late, so I sat at the back. I saw you and Lady Livia leave, so naturally I had to enquire after your health." He arched a dark brow.

"We're perfectly well, thank you, sir. Did you happen to catch the latest sensation?"

He winced. "Half a dozen notes only. They were all I needed. May I be of any assistance?"

Lord Trelawny cleared his throat. "I am perfectly capable of taking care of the ladies."

"I have a particular interest in Lady Drusilla."

He did? Dru arched her brows.

"So have I." They squared off like a pair of bulldogs spoiling for a fight.

"You are trawling the town for a bride, sir. Everybody knows that." Mountsorrel growled, so low only Dru could have heard him. The sound was thrillingly intimate.

"Is that not your purpose too, sir?" Trelawny replied. Pushing back the heavy skirts of his coat, he planted his hands on his hips. "Do you not wish for a bride?"

Thrilled, Dru took a step back.

Mountsorrel gave an easy grin that must have been calculated to annoy the staid Trelawny. "If I find one, I will not run away, but I don't wish for a woman who does not want me in return. I am willing to wait. I would also prefer to approach her first, rather than her parents." He cast an assessing glance at the baron. "Time is on my side."

A deliberate insult, which Trelawny took as one, from the way his thin mouth tightened into a straight line. "I already have a nursery full of babes. My wife would not be required to fill it, as yours must. I am searching as much for a companion as a mother to future generations."

"I have time and heirs," Mountsorrel said, his tone tighter. "I do not regard a wife as a necessity, nor will her duties involve anything she does not wish for."

Dru caught her breath. Undoubtedly he was implying that sharing a bed with the baron would be a chore no woman could wish for. His words, accompanied by the irritation he did not trouble to hide could only mean one thing.

These two men were fighting over her.

The stuff of legend. Perhaps her wishes were coming true, after all. At this late stage in her career as spinster was she finally to become a desirable woman? More than one of Strenshall's daughters, a lady sought out because of her family, not herself?

Both men were comfortably off, the duke probably much more than that, and they made their admiration apparent by their squabbling. A thrill worked its way up from her stomach right to the top of her head. Her hair prickled as if it was standing on end.

But she did not have the wit or the beauty to sustain such attention. Already she was straining to think of something clever to say. Her sister Claudia would have thought of it in an instant. Livia had the beauty to sustain attention.

"I will not squabble over a lady," Trelawny said. "Lady Drusilla, I intend to call on you soon. I trust you will receive me."

Oh, heavens! He would propose to her, she was sure of it. "Why, of course."

As if he'd dealt with the matter, his lordship sent the duke a glare of pure triumph, before bowing and turning on his heel.

"Did he mean what I thought he meant?" Mountsorrel demanded.

Dru favored him with an arch smile. "I believe he intends to ask for my hand. He has already approached my father."

"What a slow-top." The duke stared after the earl, who was beating a leisurely retreat down the stairs at the end of the hall. "To approach your parents first. Doesn't he know it's better to make sure of the lady?"

"That's a very enlightened way of looking at the matter."

"Practical," he said with a snort. "I'm seeking a life's partner. I would have thought that was the first consideration."

"Oh." Of course he was right, but she had never thought of marriage that way before. In the circles she moved in, it was a contract, like all the others people signed.

He caught her hand in his. "Do you trust me?"

What had made him ask that? "Yes of course," she said calmly, although her heart was beating a trifle faster than usual.

"Good of you to say so. I merely wanted to let you know that you are safe with me." He paused. "Safer. I would give my life to save yours, if I had to."

She recalled the deft way he had rolled when the carriage had collapsed under them, so she fell on top of him. And oh, what a sensation that had been! "You took great care of me in the park. But you do not have to sacrifice your existence to save mine."

"It's the least I can do."

His words sounded uncomfortably like love, devotion, or adoration. He could not feel that. But she could hardly bring up the subject.

"He staked his claim, you know," Mountsorrel said next. "Trelawny, just now. He believes he got there first."

"I am not a piece of land," she said indignantly, releasing her death grip on the side rail, the better to wave her hands about. "I am a person, not a member of a family, or a field to be fought over."

"Do you want men to fight over you?"

His mild tone did not fool her. "No." Or perhaps she did. The thought thrilled her, because nobody had ever wanted her that much. On the other hand, the forbidden nature of duels drew her. Val had fought for Charlotte, with all the ferocity of a man scorned. Or so Dru understood, because naturally she was not there to witness it.

He had the temerity to laugh. "Liar," he said softly.

"Sir, you forget yourself." Her hurt bled through her carefully cultivated manners. How dare he accuse her of such a thing?

"I think you would thrill to the sight of two men dueling to the death for you." His intimate tone and soft smile warmed her right through.

"But I don't want anyone to die for me." The very thought curdled her blood. Voices rose from the hall downstairs.

He muttered something under his breath, and then louder, he said, "I must deliver you back to the ladies' room, and take the utmost care, must I not?" As if driven to say it, he added, "You felt like silk under my hands that day."

She did not understand his words for a moment, as if her mind had stuttered, unused to such sentiments. But when she did, Dru heated fast. "Me?" she squeaked. She cleared her throat.

"You," he confirmed. "I wanted more. I wanted to pull you tighter and damn the consequences. I must have been out of my mind."

"Perhaps your brain was rattled in the fall," she suggested sweetly.

"Perhaps it was, but it has remained in the same position. I still want to touch you again." He turned to her with the sweetest smile she had ever seen. "Society has sketched out the way a courtship must go. I have decided to become better acquainted with you, Lady Drusilla Shaw, and let you get to know me. So do not give your Lord Trelawney an answer just yet, unless you have made up your mind."

"Sir, you—" She swallowed. What should she say? If she were honest, she'd admit that she wanted the same thing, but was such a desire a basis for a lifetime's commitment? She knew her other suitors, had met them and considered their acquaintance advanced, but she had not encountered the Duke of Mountsorrel above a half dozen times. Less. Yet she did want more. "I can't—"

"Neither can I," he said, "but I want to. I know of you, Lady Drusilla, but nothing prepared me for my reaction to you. You must know of me, about my life and how I conduct myself. I can furnish you with the usual assurances about my suitability as a life partner, your status and so on and so forth. But the truth is, marriage is more than a linking of families."

"Not for some."

"But always for your family," he pointed out. "You are notorious for marrying for love."

She pulled her hands away. She could not possibly allow him to do this. Why, there was a footman stationed outside the ladies' room. He would note everything they did. "Please, let me go and see how my sister is."

A moment later, she returned. "She's asleep. I'll leave her. The soprano will be caroling for another half hour at least. You may go into the drawing room if you wish. I assure you we are perfectly well."

A smile curled its way across his mouth. Fascinated, she watched its progress.

"Oh no, my lady, I'm going nowhere. Not unless you come with me."

"Oh, but I can't leave my sister."

"Such a pity. Not at all? Is she not perfectly safe in there? I could take you for a turn in the garden. You were feeling quite faint, were you not?"

He was offering her a chance to be private with him. Unless he meant to propose marriage to her, their times together were severely limited by propriety. But a gentleman accompanying a lady for a walk in a garden on a fine spring evening, especially with the tacit approval of her sister—that would be allowed.

How could she resist? Sparing him an impish smile, she gave him her hand. Tenderly he placed it on his arm and took her down the stairs to the garden.

A footman opened the side door for them. The sun streamed in, but she hardly noticed it as she went outside with him.

Lady Comyn had an extensive garden, laid out with care, especially for the purposes of entertainment and diversion. She even had a small maze, but when Mountsorrel led her toward it, she shook her head. "Mazes are cold and damp. Do you know the key?"

"Don't you always take the first right?"

"No."

"Shall we try?"

Doubtfully, she looked at the opening. The hedges were little more than calf-height. She could see no point in wasting her time solving puzzles she did not much care about. But when she told him, he only laughed. "Then let us move on."

She found the rose garden more to her taste. Lifting a pink bloom to her nose, she caught the scent. The perfume was often intense in the evening, just before dark fell. They had an hour yet, but they smelled sweet.

"Stay there. You make the most exquisite picture. I should have you painted like that."

Ignoring his request, she straightened and met his eyes. "You are not an incurable romantic, are you?"

"Not in general." Shrugging, he turned away. "But I was struck by the picture you made. That blue gown and the pink roses surrounding you. You should have something made in those colors."

"You are foolish." But he had made her pulse jump. She felt it in her wrist, a throb she had no way of explaining. Her breath shortened.

"You won't take that picture away from me," he said softly.

They walked on, strolling around the deserted garden. The sky glowed as the sun sank slowly, leaving pink streaks in its wake.

"Her ladyship has her guests in her thrall. They dare not leave the drawing room," she commented lightly. The well-sifted gravel stirred under her feet, and they turned a corner.

A path meandered around a few young trees, an almost bucolic scene. Apart, that was, from the sound of carriages passing and the occasional raucous cry from outside. Chairmen and street sellers trying to make a living, not sounds she had ever heard on the family estate. But she could pretend, let a little tranquility sink into her.

Except she found the task impossible with this man by her side. What was happening to her? Even when he said nothing and behaved with perfect propriety he scrambled her senses.

"You're besieged by suitors this season."

Dru bit her lip. Her suitors, no doubt egged on by her father, had pressed their case at the balls and the theater. "Four gentlemen have expressed interest in marrying me." One had dropped out, proposed to another lady. Perhaps he'd fallen in love.

They strolled a short way in silence. A breeze swept across her face, ruffling her hair.

"Are you in a rush to marry?"

Heat rushed to her cheeks. She turned her face away. "Of course not. But my parents decreed I must marry or retire from the field this season. They will not abandon me, of course…"

"But they'll remove their support. They will not actively promote your marriage."

He understood too much. Without her parents working on her behalf, she would have to take what she could find on her own. Although her family had been fortunate, she would not have that. For one thing, she wasn't as forward as her sisters. She could not sally forth boldly as Claudia had. Without the freedoms her brothers were afforded she would wilt away. She shrugged. "It doesn't matter. I will not starve." But she would keep her pride.

"Not of food and drink, maybe. But of love, concern, happiness?" He stopped abruptly.

Placing his hands on her shoulders, he turned her to face him before releasing her. "Not very well done, Drusilla."

He had never used her name like that before. Not without the honorific. The bare word thrilled her. "What? What was not very well done?"

"If you are trying to hurry me, I will have to disappoint you."

Her heart plummeted, but a thread of anger drove her to answer, "I do not connive. If I have something to tell you, I will do it directly, as I am now. We are friends, at least I thought so. I was merely telling you what my mother told me. If I am not married by the end of the season, they will choose my husband for me. If I refuse to agree, they will not actively pursue anyone on my behalf." She bit her lip, the small shot of pain pushing back her tears.

"I beg your pardon." He spoke quietly, but emotion shook in his voice. "I should have known. The truth is that I am a coxcomb, a vain fool who does not deserve to be spoken to as a friend. I didn't think it would be this bad."

"What? What is bad?" Who had hurt him? For his expression showed only somber concern.

"The pursuit. I have had women lie in wait for me. Somehow they know I came to town in search of a potential bride." He swallowed. "I do not like it."

Her anger forgotten, she laid her hand on his shoulder. The soft cloth gave under her palm, giving her a hint of the hard muscle beneath. "I'm sorry. I remember that, from my early seasons. I was the first Shaw daughter to make my entrance into society, and because of who they are, I was pursued relentlessly. Now I am taken for granted, although suitors still arrive, especially of the unsuitable variety." She gave a hard laugh. "Fortune hunters, or men wanting someone amenable and convenient." She tried not to say the words bitterly, but from his expression she had not succeeded. "Not that anyone has tried to abduct me. With my relatives, they would not dare."

"Lord, yes." He gazed down into her face, and she forgot to remove her hand, as she no doubt should have done. "I'm sorry. Walking with you, talking to you. I let out more than I should, more than I mean to. So you have to marry before the end of the season?"

"It's only fair. Livia—"

"I don't give a damn about Livia."

With a convulsive, unconsidered movement, he spread his hands over her waist, and drew her to him. Silk rustled in a rush as he dragged her close and brought his mouth down on hers, sealing them together in a way she had never known before.

Oh, she'd been kissed. She'd even kissed back. But not like this, never like this.

The warmth, the sense that he was surrounding her, holding her within him had never been so strong, so overwhelming. Dru held on and slid her other hand around the back of his neck, where small hairs tickled her fingers when he moved.

His scent swamped her in sensation, hard hot male blended with soap and a faint tinge of lavender, no doubt from his clothes. She nestled closer, rubbed herself against him. Inside her tightly laced bodice, her breasts heated and swelled, and under her rib cage, her heart pounded.

Birds sang, carriages rolled over cobbles, someone in the street shouted about chairs to mend, and still he kissed her. She never wanted him to stop. She rested her head on his shoulder, whimpered into his mouth. He stroked his hands up her back, over the box pleats, as if trying to find a way in.

He touched his tongue to her mouth, a mere flicker, in a sensation she wanted to experience again, but he drew away.

His lips were reddened, as no doubt hers were, too, and his eyes slumberous, the lids drooping over the bright irises in a way that made her shudder in the most secret place in her body. She had told herself she was no innocent. Sometimes in the dead of night she'd touched herself, but she had never done more than explore, the better to know herself. Now, sudden realization hit her with the force of a thunderbolt. The slick, wet feeling—that was for him.

He did not let her go. "Open your mouth, my sweet," he murmured. "Kiss me back."

"I am. I was." Dazed, she licked her hot, swollen mouth.

"Just like that."

When he traced her lips with his tongue, she opened them in a sigh of surrender. He licked into her, thrusting his tongue in her mouth with an insistence that spoke of his need more clearly than words. The intimate invasion overwhelmed her, made her yearn for more and yet more. He groaned into her, and she greedily swallowed the sound. She let it reverberate down her throat to her stomach and beyond, feeding the part of her that was the most lonely and needy. He tasted glorious, so wonderful, as if she could feed off him forever and never want for anything.

His big hands felt delicious on her body, making her feel delicate, cherished even. Gentle strokes turned into harder caresses. He slid his hand under her hair, searching for a way in, and she let him. Her fichu came loose, tugged out from her gown. The cloth pulled up as he explored beneath the fine fabric, tracing the edge of her gown and stomacher with firm touches.

She sucked gently on his tongue, and then with more insistence as her confidence grew. She was desperate for contact, to touch him, feel his flesh under her palms, have the right to explore every part of him. The notion of them naked, intertwined, bored its way into her brain. She would never be free of it. Moaning, she scrabbled at his waistcoat buttons.

He lifted his mouth, tore it away. "We cannot continue." He was panting, his chest heaving.

Shocked into the realization of what they were doing and where they were doing it, she stared up at him with horror. How could she have done this? She never forgot herself, never. Except that now she had.

Shyness and embarrassment swept over her in a great wave. She had thrown herself at him. He could have taken everything he wanted, and she wouldn't have fought him off. What had she been thinking?

Nothing, that was the trouble. She hadn't been thinking anything, only gone with the emotions of the moment.

"Well that takes care of that," he murmured, smiling down at her. He was still holding her tightly, and Dru didn't try to break away.

His words made her frown. "What?"

"I wondered what it would be like to kiss you since I first laid eyes on you." He dropped a light kiss on her forehead, lingering as her father and brothers never did when they kissed her there. "Now I know. It was better than I imagined, and I've imagined it far too much recently."

"You have?"

"What do you think? How could I spend time with you without wanting to do this?"

Eagerly, she stretched up when he kissed her again, but he did not linger to taste and touch. "We cannot indulge here. Come to the theater tomorrow, Dru."

"What?" she said, bewildered by the abrupt change of subject.

"I'll bespeak a private room."

Even that did not evoke outrage, as it should have. She was not the kind of woman to engage in secret trysts in private rooms, and she said so.

He touched her nose, but still held her close to him, one arm lashed around her waist. "I know. It was wishful thinking. But come anyway."

She swallowed. Was this what was meant by bringing a man to scratch? She had no idea, since she had never tried to do it before. "Sir, we've been seeing each other quite often recently. Every day, I think."

"Sometimes," he admitted.

"Twice today." She had seen him earlier on Oxford Street, and he'd stopped to speak to her. Every time she saw him, he warmed her heart, but not like this. No, she could not do it, could not push him. She hadn't meant to earlier, and his reaction had been harsh. Whatever he was thinking, she didn't want to provoke that reaction.

"I knew you were coming here tonight. It's the only reason I accepted the invitation. I wanted to see you again, Drusilla. I admit it. And when we are in private, like this, please call me Oliver."

"Oliver." She tried the word, rolled her tongue around it, tasted it. "My family calls me Dru."

"I am not yet family." A smile flashed across his lips. "But thank you."

That "yet" made her wonder what he meant.

But he did not do anything more or say anything. Did he mean to propose? Because she would accept before the words left his mouth, as long as he kissed her again. Instead, he released her and stroked her fichu back into place. If the neat pleats Forde had put it into were disturbed, they were not in such disarray that people would notice. Her lips, though—they were another matter. They felt full and hot. When she touched them, she was surprised to find them no different to usual.

"Don't do that. Or I'll kiss you again and someone will find us. That soprano won't warble forever."

"And Livia is waiting." Dru had no idea how long she had wandered around the garden with him. The windows stared down at them blankly, but who knew who had seen her indiscretion?

But Dru discovered she did not care. She only wanted more. She had never known such aching urges, things she didn't know about waited for her on the horizon, she just knew it. But only with this man.

He chatted, about what she did not know. He'd given her a chance to recover from the assault he'd inflicted upon her. But such a welcome assault! The effect felt that way. He'd reached every part of her with his kisses and caresses. Her whole body tingled, and he had awoken her to possibilities she'd never thought of before.

Marriage was for linking families and interests. It was for the procreation of children, heirs, to be precise. Not for personal pleasure. Did her parents experience this? Her mother had said she fell in love with her father after their marriage. Could this be why?

"Ready?" His gentle smile reflected none of the turmoil she was feeling.

She let him take her back indoors.

* * * *

Even the screeches of the soprano didn't rouse him from his shock. Oliver had no idea how he had kept a calm demeanor after those kisses in the garden. Just kisses. Gentlemen stole kisses from ladies all the time.

But he'd taken her indoors, restored her to her family, and repaired to his own seat at the back of the room. He would have left, but Lady Comyn would probably take it amiss, and she was a particular crony of his mother's. Better suffer half an hour of excruciating singing than several weeks of his surviving parent's opprobrium. Even though she did not live with him any longer, she could write, and she did. Screeds of the stuff.

Besides, the respite gave him a chance to recover from the overwhelming experience in the garden. |He'd wanted a flirtatious kiss. Not this... devastation of his senses. Did she know what she'd done? He guessed not, because apart from the disarray of her clothes, which he had caused, and the reddening of her lips, she did not seem as perturbed as he.

At least his heart rate had returned to normal by the time the woman finally finished murdering opera.

The applause sounded like relief to Oliver. From his neighbors he gathered that she'd been warbling for two hours.

Lord Osborne commented, "I generally turn off my watch, but it came as a relief to hear the chiming. Two and a quarter hours, by my reckoning." Drawing out the watch from his waistcoat pocket, he touched the button at the top and let the lid spring up. The instrument had a particularly interesting way of marking the hours. A man was busy driving his cock into a woman, who had flung her skirts up to receive him.

"Midnight must be interesting," he murmured.

While he admired the ingenuity of the maker, he'd rather have a watch he could take out whatever the company. But the gentlemen sitting on the back row snickered and exclaimed on the item. Lord Osborne had to snap it hurriedly shut when the lady in front turned around to demand to know what had amused them so much. When Lord Osborne restored the item to his pocket, she flushed beetroot red and returned to her friends.

Oliver smiled at her rigid back. The floral fabric strained at the seams, but he was too much of a gentleman to say so. Only to think it.

At least the soprano did not perform an encore. Unless Oliver had entered during the extra pieces. Funny that he had not anything at all in the garden. The woman's voice would have carried considerably, but he had been aware of nothing except the lady in his arms. Dru had taken him over completely, swamping him with sensation.

He stayed seated until the company began to disperse. Lady Comyn had refreshments laid out in another room, but he didn't intend to stay. He had too much to think about.

He merely nodded to Drusilla as she passed him. She jerked, but only slightly, and then returned his greeting. Oliver didn't leave until he was sure everyone was gathered in the other room, then he took his leave of his hostess. She asked after his brother, but as usual he answered in a noncommittal way and left.

When he got home, he headed upstairs.

Charles responded to his gentle tap on the door.

"I think I will propose to Lady Drusilla," he said as soon as he had poured himself the sherry Charles insisted on.

His brother nodded. "I thought you might. Mama may not approve. You know how straitlaced she can be!" He laughed, but Oliver didn't join in. "Once she hears, she is bound to come straight up to town."

"I'm sorry, I don't understand. She's from one of the premier families in the country."

Charles's hand tightened on the arm of his chair. He was wearing a nightshirt and robe, but he didn't sleep much. His wheeled chair would be pushed to the bed by his valet when he rang the little bell that he carried everywhere, and then he'd be lifted into it. "The scandals, dear boy."

Oliver couldn't imagine living that way, or with the utterly terrifying fits that exhausted Charles for days afterward. He admired his brother for his stoicism and his constant cheerfulness. So he answered mildly. "They are, however, still extremely influential. Nobody wants to upset them."

"The Shaws or the Emperors?" Charles enquired mildly. "It was the Shaws in particular I was referring to. Their relatives have helped them cheat the gallows, survive a runaway marriage, and Lord knows how many duels and gaming debts."

"Gaming debts? I was not aware of that." Were they fortune hunters in disguise? Many a family lived extravagantly while owing thousands.

Charles grunted. "They tend to win, so the debts are usually temporary. The people who do not need the money always do win, don't you find?"

Oliver shrugged. "I don't gamble very much. After an hour at the tables, I grow bored." He had too many things to think about. Simple games of chance failed to hold his attention for long, but everybody played, so he indulged for an hour or two on occasion.

Charles shifted, moving his body from side to side carefully.

Oliver swallowed. He knew the problems Charles had, and what was entailed in caring for him, although Charles never allowed him to help. Or even to be in the room when his attendant did what was necessary. He knew better than to mention his brother's obvious discomfort. Charles would poker up and order him not to talk about it, that he was perfectly well. Oliver gleaned what he could from his brother's attendant and companion, Burnett, who was utterly devoted to him.

"Not to mention the younger brother's sins," Charles said in a low voice, as if someone were listening.

Oliver knew exactly who Charles meant. "Lord Darius has allied himself to a lawyer and set up in business with him."

"We know that is not all."

Yes, he did, but he had never seen Lord Darius become over-affectionate in public with the man people assumed was his lover. The pair did not make too many appearances in society, either. As far as he knew, no outright scandal had ensued, even though there had been a great deal of gossip.

"I would think seriously about allying yourself to that family," Charles advised now. "I'm not sure one of them would make you happy. And above all, Oliver, you deserve to be happy."

Oliver did not cry, but the closest he ever came was in his brother's company. "I'm not sure about that," he said gruffly, and cleared his throat. "I do what I can."

"Would Lady Drusilla make you happy?"

Yes, so much. "She is young, pretty, and eager." He was still processing their astonishing kiss. No kiss he'd ever had before had affected him that way. He could still feel her hands on his shoulders, her fingers in his hair. She'd marked him for life.

"The worst woman is the one who gets her claws into a man and turns him into her pet," Charles observed casually, picking up his hand bell.

Oliver had not thought of his relationship with Dru in that way. But yes, he would do almost anything to get her into his bed. Perhaps Charles was right. Was physical attraction, even something as powerful as what he shared with Drusilla, enough?

He should let matters between them cool down a little before he found himself caught in a trap he might come to regret.

Chapter 6

A week later, Dru had given up on Oliver. She had gone to bed every night reliving their kiss, the way he'd held her so close. She tried to imagine what it would be like to share a bed with him. Or a couch, for that matter. Or a table. She wasn't so innocent as to believe all personal relations happened in the bedchamber.

And the proof of passion was around her every day. Even her brother Darius, who brought his partner to dinner that week, was deeply in love. When nobody, least of all Darius, had believed such a thing possible, by dint of a few sacrifices Darius had found bliss. Although Dru could not begin to understand what he shared with Andrew Grey. Some things were beyond even her vivid imagination. For all she knew, they did not share a bed or engage in the most intimate of exchanges.

While society and the church disapproved what Darius had done, Dru had grown up seeing her brother grow ever more unhappy and distant. Now he'd returned to the carefree boy she had played with in their youth, happy and fulfilled in his new life. Again, the Shaws had skirted scandal and escaped the cut direct, the way society sliced someone out of its midst. If they had done that, the family would have followed them. Because of their wealth and influence, society tolerated them.

Such reminders only served to make Dru more uncomfortable as the week wore on and she heard nothing from his grace the Duke of Mountsorrel. His partiality to her seemed to have disappeared, as had his presence. Yet she read of reports of him visiting this ball or that performance at Drury Lane. Just not when she was there.

If he had decided to cut the connection, she could not force anything. Just mourn what could have been. And move on to a new suitor, even though her heart would break when she did so.

After breakfast one morning, her mother called her to her side. "Go into the drawing room, dear. A gentleman wishes to have a word with you."

Dru's throat closed. "Who?"

"Lord Trelawny."

Oh, no. Why did it have to be him? Of all the gentlemen vying for her hand, he was the one she liked most. But only liked. Perhaps that was for the best. It might be a sign, that he was the first of her suitors to come up to scratch. He had intimated as much when he put his primitive claim on her at the musicale. "Oh. Has anyone else spoken to Papa?"

"Not since the last time we spoke."

Her final spark died. The fire that Oliver had set last week was now completely extinguished. She would not think of him, would not speak of him ever again. When she saw him in public, she'd grant him a distant nod. That was all. She would be the first member of this generation of her family to enter into an arranged marriage.

Her only married sister, Claudia, had done well, but her love affair with her husband displayed itself whenever they met. So did their frequent quarrels, which both appeared to thrive on.

Dru would have a perfectly conventional, calm marriage. She'd bear children and sail through the rest of her life with tranquility and absolutely no violent emotions.

What a prospect to anticipate! Every bone in her body revolted at such an idea. But she would do it. Perhaps she would find the same connection with her chosen husband as she would have with the Duke of Mountsorrel. For all she knew, that incredible reaction could happen again with someone else. How did she know how these things worked?

Outside the drawing room, she smoothed her voluminous skirts with a hand that had become sweaty. Lifting her chin, she smoothed back an errant curl and prepared to meet her fate. The footman, at his most stiffly formal, probably aware of the decision she was about to take, threw open the door.

She walked through, ready to take the step that would alter the rest of her life.

* * * *

Oliver had not realized how small the London house was before. It had been a convenience, a place he could enjoy because there were no childhood memories to trip him up. Now, he felt penned in, like a sheep waiting for the knife of the slaughterman. The whole place reeked of sickness.

The day after his conversation with Charles, his brother had fallen into one of his fits. Three men had to hold him down for fear he would hurt himself. After he had recovered he had vomited the contents of his stomach and continued to do so. He'd run a dangerously high fever. Oliver was beside himself. Would Charles's sufferings never end?

He sat with Charles when his brother allowed him to, but he was still annoyingly independent. He insisted Oliver attended a few functions, to demonstrate to the outside world that everything was well in his household. He kept his attendants to their usual minimum, which meant the three men were more than busy in the hours and days following.

When he visited his brother just after lunch, Oliver found one of the men asleep in a chair by his brother's bed and Charles tossing and moaning. Oliver did not blame the man who had been up for three days straight through, but set to helping his brother himself.

Stripping off the bedcovers and Charles's nightshirt, he'd found the bowl of water put ready and set to sponging him. He tucked towels around Charles's poor body and bathed him in cool water until Charles opened his eyes with a snap. Shock made them wide.

"I don't want you," he whispered hoarsely, reaching for the sheet. "Wake Latimer."

"No. He is exhausted. Let me do this, Charles. It's me or no one."

Charles groaned and gave up, obviously too tired to do anything more to stop him. He watched listlessly as Oliver smoothed the damp sponge over the hottest parts of his brother's body. He soaked a cloth and draped it across Charles's eyes. Charles sighed, relief probably.

After, he covered Charles's naked body with a light sheet and blanket. Whoever had tucked him in before had done their job too well. There was no need for heavy blankets and quilts.

By the time he'd finished, his brother was asleep and Latimer had woken.

Oliver nodded to him. "I think he'll do now." He glanced at the various potions laid out on the dressing table, sighing when he found the laudanum. A necessary medicine, but not one he wanted his brother to take on a regular basis. But it helped with his crippling headaches and gave him relief from the constant agony he suffered.

Every time he saw his brother's body, guilt racked Oliver, but he refused to turn away. The twisted legs, the useless arm. Without the disguise of his elegant clothes, Charles's slim, white body spoke of his daily agony. He softly drew the sheet up and left the room.

Oliver had done his duty, and he would continue to do so. Was it so terrible for him to ask for a little pleasure for himself?

With his brother asleep, he saw no reason not to continue with his plan. After all, nothing ventured, nothing gained. If the lady had promised herself to another man, he could do little. Charles had kept him busy this last week, and he could not do anything but care for him.

Half an hour later, resplendent in dark green velvet, he left the house. Deciding to walk, he ignored the chairmen gathered at the corner of the square and nodded to the watchman. Midafternoon, the visiting hour. He should probably seek an interview with Lord Strenshall, but he rebelled against it. As he'd told Drusilla in Lady Comyn's garden, he wanted to be sure of her before he sought formal permission. After all, he would be marrying her, not her father.

As he strode through the streets of the West End of London, his heart lifted. With the sick room behind him, he could finally continue what he had left off last week. Here the air smelled as fresh as it ever got in the city. The tang of coal smoke was nearly undetectable but served as a constant reminder of the thousands of people here. While he had to nod to several people on his way, he did not stop to chat. He wasn't in the mood for chatting. Exchanging the time of day was completely out of the question.

Tension did not affect him, but even as he steeled himself, he knew he was lying. Of course he was tense. He'd made a decision that would impinge on the rest of his life. But although he felt tension, he had no regrets or misgivings. Not where he was concerned. He'd accepted the doubts his brother had imparted, but he would not allow them to rule his life.

Even less now. The only person who would do that was Lady Drusilla Shaw. His fate was completely in her delicate hands. Her delicate ink-stained hands, he recalled with a smile.

The London house of the Marquess of Strenshall was always a hive of activity. The glossy black front door lay open. Oliver tipped his hat to the couple leaving, barely registering their presence, before he strode purposefully inside.

The hall contained two liveried footmen and a butler, distinctive in his dark coat and superior demeanor. Much like his own man. Perhaps that air was required of them. Maybe somewhere was a family that schooled them.

Planting his mind firmly in the present, he handed his hat and gloves to the tallest footman and asked if Drusilla was at home.

"I'm afraid she is otherwise engaged, your grace," the butler said. He stood a head shorter than Oliver, his hands loosely by his sides, a smooth almost-smile on his face. Oliver took an instant dislike to him. "Should I inform her that you have called?"

A suspicion took hold of Oliver's mind. "Who is she with?"

"I'm afraid I cannot vouchsafe that information."

No, and Oliver would not want him to. Until he produced a couple of guineas from his pocket, and let them click in his hand. The butler remained silent. Oliver added another gleaming coin.

The butler sighed. "Her ladyship gave permission for her to speak to another gentleman in private."

Oliver handed over the coins. That was all he was getting, but it was all he needed. He nodded. "Is her ladyship at home?"

"Not receiving today, your grace. Would you like me to inform her of your presence?"

Oliver considered. He had moved well into the hall and stood at the base of the stairs. Another ten minutes and his mission could be rendered useless. A gentleman would withdraw, leaving the field to his rival. Oliver had learned that a gentleman had his limits. He could also appear and disappear at will.

Turning, he took the first stair and then the next two. "I'll inform her myself," he threw back, without slowing his pace.

A shout went up from behind him, and feet thumped behind him. He thought that might happen, which was why he was taking the stairs two at a time. At the top, he turned right, racing across the short, though gracious landing. Another footman stood outside the door to the main drawing room.

Oliver nodded to him. "Let me in. Now."

The man flung open the door. Oliver would give him five guineas before he left. Ten.

Inside, a man knelt in front of the woman on the sofa. Drusilla made a magnificent picture, the sun lighting her hair, revealing the golden glints, her ultramarine gown spread around her. The man, not so much. He should be out of the picture.

He leaped to his feet and spun around as Oliver made his precipitate entry. "Sir!" he exclaimed indignantly.

Oliver straightened his coat. "My lord." He spared the man a brief nod. "May I have a word with Lady Drusilla?"

* * * *

Dru had not understood what a prosy bore Lord Trelawny could be until she received his proposal of marriage. He'd reached his fifth paragraph when she heard the noise outside.

The door burst open, and if it were not for the stop it would have crashed into her mother's precious lacquer cabinet. As it was, the duke was ready for the rebound and caught it on the flat of his hand as it sprang back at him. She had to admire his presence of mind. Even as she leaped to her feet and wondered what the right response should be, she noticed little details about him. She took them in like a woman dying of thirst gulped water. She saw the way the end of his neckcloth was thrust through the buttonholes of his coat in the latest fashion and how his hands were clenched by his side. And how well his green velvet coat and waistcoat would compliment her blue gown.

Unfortunately, Lord Trelawny had chosen a shade of apricot that made him look bilious, but she had done her best not to hold his choice of finery against him. Nor his pomposity. He'd made a speech at her.

But if he had not prosed on, she'd have accepted him by now. As soon as she saw Mountsorrel, she knew that she would have made a terrible mistake. Choosing mediocrity over taking a risk and living. Even though mediocrity could be comfortable and easy.

Comfortable and easy were no longer good enough.

She decided on a moderate remark, considering Mountsorrel was breathing enough fire for two. "Did the footman not tell you I was not at home?"

The duke's eyelids drooped, but not before Dru had caught the wicked gleam in the depths of his eyes. "And yet, you are. Do you pay your servants to behave mendaciously?"

"Of course we do." Didn't everyone? The world would be interesting if they did not. *I'm sorry, but her ladyship is entertaining her lover. I'm sorry, the earl's latest tantrum destroyed the drawing room. I'm sorry, but nobody in this family likes you, and they've told me not to admit you.*

"Of course," he repeated, and joined her in watching his lordship ungracefully scramble to his feet.

"You should have planned that part before you got on the floor," Mountsorrel observed.

He received a savage glare from the earl in response.

"I would prefer that you leave me alone with my betrothed." Trelawny reached for Dru's hand.

She clasped her hands tightly in her lap, indignation making her stubborn. "I fear you are mistaken, my lord. We hadn't got to that part yet."

A grown man should not scowl.

Mountsorrel closed the door much more softly than when he'd entered. Leaning against it, he folded his arms across his chest. She couldn't help noticing the way his shoulders flexed.

"Do go on, my lord. I would hate to think I had interrupted something…important."

That was unkind of him. But undeterred, Trelawny turned his back on the duke. And at last, got down to business. "I have long admired your beauty and dignified behavior in sometimes difficult circumstances. Your beauty outshines the sun. I would be honored if you would accept my hand in marriage, so I might care for you for the rest of our lives."

"And bear your heirs?" she prompted. What did he mean by "difficult circumstances"? Did that imply he would not wish her to contact her family?

He nodded. "That too, although you are probably aware my last wife presented me with three children. You would be the perfect mother to my poor babies."

"He wants a drudge," Mountsorrel put in. "And somebody to warm his bed."

Dru shot the duke a quelling glare. "And you don't?"

"I'm waiting my turn," the duke said. "I am fortunate to be second in the queue."

"There are a line of men waiting to ask for my hand in marriage?" Scorn infused her voice. "After all these years?"

When the duke would have replied, she held up her free hand. Fortunately, he did not reply to her last question. She addressed the earl. "Lord Trelawny you do me great honor. Indeed, I thank you most sincerely for your kind offer. However—" As Mountsorrel sucked in a breath, no doubt to start again, she gave him another stare. "However, I am concerned with your remark about difficult circumstances. I've been carefully reared, I come from the best stock in England and received the finest education. I do not consider anything difficult about that." She'd made herself sound like a horse, but she couldn't help that now. Her breeding was the least of her problems.

"Madam, your family is one of the most prominent in the country, but not always for the best reasons." Trelawny kept wading deeper into the mire. "I would care for my wife—you—with the utmost attention, and I would remove you from this den of iniquity."

Dru ignored Mountsorrel's snort of derision. She would scold him for that. And she would make him suffer for standing there instead of retreating gracefully.

Except in that case she might have been forced to accept Trelawny's offer.

"Sir, you are speaking of my family," she said, as sternly as she could. "I am deeply grateful for your kind offer, but I fear I must refuse. Anyone who marries me also acknowledges my strong connection to my family."

"I see." He stepped back.

She took a deep breath.

"I am very sorry to hear that."

But also relieved, she guessed, from the expression on his face. His slight, superior smile had returned, and he held his head in the haughty way she recognized in him.

"I am forced to accept your refusal. I will not renew my request." He took a step back and bowed to her.

She didn't offer her hand. She might not get it back.

Turning smartly, he went to the door, which the duke obligingly opened for him.

She turned around and went to the window, staring out at the street below, folding her arms under her breasts. She felt rather than heard him come up behind her.

"My turn," he said softly.

"To do what?"

"Don't you know?"

She lifted one shoulder in a careless shrug. "I swear I do not have the faintest idea. And for your information, I had decided to reject the earl's offer before you'd even entered the room."

"Good. But I wouldn't have let you do it. He's not suitable for you. You must know that."

"I didn't, until he started talking to me. Then I realized I wouldn't abide more than a year with him. We just do not suit."

"Your family won't abide him, either."

"Careful." She added a warning note to her voice.

He grazed his hand along the silk of her sleeve. Even that slight touch affected her, although she tried not to let it. She continued to stare out of the window. Trelawny crossed the road, dodging the traveling carriage that swept past as if it had been laying in wait for him.

"Lord Trelawny is not having a good day," she remarked.

"I have yet to discover if I am to follow suit."

Mountsorrel sounded grave, but she wasn't done. "You should speak to my father. Have you done so?"

"Not yet. I would rather speak to you first."

"What if my father says no?"

He paused. "I will have to pray that he doesn't. But the decision is yours. You are the person who will have to live with the consequences."

She turned then, facing him, her astonishment not hidden. "The consequences? What do you mean?"

His face was bland, completely devoid of expression. What was he hiding? What consequences? "Of taking me. I am not a paragon. If you have waited to find a perfect man, I am far from that."

"Thank God," she said fervently. "I couldn't live up to the expectations of the perfect man." He was dancing around the subject, as he always did. Was she then expected to push him? She would not. She absolutely refused. "Lord Trelawny told me that he would provide for me. He assured me he would not touch the settlement my father wishes to give me. Will you promise the same?"

"Just that?" He shook his head. "Paltry. I could buy you the moon, except it wouldn't do you any good. I could find the largest diamond in London for you. But you don't wear diamonds often. You prefer sapphires."

He'd noticed that much about her. Trelawny probably wouldn't have discerned that in ten years. She would have been a status symbol, an accessory he could wear on his arm at important events. But Mountsorrel noticed her, Drusilla, not the daughter of the Marquess of Strenshall.

"You're not serious now."

"Not entirely. But if you want the diamonds, say the word."

"Even if I refuse you?"

"Even then." His smile melted her. "May I ask now?"

Her heart thumped far too hard, but she kept her control. Just. Because she wanted the answer to another question. "Why did you keep away from me?"

He closed his eyes, and an expression of pain crossed his face. Opening his eyes again, he reached for her hands, and held them between his own. "I will tell you nothing but the truth. I confess I have been caring for my brother who has not been well recently, but even then I could have written to you. But I did not. I didn't know if you would want to. I backed away. Our previous meeting in the garden at Lady Comyn's... It unnerved me, I confess. I came to town to look for a wife, but only halfheartedly, to please my mother, who wants to see me wed. Then I met you." His smile deepened, grew more intimate. "I was taught that great ladies are reared to do their duty but no more. While I have seen enough to cast doubt on that, I still saw marriages made cold-bloodedly. I assumed the arrangement was a business transaction, and I would have the same when the time came. Then I met you."

"Oh? And you can't engage in a business transaction with me?" She wasn't sure what to think.

"I daresay I could." He shook his head. "No, that is wrong. I can't. Not with you. If you stood here in nothing more than the clothes you wore, I would take you and care for you much the same. That is not what I should feel. I should care about dowries, connections, Parliamentary influence and the rest. But I do not, not when I'm with you. I only think about those things later."

"That's the best thing anybody has ever said to me." She breathed through the words, trying to control her wayward body. Her heart pounded against her ribs, her breath came shallowly. He really thought those things about her? He wanted her, not what she brought with her? Dru knew she brought a lot. Her father had taken her through the settlement, the lands and money she would bring to the marriage, and what he would expect from her future husband. Now she wished she had listened with more attention. He, clearly, did not.

"I don't care about land and all the things that should be forefront in my mind. That unnerved me. I needed time to think. I beg your pardon if I did not immediately rush to your side, and I see I barely stopped you making your choice."

"Is that why you shoved your way in here?"

He nodded. "I've never behaved so badly in my life before. But I'd do more than that for you."

"Would you fight a duel for me?"

"Like your brother did for his beloved?" He nodded. "Probably. Especially given the circumstances of your brother's challenge. Do I have to?"

Mutely, she shook her head.

"Do you want me to wait longer?"

She found her voice. "If you do, my mother will have me married off quick smart. She says I must decide."

"Have you decided?"

She wanted more. "Kiss me," she said, more daring than she'd ever been before.

So there, in front of the window where the whole of fashionable London could gather and watch, if they wished, he did as she asked.

Drawing her closer, he released her hands. Immediately she clasped his shoulders, needing the solidity of male muscle to steady her. He wrapped his arms around her, gazing into her eyes before he let his heavy-lashed lids drop as he brushed his lips against hers.

That first gentle touch slowly increased, and as if the progression was natural, she opened her mouth and accepted his tongue, giving him hers in response. They tasted each other, warmth flowing from one to the other and back again. Lifting one hand, she cupped his cheek, thrilling at the rough male flesh under the delicate skin of her palm.

He grunted, such a masculine sound. She would have smiled, had her mouth not been engaged in responding to his increasingly passionate embrace. He ran his hands up the heavily ribbed fabric covering her back to the high neckline and traced the edge, just as he had before. Cradling her head as if she were the most delicate thing in the world, he attacked her mouth with passion and vigor, teaching her how to respond. She had so much to learn.

He lifted his head. "Perhaps we should take this somewhere a little less public." He glanced at the window.

"I don't care."

"You should."

His reddened lips shaped the words but she took a moment to catch up with the meaning. She didn't care for anything except this.

"Come, my sweet. We have a lot to discuss."

Taking her hand, he led her to the sofa, where she sank in a froth of silk and lace, her skirts shushing around her. Unceremoniously, he lifted one side and took his place next to her, draping the excess fabric over his lap. That way he could stay close to her, and she wanted that above all things.

"My mother will send someone in here soon," she warned him. "She will know when you arrived, and she won't give us more than half an hour together."

"But you can do so much in half an hour!"

She blinked, shocked at the deep, wicked tone infusing his voice. "We can't do anything. Can we?"

His chuckle reverberated around the room. As if to remind them, the clock banged out the quarter-hour. A quarter past what, she didn't know or care.

His slight jerk made her laugh. "Everybody reacts like that to the clock."

"It's hideous," he said, without turning his head to look at the monstrosity. The cherubs would be smirking at him. They always did.

"But expensive. And it does remind people when it's time to go."

"Do you want me to go?"

Hastily, she shook her head. "Not yet. I want you to kiss me again."

"Willingly."

He cradled her so tenderly, he made her feel precious. In his arms she didn't feel inadequate or clumsy. She came from a large, loving family, but as the middle child between two sets of twins, she'd often been left on her own.

This time he kept the embrace gentle. He gave her several small, sweet kisses, peppering them over her face and lips, before taking her earlobe into his mouth and nipping it lightly.

"Oh!" Who would have thought the earlobe would be a sensitive place? Not she, for sure. She adored being this close to him, feeling his breath hot on her skin, and his body pressing against hers. He did not try to move her neckcloth, and she was sorely tempted to do it herself. All of her against all of him.

But they would have to wait for that. The prospect of having him to herself filled her with joy. Was this love? She had absolutely no idea, but she would accept it. "What is love?" she said, before realizing she'd said it aloud.

"Love?" Abruptly he drew back. "Why did you say that?"

He'd withdrawn, and to her surprise she found that it hurt. She didn't want him to do that.

"I mean, I love my family, of course. But some people do astonishing things in its name." She'd wanted to say it, but his withdrawal warned her she was treading on delicate ground.

"I don't know," he confessed. "I take it for granted, I suppose. And yes, they do, but I suspect their reason is not always love. Maybe they wanted to escape from a difficult home life. Maybe they want to be in love. I don't believe it is necessary for a happy marriage."

She swallowed her disappointment. "I wasn't sure. That's all. This is so new to me."

"Good," he said with emphasis.

"Would you not have preferred me to know more about…kissing and such before I met you?"

"And such?" A smile tilted his mouth, and she wanted to forget any conversation and kiss him again. "No."

He would not let her draw him on the matter, however much she teased, so she asked him the other question that burned at her. "Do you have a mistress?"

His arm, which was draped over her shoulders, stiffened. "You know that is none of your concern, don't you?"

"I know no such thing." The very notion of him kissing someone else as he'd kissed her repelled Dru. She sat up, pushing him away.

"Then you should not have asked. Do you want the answer?"

She nodded. Of course she did. If she had to share her bed with an invisible third person, she wanted to know it. "I won't be fooled."

"Some women dislike the intimacies necessary in making a child. That's why men take mistresses. Some of the time."

"Well, I'm sure I will not dislike them." She remembered something he'd said. "You wanted honesty from me. That should go both ways, or it will not work at all." She did not look at him, but she heard his sigh.

"You are right. I don't want an obedient, meek wife who endures my presence in her bed for twenty minutes every year. No, my dear, I do not have a mistress. I had one, but I presented her with her congé before I came to town. I knew I would most likely return with a wife. To my mind, it would be an insult to expect a wife to tolerate someone else so early in the marriage."

Turning, she met his eyes, still dark with the passion they had just shared. Relief flooded her, so she wanted to fall back into his arms and forget what she'd said. "Thank you." She bit off her next question. Did he plan to take another, when he considered the initial stage of their marriage done? Or when she was pregnant and unable to receive him in her bedchamber?

He took her hands between his, as he had before, warming them, stilling their trembling. "My dear, I want a partner, a friend, a companion, and a lover. I thought I would not find all those things in one person, but I am beginning to believe that in you, I have found it. You make me laugh, you are deliciously responsive, and I already know you are intelligent."

His last compliment delighted her the most. "I'm not sure, but I try."

"You come from a very bright family. They did not reach their current altitude on birth alone." He huffed a laugh. "Although I daresay that helped."

"Julius married a governess, and my oldest brother married the daughter of our land steward." They married for love, she reflected with melancholy. True, the two ladies in question had other more private identities, but the men would not have married them had they not fallen irrevocably in love.

She had always dreamed of that, but now she had to put away childish expectations. That, she realized regretfully, included the stories she spun for her own amusement. They would have to go. All of them.

As the clock hammered the half hour, the door opened and her parents came in. Her new life was about to begin.

Chapter 7

Dru had seen the marriage rituals before, but she had never been a part of it. Two of her siblings had married in an irregular way, but this was to be a society wedding, with all the trappings. They would marry by special license at St. George's, since having the banns read was considered unnecessary, and more importantly, unfashionable, but they would wait the requisite three weeks. That would give her time to assemble her trousseau. As if she didn't have enough clothes already.

But her mother ordered the entire contents of her clothespress emptied, and she called a mantua-maker in. To make matters worse, she held a levee. That meant tradesmen, friends, anyone could come and share the filtering of Dru's wardrobe.

And they did. A pile of clothes Dru was fond of but were, admittedly, out of date, grew as the morning advanced. Some would be altered to the latest style, a few would go to the maid. Of course Forde was quietly overjoyed because a perquisite of her position was to take rejected garments. She usually sold them to a shop where she did regular business, so Dru supposed she was helping London's economy with her sacrifice.

In return, she was to receive a plethora of new gowns in the latest colors and styles. That included the smaller hoops currently in fashion, so she could be grateful for small mercies. New lace and ribbons, trims exploding out of their boxes in glittering perfection, embroidery samples that astonished. The large, bold patterns in style when she bought her coming-out gowns, that she'd had made over, had been replaced with smaller, more delicate ones.

Dru committed to a week of choosing and trying on. She would not have been human had the display not thrilled her, but the extra comments did not come as particularly helpful.

She lingered over a ruffle of French lace that bore a dull gray stain, the remains of ink. Her mother sighed when she saw it. "If you insist on writing, we will order more linen and an overgown." Dru swallowed, but kept hold of the scrap. Constant washing had dulled it and it fell limply in her hand, but she didn't want to lose it. Pretending to drop it on the pile of discards, she shoved it into her pocket. A souvenir of the night she'd met her future husband.

The one she had disparaged in her novel. She could smile about that because the evidence was consigned to the kitchen fire. Instead, she'd made her villain the opposite of Mountsorrel—Oliver, as he had bade her call him. She still stumbled on the word. It seemed so…intimate, and when she thought of how intimate they would become, she grew flustered and confused.

She liked the name, though. It suited him. He had an integrity she associated with the old Lord Protector and a stillness that suited him, rather than the more frivolous and vain Charles. Her family had supported the Commonwealth. It had done very well during its short reign, and thanks to the magnanimity of King Charles the Second, had not suffered for it. The Shaws had prospered and even provided the king with a mistress.

Fingering a length of amber satin that everybody had agreed did her no favors, Dru sighed. The well-meaning friends had probably helped her to not make an expensive mistake, but she loved the fabric. She would probably look terrible in it. "I'd like a yard of this put by, please," she murmured.

"We agreed it was not for you," her mother said, and would have waved her on to the next piece.

"I have an idea for an embroidery."

"Ah. Yes, a yard," her mother agreed reluctantly.

That way at least she would get to handle the pretty stuff. Like most ladies she embroidered, but she had no idea what to do with the pretty fabric. She would keep it and stroke it, perhaps make a simple pincushion of it. All her life she'd made protests that nobody noticed but she found satisfying. Sometimes they had worked out nicely, and others, such as when she'd climbed the old oak in the Home Park and fallen out of it, not so well. She had broken her leg, but the break had been a clean one and had healed well.

The next fabric, a crimson silk, received general approbation from the company. The sample was passed around, and everyone said how pretty it was. Then her mother came to the subject of her court gown.

Damn. Of course one presentation would not be enough. She'd have to return after her marriage. The old King rarely received anymore but left it to his oldest surviving son and his wife, the Duke and Duchess of Cumberland.

The gown would be a mantua and would have hoops so wide she would take up a whole corridor all on her own. Dru let her mind drift as they discussed it, taking very little interest in it but smiling and nodding. Was that why she had passed unnoticed for so long? Her book was a kind of revenge. She'd written people into it, made them easily identifiable. Then she'd acted as a god and made terrible or wonderful things happen to them, depending on her reaction to them in real life.

The main tale had followed a man and his drive to become king of his country. He had murdered his way there, starting with his brother. Dru had seen Garrick's *Richard the Second* and loved it. That had started her on her trail. Some nights she could hardly wait to get home to write the latest installment. Her hero and heroine were saintly individuals who could not exist in real life. Far too good, far too perfect, and most people would want to slap them silly.

Secretly she'd given them love scenes that went far beyond the acceptable. Knowing her story would never see the light of day, she'd let herself go, pushing her imagination as far as she could. When she found a secret trove of very wicked material that must have belonged to her grandfather, she raided them for passages, thrilling to what she found. Obviously most of the descriptions and pictures were impossible. Who would agree to have such things done to them? A woman receiving seven lovers in one night, sometimes two at a time?

Hastily, she turned her mind away from the books and engravings she'd uncovered. Now she was facing such a fate, she had no wish to imagine herself out of them. Scurrilous though they were, they made her uncomfortable in a good way, something she was not sure she understood. But instead of faceless, anonymous men she thought of Oliver in them—in every one. A yearning she barely understood filled her, heating her and bringing moisture to the place between her legs. She knew no words for it except the forbidden, wicked ones she'd read.

Then she saw the horror they had nearly chosen for her court mantua. Extremely expensive and exquisitely embroidered, but horrible for all that. "No," she said firmly. "Not that."

Her mother turned to her, hands on hips, outrage in every line of her features. Not that there were many of those, because she painted her face every day. "You just agreed to it. You'll make a show in this."

"I'd look like a walking sofa," Dru said bluntly. It was high time she took control of the way she looked, even if she did not care for the occasion. "I'll take something in dark blue, with pink embroidery, perhaps enhanced in pale gold." Recalling the garden, and Oliver's comments, she wanted a reminder of the occasion. "Make the embroidery of roses."

Lady Strenshall sighed. "Very well. I daresay you will look superb in it."

"And make the embroidery delicate, not something that looks as if I'm wearing a trellis. I am not a large woman, and I can't take those huge designs. They might be spectacular, but they are not for me."

This time her mother smiled. "It's very good to see you taking an interest at last, Drusilla."

Yes, it was. She would go through her wardrobe and leave everything she didn't like behind.

When everyone left the room except Dru, her mother, and their maids, they viewed the pile of samples with some misgiving. "I know we are not to think of expense," Dru said doubtfully, "but is this not outdoing what I will need?"

"Do not think of it," her mother declared briskly. "We have saved on extravagance with your sister's wedding, which she insisted should be quiet, and your brother is never likely to need anything of the kind. Livia will certainly receive this and more." Her sigh reminded everyone of Livia's unmarried state. "I want to see at least one of my daughters married with due circumstance. You will go to your husband in magnificence, Drusilla, if I have anything to do with the matter."

The cost of her gowns alone would feed a large family for several years. Not that Dru said that aloud. She knew better. Her father made generous donations to good causes, even founding an orphanage. They would scoff at her concerns. Sand she could not deny that she had at times become intoxicated by the possibilities.

But she had something else to do before she went down to breakfast. Excusing herself, she hurried to her bedroom and fumbled around her neck for the key she always kept with her.

Her desk was unlocked. Strange, she never left it that way. Sliding up the top, she stared at the clean, empty space that met her horrified gaze. She spun around guiltily when the door opened but discovered her maid coming through with a gown draped over her arm.

"Where are my papers?"

Forde carefully laid the green silk on the bed, pausing to smooth out a crease before turning and answering. "Your lady mother expressed a desire to get rid of them. I took them down to the kitchens this morning."

Anger seared Dru. "Without consulting me?" How dare her maid do this?

"If I recall correctly, ma'am, you expressed a similar desire recently. Two nights ago, I believe."

Oh, damn. Yes, she had. "I would have expected you to consult me first. However, it is done." Another thought struck her as horror followed quickly on the heels of her anger. Even though she had eliminated mention of Oliver, many other prominent members of society featured in her story. What had she been thinking? Ignoring the many hours she'd spent chuckling over her work, she recalled the vicious pen portraits she'd made and groaned aloud. "Go now. I want those papers destroyed instantly, not kept for weeks for kindling. I do not want them to exist any longer."

The destruction would be a symbol of the way she intended to change her life. She would put childish things away and become the best duchess she could possibly be.

Forde dropped a curtsy. "I will go directly after I've helped you to change, or you will be late for breakfast."

Dru stamped her foot in frustration, but the maid was right. She couldn't lace the green gown on her own. It had adjustment cords at the back, under the skirt. "Of course."

Although she tried to play down the importance of recovering her story, she feared she had not done a very good job. To allay Forde's suspicions, that she might realize how important recovery of the book was, she allowed the maid to help her into her gown and style her hair. She refused powder or paint.

When Dru became a duchess, Forde would probably have an assistant. The marchioness had two maids. Maybe then Forde would obey her more readily. Or perhaps Dru would not take the provoking creature at all. She did not need the silent rebukes and the palpable resentment any longer. But Forde was superb at her job, and fast. She could array Dru for a grand ball in less than an hour, and Dru, who often grew irritated with the dressing rituals required of her, appreciated that. Forde might be satisfied with her change in status and become the perfect maid.

Or she might not. In which case Dru would sack her. But she wanted to clear up a few things. "Forde, a moment." Lifting her chin, Dru did her best to act the part of the duchess she must become. Inside she was trembling, but she'd learned long ago to conceal that.

Forde dropped another slight curtsy, not bothering to hide her tightly pursed lips and the look of impatience in her eyes. "We must make haste, ma'am."

Dru clasped her hands in her lap. "When I am married, I will become a duchess. You are aware of that?" She didn't wait for acknowledgment. "I will require a higher standard of service from you. While you are excellent at caring for my clothes and my person, I wish for more."

"You wish for a confidante, ma'am?"

That was deliberately insulting. Dru knew, as did everyone in her position, what she could and could not expect from a maid. Certainly not intimacies. Maids were close to their mistresses as it was, and to insinuate friendship would have made the services they rendered untenable. Who would like their best friend taking care of them every month? But she restrained herself, knowing this as typical of Forde, who would behave with seeming docility while radiating aggression from every pore. "No. I wish for fewer comments. I will accept your opinion on what I should wear. A good lady's maid knows the latest fashions as well, if not better, than her mistress. I am aware my interest in fashion is desultory. But that is for you to supplement, not for me to redress. I will have more duties and a higher status. I will probably need another maid, who will be under the direction of the principal maid, and I am aware that my maid's place downstairs will be considerably enhanced. So will the salary of anyone I employ as principal lady's maid. I will be reviewing your situation, and I trust I will be able to take you with me. However, this is no longer the decision of my mother. It is mine. I trust I make myself clear?"

She'd made the threat as lucid as she could. She would look at Forde with a view to either dismissing her or putting another maid over her. Since the announcement of Dru's engagement to Oliver, Forde had put on more airs. She had attempted to swamp Dru with her instructions, threatening, as she always did, to go to Dru's mother to "clarify" any orders she didn't agree with.

The maid sucked in a breath, her bosom moving convulsively as she attempted to regain control. Dru had not been the recipient of Forde's hasty temper, but she'd seen it and heard it a couple of times. That would stop, too. She would not employ a bully as a maid, however clever and fast she was.

Forde's curtsy this time was of the required depth. She rose smoothly to her feet. "Of course, my lady."

"Now go and ensure those papers are totally destroyed."

"Yes, my lady."

Her first experiment at being a great lady. Not at all bad.

* * * *

"The breakfast table is not the place for sniggering," the marchioness said a few mornings after the day Dru had named "the Taming of Forde Day." "I would go so far as to say nowhere is the correct place." She directed her glare at the offender, who happened to be her husband.

He looked up from his morning paper and adjusted the gold-rimmed spectacles pinched on the end of his nose. "I beg your pardon, my dear. It appears a new sensation is about to make its appearance, at least if this advertisement is to be believed."

"Do tell," said the marchioness, stifling a yawn.

Dru applied herself to her breakfast, lending her father half an ear. When he read aloud, he expected comments, or for his family to laugh in the right places. Val and Charlotte were still here, so the breakfast table with an extra leaf added, was full. The first true meal of the day was an informal affair. People arrived dressed in whatever they pleased. Val and Charlotte were in loose undress, Val in an eye-watering banyan and Charlotte in a pretty pink gown. Dru wore her best riding dress, since she was due to ride in the Park with her betrothed. Livia was wearing riding dress too, but she refused to say who was accompanying her. No doubt their mother knew.

Excitement simmered in Dru, but not enough to quell her appetite. She felt like a mineral spring when she thought of him—all bubbles.

Her father cleared his throat and settled his spectacles more securely on his nose. "Mr. Wilkins of Conduit Street is honored to announce the acquisition of a most interesting new manuscript, to be published in three volumes. It describes the history of a most heinous soul, a man who will surely be condemned to the vasty pits of hell. His adventures in the society of his country are many and sinful. By far the worst is his attempt to seduce and blacken a woman who is his ward, and so should be sacred to him."

It started like Dru's story did, but then, since *Pamela* had been published, so did many. Pamela had been a maid, but other tales had followed hard on the heels of that one. Its unprecedented success has swept the country, and a few years ago, Mr. Fielding's tale, *Tom Jones*, had similarly reached a wide audience.

"Money will follow," the marchioness said.

"I have no doubt it will, especially with these three volumes. Just listen." He continued to read. "A young man comes to the rescue, but as he pits himself against the dastardly Prince of Tirolly, he suffers cruelly."

The marquess broke off, turning his attention to Dru. "Why, whatever is the matter, daughter?"

Dru had allowed her silverware to fall with a clatter on to her plate, taking a chip out of the edge of the pretty porcelain.

She couldn't speak, could only repeat the name that her father had quoted so matter-of-factly. "The P-Prince of Tirolly?"

"Yes, my dear. Are you feeling quite well?"

"Merely clumsy." They would understand that.

Dru sat trembling while a footman removed her chipped plate and replaced it with a clean one that Dru had no use for. Her appetite had fled with the mention of the name of her dastardly villain. But perhaps two people had chanced on the same name. Of course, that would be the reason. Forcing a smile that stretched her lips but did nothing for her churning stomach, she helped herself to a slice of toast, the smallest in the rack. "Do go on, Papa." She needed to know more.

After a doubtful glance, her father resettled his spectacles. "Our heroic couple suffer many adventures, and they learn much that is good for their souls. But the Prince is too much for them and imprisons our beauteous heroine, Drusetta, in his mountain-top castle. To discover if she escapes the dastard, you must purchase the book which will be released next week, the twenty-fifth of May."

The marquess removed his spectacles, which left red marks on his nose, and put them by the side of his plate. "That was why I thought the story might amuse. The heroine's name is remarkably close to your own, my dear. Should we order a copy of the first volume? The man is releasing the three volume set before the end of the season. Every two weeks, in fact."

"We should buy a copy," the marchioness said, tight-lipped. "I am not sure we should allow a book that mirrors Drusilla's name so closely. After all, the name is rare. In a society of Annes and Charlottes and Amelias, Drusilla stands out."

"I agree." The marquess frowned at his wife. "I opposed such outlandish names from the start, but you and your siblings would have it so. Now you have to bear the consequences of such singularity." He glanced at the paper. "The first volume comes out on Monday. I shall pass by the shop and pick up a copy."

The twisting turmoil that was Dru's brain settled on one thing. Someone had found her manuscript. They had to have done so. But at least she had changed the name and appearance of her villain. Clearly she could do nothing about others reading it, but they might consider it ill-written or foolish. The fashionable mind was capricious. It did not always reward merit but sometimes celebrated the mediocre. Her book must be in the mediocre category. If only people did not recognize the pen-portraits she had made of them, she would be safe. And after all, who would consider for one moment that she was the author? Merely that the heroine of this book was a little clumsy, like she was, and quiet-natured, like she was. That could be said of many young ladies in society. Unfortunately, other portraits were drawn with a more accurate, if not always kind, pen.

Dru forced herself to eat the slice of toast, but every crumb choked her. When she received word that Oliver waited outside for her, she went to him with a heavy heart. She had no choice but to wait until Monday.

Who had betrayed her by selling her book? She had no way of knowing, and if she asked, someone was bound to suspect something. As Oliver cupped his hands to throw her into the saddle, Dru stared at him, still in numb shock. Three weeks until their wedding—less than that now—and she could have destroyed all her dreams. If anyone found out she had written the story.

Forde had taken the papers to the kitchen, or so she said. But would she risk her lucrative position, with the prospect of such advancement, to steal the book? Dru didn't think so. Or had a maid seen the papers and taken them away to read? Had she decided to sell the stories?

Dru's stomach tightened, and she was close to losing her breakfast. How on earth could she find out who had sold the book? And what would she do then?

The day was fine, if overcast, the gray clouds matching her mood, but the Park appeared the same. People paraded. A few horses went at a quicker pace around or between the carriages but never more than a canter. Her posture came as second nature, and she sat, if not gracefully, then in the approved manner, nodding to whatever Oliver was saying. When he called her name, she blinked, and stared at him. "I'm sorry, what was that?"

"I said, would you like to come to the theater tomorrow night? I will of course ask your mother, but I might at least have a chance of snatching a kiss."

"From my mother?" Her brain, slow to move from the subject obsessing her, had pushed words to her mouth before she had a proper chance of working out what she was saying.

"I'm sorry? No." He barked a laugh. "Sometimes, my dear, your sense of humor defeats even me. That should make for a lively marriage." He sidled his mount closer. "You, Drusilla. I want to kiss you. Rather more than is respectable. I am discovering new delights about you every day."

"Thank you." Dru could not help but be charmed by her handsome betrothed. Even despite her turmoil, she recognized the effort he was making and tried to match it. "Will we stay in town when we are married?"

He sighed. "Much though I'd love to whisk you off to a quiet villa in the country, life must go on. For a short time, we have to remain in town. Land disputes." Taking his reins in one hand, he waved the other expansively before controlling his frisky mount without any apparent effort. "Soon over, I promise. Perhaps I should have arranged our marriage for two months, instead of one, but I find I'm unaccountably eager to claim my bride for myself."

She adored his gentle tease. Already she could see through the stern exterior to the man beneath. She was not sure if that was because he allowed her to, or if she could do it all on her own. Little changed in his outward demeanor. Only the slight movement of his lips, or a narrowing of his eyes, or even the way he held himself transmitted the information to her. Today, although his seat on his mount was perfect, he leaned infinitesimally toward her, even when they were not conversing. Dru couldn't deny that she liked it. He made her feel as if she was somebody worth listening to. Her boisterous family had talked over her so many times that Dru had given up trying. She loved them, naturally she did, but having someone who listened to her made her want him even more.

"We could have gone to another park, maybe taken the carriage and left it outside," he commented after they had ridden up one side and were preparing to ride down the other. They ambled at a comfortable walk.

"Oh, yes!" Perhaps she'd shown too much eagerness. Her mother would certainly say so.

He didn't seem to notice. "Tomorrow, then, unless you have an appointment elsewhere."

"I'd like that."

When she leaned into her seat, she became aware of a slight list when her horse walked forward. Paying more attention, she confirmed her suspicions. Without thinking about it, she pulled her mount to a halt, swung her leg off the pommel, and slid off the saddle.

When she turned around, he was standing behind her. "What is it?"

She was impressed. He'd dismounted and come around to her before she'd had time to register that he'd done so. His groom was holding both his own and Oliver's horses, but had remained mounted. Their family had people like that who had served the Shaws for generations, but they mostly stayed in the country.

"I think Misty has thrown a shoe, or maybe she has a stone in her foot. I don't want to make it worse by riding her." Biting her lip, she turned to discover what was wrong.

Oliver forestalled her. "Let Halford take a look. I'd trust him with any horse in my stables."

The groom dismounted and handed the reins to his horse and Oliver's to his master. Misty was standing on her own now, dipping her head to the grass verge.

The man, Halford, dealt very crisply with the animal, tapping her hock. She raised her hoof as she'd been trained to do. He took a stick from the ground and explored before tossing it away. "It's a stone all right, my lady, but it's a bit deep. I can't get it out with my knife. I might hurt her. I'd rather do it with the proper instruments to hand than try to get it out here. It's an odd one."

"In what way odd?" she asked sharply. "I'd hate to lose her."

"Oh, I don't think it will come to that, ma'am...my lady."

The duke exchanged a sharp look with his groom. "What is it, Halford?"

"I daresay nothing, your grace, sir. But I'd like to take care of it myself. That stone has sharp edges. But I can do it easily enough."

When she turned to Oliver, he took her gloved hand and patted it. "The mare will be fine. I take it you've had her for many years?"

Dru smiled ruefully. "Yes. I named her when I was fifteen. I sat up with her mother all night. Papa insisted we all had experience of such things, even the girls. When Misty was born, I knew she belonged to me, and the mist was rising over the fields." She remembered that day as clearly as yesterday. The magical sight of the new foal struggling to feed, the tender care her mama took of her, and the morning mist caused by the sun evaporating the dew on the grass all blended into a perfect memory.

He nodded. "If you allow Halford to look after her, I promise she'll get the best of care."

"Nevertheless, I'd like to take her back myself," she said.

"We can do that, but we have to walk."

She gave him a tentative smile. "Then it's as well we're betrothed. People won't mind that. May I lead her?"

"Of course." He nodded to Halford, who passed her the reins.

A simple stone rarely caused such trouble, but she did not want to take a chance that riding the mare would make her worse. Pausing only to pull a couple of pins from her pocket and fasten up her trailing skirt, she took Misty's reins, spoke softly to the mare, and led her.

Her boots were not made for walking in, but she managed well enough. However, after they had gone the half-mile to the park gates, she had to tackle the harder pavements of the squares bordering Hyde Park. They crossed into Tyburn Street, heading in the direction of Oxford Street. They nodded but didn't stop to talk to anyone, passing the fashionable shops and a shabby one Dru briefly wondered at. She liked the hats displayed in the window.

But she had no time to linger. Instead, she led Misty steadily in the direction of their house. Remembering her manners, she conversed in a desultory way with the duke, more concerned with her poor mare. "I have her brought into town every year, but soon I fear I shall have to leave her behind."

"Will you bring her with you when we marry?"

Would she ever become accustomed to marriage and the twist of fortune that had brought her to him? Somehow she doubted it. Not until she had actually spoken the words and heard them repeated back to her. That jolt she felt every time anyone referred to her coming nuptials was as nothing when compared to her reaction as he said it, especially in such a calm manner.

An unwanted flush rose to her cheeks, but she turned her face to his. "I would like to."

His smile did not appear to be connected to simple information about a horse. "I do like that expression. So open, so sweet. It makes we want to do things that would have London talking about us for years to come."

Her jaw dropped. "Oh." Recalling where she was, she glanced ahead to the groom leading his horse, with Oliver's mount tethered behind.

"Don't worry. Halford has been with me since I was a boy."

"He's not a London servant?"

He shook his head. "I don't use them, as a rule. I bring my own staff on the rare occasions that I come to town." He hesitated, gazing down at her, his eyes narrowing slightly. "It is because of my brother. He dislikes strangers about him."

"I see." She could not visit his house until his mother arrived in town, but she knew where he lived. Close to the Strenshall house, in fact. "I didn't know you'd brought him to London. Will I meet him?"

"Presently, yes, you will." His voice lowered. "He does not go into society. I will prepare you, tell you what to expect, but this is not the place to do it. Don't you agree?"

Hastily, she turned her gaze to the road before them. They were on the relative cleanliness of the pavement, an innovation in the more fashionable streets of the city, the horse walking next to them. "Yes, of course. I understand."

A pair of chairmen with an empty sedan chair between them trotted past.

Dru had not heard anything about his brother of recent date. He lived completely secluded. The few rumors she'd heard depicted him as simpleminded, cared for by a fleet of servants, irreparably damaged from the accident many years before. Some said they thought it a shame he had survived the overturning of the carriage, because he would be out of his pain by now. The rumors varied from drastic to simple—that he was scarred but preferred not to go out in public, or he was completely incapacitated and did not understand even how to care for himself. The truth was nobody knew, which was remarkable for a set of people who shared gossip like air.

They walked slowly, but it took them little time, since she lived barely half a mile from Hyde Park. She took him to the mews that ran along the back of her house. They had to walk in single file for safety, in case a carriage swung out of an opening. There was no pavement or even a guide for walkers here.

However, he led her past her gate and to one on the other side. He walked through without hesitation.

"Why, we are barely a hundred yards away from each other!" she exclaimed when she realized he'd taken her to his mews. After all, his groom had offered to deal with Misty.

"Indeed." He waited until Halford had given the two horses he led to a groom and came back for Misty.

Reluctantly, she allowed the man to take her. The mews appeared as busy as the Strenshall one. A traveling carriage had a stall of its own, and several more vehicles were visible in the dimness of the carriage house. "These places could house several families," she commented.

He turned to her, his brows lifting. "You're interested in housing the poor?"

Shamefaced, she shrugged. "Not exactly. Yes, in a way, because my family have been housing them for years. My parents sponsor an orphanage, but that is not enough, is it?"

He took her hands. "No, it is not. Nothing will ever be enough, but we can do what we must."

Gazing at him, she lost track of the conversation and had to admit it. "You must think me a complete booby."

"Not one bit. You are, as always, perfectly delightful."

"You didn't think so once."

He smiled. "I was foolish. I know better now."

Was it any wonder she was falling in love with him? She had not expected to fall for her future husband, especially one so absolutely suitable, as her mother put it. But she found the experience so much more than she had ever written about. Her imaginings had fallen far short of what she was going through now.

He was gazing back as if he felt the same thing. The warmth, the increased heartbeat, the hair prickling. But he said nothing, and Dru did not know how. Revealing her heart did not come naturally. It had not come at all. She'd told her parents she loved them, and she did. It was her duty. But nobody expected her to love her husband. Even her mother's confession that she had grown to love Dru's father had not prepared her for this overwhelming sensation—the warmth, the urge to fall into his arms wherever she was, the longing for his kiss.

Being the person she was, Dru tried to analyze the way she felt, but for the first time in her life she came up short. She could not imagine anyone else feeling like this, ever. Least of all her mother.

"Y'r grace, sir." The wizened groom—Halford—was back.

"Yes?" Oliver appeared to move reluctantly from her gaze to his.

"The stone. It will take a bit of effort to remove."

Something passed between them, but Dru couldn't discern what the groom was trying to communicate. "Will Misty recover?"

"Oh, yes, my lady. Most certainly. But I want to be sure the stone is completely gone. I would like to keep her for an hour or two."

"Halford has a most excellent receipt for a salve," Oliver put in. "He will ensure the mare is perfectly well." He glanced toward the exit. "And delivering her will not prove difficult."

They shared a smile, all three. "Yes, of course you may keep her."

"She will be coming here soon, anyway," Oliver said.

Dru ducked her head, embarrassed and warmed by the expression in his eyes.

"I will escort you home," Oliver said. "If you will permit me."

"Of course." She said goodbye to Misty, and they went on their way.

In this hidden part of London, the smell of fresh horse manure mingled with the smoky scent of hay. Stacks of it stood in every yard. As they passed the mews to her house, she paused. "If we go this way, we can walk through the garden."

He agreed, and she inwardly rejoiced. She had plans for their stroll through the garden.

* * * *

Oliver had meant to take Dru straight to her house. He really had. The garden was large, well-kept, and visible from the house. However, when she caught his hand and tugged him in a different direction, he went with her and found a small pavilion. The charming confection was plainly meant to display climbing roses. A veritable thicket wound its way around the six white columns to the domed roof, which was mostly open to the sky.

Dru appeared to advantage in a riding habit, the mannish jacket, and cocked hat softened by the skirts. And that shade of crimson deepened the flush in her cheeks. Her eyes sparkled as she turned to him, a naughty smile on her lips. "They can't see us from the house here."

Willingly, he followed her into the bower. "We can't be long. Someone will already have seen us."

"Oh, yes, a gardener will interrupt us shortly."

Oliver hated to admit how much the subterfuge aroused him. Sneaking around to snatch rare minutes with a girl reminded him of his first passion, a dairymaid called Alice. Goodness, he'd had to stretch his mind to remember her name. They never went beyond kisses and caresses, but she had wanted more. If she'd led him on any further, he might have found himself in a much stickier position. One he would welcome with Dru, but they could hardly go that far here. Even if it would speed the wedding process. Already, waiting two weeks to possess her was driving him to heights of frustration he refused to assuage, except for the occasional relief with his hand. Otherwise, he'd go around in a state of permanent arousal.

Still, the relief of taking her in his arms and kissing her gave him some peace. Until it did not. He'd shown her how to respond. Now he had reason to wish he had not, when she spread her hand over his waistcoat and wickedly slid it down to press his aching erection.

He pulled slightly away, groaning against her lips. "Have mercy. You don't know what you're doing."

"But I will soon, won't I?"

Giving in, he resumed the kiss, claiming an intimate caress of his own when he cupped her sweetly curved little bottom, pulling her tightly against him. "Feel that?" he murmured to her. "It is waiting for you, as is the rest of me."

Her shudder evoked a response from him, one that hardened the shaft she had her fingers curled around. "I want it now," she said. "I couldn't bear if all this was taken away from me."

A thread of uneasiness curled into his mind. "Why should anyone take our happiness away?"

She smiled, but he felt the tension in her lips, since his were a breath away. Something concerned her. "Has someone in your family created trouble again?" He stepped back, although it nearly killed him to do so, and gathered her hands between his, warming them. "If they have, we will go into the countryside and marry quietly. We have a special license. We may wed anywhere we choose."

"Then let's go now." Her voice grew urgent. "Please, Oliver. We may elope. Our families will make it right. I want you. Now."

He groaned. "You look at me with such eagerness. But no, Dru. Two weeks, sweetheart. That's all. Let's please our families and let them turn our union into a social event. Once we've attended the wedding breakfast, we may go where we please. I have a small villa in the country nearby. We could go there. It's a day's ride from London, and few people know of it."

"Oh. Can we not go tomorrow?"

Laughing softly, he drew her close, looped his hands around her waist. "I love your eagerness. I feel it, too. But we should do our utmost to wait. We will see one another often and maybe snatch more interludes like these." He touched his lips to hers, and they opened eagerly, inviting him to explore.

He would have lost himself in her then. However, the gentle throat-clearing and the perfectly unnecessary crunching of feet on gravel told him of the imminent arrival of the promised gardener.

Their enjoyable interlude was over for today.

After seeing Dru home and having a quick word with her father about the mare, Oliver returned to his stables, a pleasant smile wreathing his features. He loved the dreamy look when she finally opened her eyes, and her kiss-stained lips ensured that he had made his mark on her. She'd wear his brand for an hour or two yet.

Previously he'd had no intention of something as basic as marking any woman. Some men delighted in it, often with marks more permanent and brutal than a kiss, but he had never understood the urge before. He did now. He wanted her known as his, belonging to him, so that nobody would touch her.

A strange urge. No doubt he would understand it before long. Oliver set to understanding everything that happened to him or to the people around him. He was never satisfied unless he knew and could claim it as his own. Ever since the act that had changed his world, he never took anything for granted.

This phenomenon, his urgent and strong reaction to Drusilla, fascinated and alarmed him. He wanted no one to have jurisdiction over him or his emotions. That must never happen. He had too many responsibilities, too much on his mind to allow himself to become obsessed by one person.

Yet it was happening.

His sunny mood lasted until Halford met him, his eyes mere slits under his furrowed brow.

"What is it?"

Halford glanced around, marking their solitude, and lowered his voice almost to a whisper. "I can't be sure, sir, but I think that stone was put there."

The man must be imagining things. "That is foolish talk. Who would want to put a stone in a horse's hoof?"

"Someone who wanted that horse to stumble. Fall, I'd say. Could have delivered a dangerous tumble for whoever was on her back."

Shock throbbed through Oliver, a dull thud that swiftly escalated to pure anger. "You mean someone intends Lady Drusilla harm?"

"It looks that way, sir. I can't be sure, now, but if she was hurt, the wedding would have to be put off."

Oh, no, it would not, he thought grimly. He would marry her the sooner, so he could take care of her. But an injury would necessarily deter more intimate exchanges. The delightful interlude he'd just shared with Dru put him in mind of that part. Because she was injured, he could not possibly consider inflicting her with an experience that, despite her teasing, would probably shock her, although he intended it would also please her. Perhaps deter him from marrying her.

Who did not want him to marry Dru? The match was eminently suitable, and all parties appeared pleased with it, he and Dru not least of those.

Who would do this? The only person he could think of was his previous mistress. But she would not care. Already she'd found a new protector, and Oliver had left her well provided for.

A servant? A member of his family? No, his brother was overjoyed. Only this morning Charles had warmly congratulated Oliver and asked when he would have the pleasure of meeting Dru. He'd taken Oliver aback. Charles never saw anyone except Oliver, their mother, and his three personal servants.

Or perhaps another agent. Someone who wanted Oliver to look elsewhere for a bride. That broadened the field considerably. Many ladies of society must have been aware that Oliver was in the market and had pushed their daughters his way. Perhaps one had arranged a little subversion.

Anyone could get access to a stable, if he knew a groom, or if he delivered material.

"Have you noticed any unusual activity?" Oliver asked his groom. He had, after all, set a watch after the carriage incident.

Halford jerked his thumb in the vague direction of the Strenshall stable. "Over there? I've not been looking, sir. Perhaps I should, but I can't direct who comes and goes in another stable. In ours? Not a blessed thing, and I've set careful watch. Even let people in to see what they would do, and the answer was nothing they shouldn't have been doing. Our servants sometimes use the stables as a short way to the house, like they all do. It's a way between houses, too, one that isn't as well observed as the front entrance. Even the kitchens are better guarded."

"Hmm." Oliver stroked his chin. His morning stubble rasped his fingers, and he was reminded of the reddened spots on Dru's delicate skin after their kisses. Damnation, he would have to take care with that. Ensure his valet shaved him closely, perhaps twice a day, like a blasted dandy. "A direct attack on Lady Drusilla. That answers the questions we had about the carriage accident."

"I don't like to say it, sir, but that family has its enemies."

Halford was right. Dru had five siblings and belonged to a big close-knit extended family. That could prove a problem. Perhaps he should consult with Drusilla's father, inform him of what was going on.

His instincts went against taking that course. The fewer people who knew his suspicions the better, as far as he was concerned. He trusted the marquess, but he could not say he knew him very well. And Strenshall would tell the rest of his family. Then, who knew who would come to know the unfortunate accidents that happened recently were of a more sinister nature?

No, he would deal with this matter himself. He was used to keeping secrets, and he would keep this one, but the sooner he had Dru under his own roof the happier he would feel. Once she had separated from her family, the attacks would likely cease.

Swiftly, Oliver made his decision. "Do not tell anyone about this for now. Keep a watch as much as you can of the comings and goings here and the other stables. I will continue to look into this." One last try. "Are you certain these incidents aren't accidents?"

"Somebody else would have missed them. But that stone was pushed into place. It would have worn on the poor animal the longer you traveled, but the mare couldn't have picked it up on the way. And the carriage—yes, sir, I'm certain about that now I've had a better look at it."

Oliver thought of all the curse words he had in his vocabulary, and he had quite a few. He would let them all go once in the privacy of his bedchamber, but not now. His protective instincts rose as never before, and that was saying something. For years, he'd jealously protected Charles and his mother from any scandal or hurt, but his urge to care for Dru superseded even that. He would not willingly let her out of his sight until he had her to himself.

Chapter 8

Dru couldn't allow anything to come between her and the man with whom she was rapidly falling in love. She had to get to that manuscript before it was published on Monday, and she had three days to do it. Tonight she was to attend the theater with Oliver. Sunday was church and preparation. She'd have no chance then. And today, she had to sign the contract for her marriage settlement at the lawyer's office.

Her attempt to get him to elope had fallen on stony ground. That would create a completely unnecessary scandal in the eyes of the world. In her view, it was the perfect solution. The book would come out, be a nine days' wonder, and disappear by the time they returned to town.

The carriage took them to the solicitor's office. The Strenshalls had used the same solicitor for generations. Their current man of business was the great-grandson of the founder of the firm, and he considered the Strenshall business the most important he had. His office was located in the City, a place that fascinated Dru, full of narrow streets, shouts, and the occasional grand space that had seen better days. As the fashionable world had moved farther west, wealthy Cits had taken over the houses until they dominated the City.

The carriage took Dru, her parents, and her brother Darius with his business—and personal—partner, lawyer Andrew Grey to the busy cramped offices. They alighted to be met by Mr. Carter himself, who, with due ceremony, ushered them up the narrow bare stairs to his office. There, Oliver and his man of business awaited them.

Dru tried to behave like a society lady and coolly offer her hand. However, when Oliver glanced at her as he rose from his bow with a wicked grin, he tried her self-control. She would have preferred a more intimate greeting, and from his expression, he would, too.

She listened to the explanations of her marriage settlement impatiently, even more to Andrew's translation of the legal language to normal everyday words. Andrew had a gift for making people understand, and he'd used his eloquence to great results when he had acted as her brother Marcus's advocate. That was why the family trusted him. His work for the Shaws had marked the beginning of the love affair that had shocked the Shaw family. They'd always known of Darius's preferences, but he'd never lost his head as he did over Andrew. Or sacrificed so much. He rarely appeared in society these days and preferred his City friends. His business was prospering, although Dru didn't understand the half of what he did. He'd soon be wealthier than anyone except her father.

He certainly appeared to be happy in his new life. Nobody knew how he'd persuaded Andrew to join him, especially when Andrew had so much more to lose, but they both seemed content. In fact, they exuded the happiness of a newly married couple, although of course that would never happen. Neither could anyone acknowledge what Darius and Andrew truly meant to one another. The world was given to believe that the couple were business associates and shared the same roof for convenience. That thin excuse kept most people happy.

Now Dru wanted her own slice of happiness, but if her book was allowed to see the light of day, she feared that would never happen. Oliver guarded his privacy carefully—she knew that—and he also expected honesty from her. She shivered when she thought of what might happen if he ever discovered what she'd done.

She had worn her plainest clothes in preparation for the plan she was determined to put into place today. It would be her only chance.

The contract explained and signed, she breathed a long sigh of relief. She did everything expected of her, spoke warmly to her brother and his friend, expressed her pleasure, and then saw her betrothed frown.

As they sat together on hard chairs in the crammed office, he managed a private word with her. "Is there anything wrong?"

"No, of course not. Why?" Alarm spiked in her.

"You seem on edge. Too bright." He frowned. "I can't quite explain it. But I can feel your tension."

Forcing a smile and smoothing her expression, she faced him. "Is it any wonder? My whole life will change in a matter of two weeks. I have a lot to think of."

He stroked her palm, sending responsive warmth through her. "Then I insist that you rest. I want you rested and happy on our wedding day. Are you happy?" He let her see his concern, his expression soft and caring.

For a man who kept his emotions so carefully shielded from public view, he was letting her see so much. "Yes," she replied immediately, and dropped her gaze, for fear he would see more than she wanted him to. Aware she was withdrawing while he was advancing, she set her expression and lifted her head again.

His steely gaze bored into her, seeking her deepest secrets. "You are well?"

"Perfectly." Then she decided to tell the truth, at least some of it. She could soothe her raging conscience. But he must not know what she had planned. "I am visiting the mantua-maker after this. I have something I particularly want her to do to my gown, and I have had no time to tell her."

A seductive smile curled his lips. "I'm intrigued. Would you like me to escort you?"

"No!" Her reply was so vehement that her mother turned her head and arched her brows in query. Dru forced the smile back. "Livia has promised to accompany me to the mantua-maker after this," she explained. "Merely a detail I want to clarify."

"I'll send James with you," the marchioness said.

Take a footman who would report directly to her mother? No, she could not have that. She had only let Livia into her confidence reluctantly, and for two pins her sister would betray her and blab the truth.

"Really, there is no need. We'll take a hackney."

"No, you will not." Her mother sucked in a breath. "A hackney indeed!"

Dru exchanged a glance with her sister.

Livia grinned back. "James would be a great help. Then we can walk. It's a fine day," she added, glancing out of the window. "And Dru is a cat on a hot bakestone these days. A walk would do her good."

The marchioness agreed, and Dru could breathe freely again. She had a plan. She knew exactly how to deal with James.

Half an hour later, the contracts were signed. Despite Dru refusing to allow Oliver to accompany her to the dressmaker's, he accepted her father's invitation to return to celebrate the forthcoming marriage. With a fond smile, which for the first time she had to force, she left the building. With Livia by her side and James striding before them to clear the way, she walked the short distance to the mantua-maker's. Although she usually used Celine's, Dru had her riding costumes made by a specialist in the City. She had everything she needed, and she had no intention of staying at the mantua-makers.

She ordered poor James to carry on. "I intend to buy my betrothed a gift," she said loftily. "A book. But I could hardly say that when he was there, could I?"

Livia giggled. Dru glared at her, but that did not help a great deal. Livia still grinned.

Many booksellers had stalls and small shops clustered around St. Paul's at the bottom end of Ludgate Hill. Dru enjoyed the walk. They went down Fleet Street, past the coffeehouses and inns full of people—mostly men—discussing everything from literature to politics. Once Dru had longed to go there just to listen, but of course she could not. Her father guarded all his children most carefully. He'd have a fit if he knew what his eldest daughter was doing now. Dru shuddered at the very thought of him finding out her exploits today.

Her pockets weighed heavily under her gown. She'd scraped together every guinea she could find.

She found the bookseller and dived inside, followed closely by Livia. But she ordered James to stay outside. She'd chosen this one because it was full of narrow crammed shelves, with no room for all three of them. And because it had an exit on the other side of the shop. That wasn't normal for the tiny establishments here, but the proprietor had met with a degree of success, and he'd used his good fortune to expand his premises.

In fact, Dru went there rather a lot. Pausing inside the front entrance, she took a deep breath of the musty, inky smell that she loved. It welcomed her. She felt like she was coming home.

"Lady Drusilla, I'm delighted to see you! We have your latest order ready."

"Yes, thank you." Fumbling in her pocket, she found a guinea and pushed it across the scarred oak counter to Mr. Pinker. "I need half an hour to myself," she murmured. "My sister will accompany me, but I don't want the footman outside to know."

Mr. Pinker raised a bushy gray brow. "I will not ask, my lady, only that you take great care."

"Thank you. When we return, we can load James with books and get a cab back."

Mr. Pinker nodded. "But I will not be responsible if he finds you gone, my lady. I will disclaim all knowledge and help him raise the alarm." Her father would ruin him if she was discovered and he was revealed as a coconspirator.

"But you won't start the alarm yourself."

He inclined his head. "As you say, my lady."

She turned toward the small door at the back of the shop and then glanced back. "I'm looking for a gift for my betrothed. A beautiful atlas, perhaps."

"I have just the thing."

No doubt the book would be expensive and would cost her most of her next quarter's pin money. Except she would command considerably more, come next quarter, but only if her plan worked. "Make sure it's big and heavy," she said over her shoulder as she and Livia headed for the back of the shop.

The door opened with a creak on to a narrow alley. Such places honeycombed London, sometimes hidden by later buildings. This example stank of piss and tobacco, and underfoot the stone floor was considerably sticky and muddy.

"Ugh," Livia said, lifting her skirts high.

Dru followed suit, glad of her sturdy outdoor shoes, and carefully sidled out of the noxious place, only to come face to face with the glories of St. Paul's Cathedral.

The great dome soared above. The walls had once been white, but thirty years of London coal fires had turned it to dull, furry black. Dru and Livia took care not to allow their skirts to brush against the limestone, tiptoeing past until they could walk clear.

Livia sighed. "Are you sure you want to do this?"

"Yes," Dru snapped. "After all the scrapes you got into with Claudia, this is small beer. But if you feel you need to go back, just say so. But never call me sister again."

Livia laughed, much to Dru's irritation. "Do not be over-dramatic. If you insist on doing this, let's get going."

Dru had looked up the address on her father's copy of the map of London, so she knew exactly where she was going, even with the bookstalls and other detritus piled up on all sides. Although the atmosphere was relatively quiet, that did not mean constant conversations, discussions, and the occasional raised voice didn't go on around them. Dru took comfort in the sounds and smells of London. Nobody cared about her or what she was doing, bar the odd pickpocket. She kept her hand shoved through the slit in her skirts and into her pocket, where she clutched the purse holding her money.

Past St. Paul's, more shops and offices awaited them. There, the Fire of London had raged hardest, so the buildings were relatively new, although not as modern as the house she lived in. They were crammed together, three and four stories high, some only a room wide.

Dru led the way to one of the establishments. A few dusty tomes were visible through the grimy cracked windowpanes. When she plied the iron knocker against the plate, the door shuddered, so she wondered if the bricks were held together by much more than spit and birds' nests.

The door opened.

Dru lifted her chin. "A word with the owner of this establishment, if you please." She put on her best aristocratic expression, all disdain and expectation.

After a minute, the man who had opened to them stood aside. He was tall and thin, dressed in a black coat that was turning green from age and over-laundering. He had a pair of pince-nez hanging from a cord around his neck.

He crossed the room, his feet clicking against the hard wooden floorboards. He must have nailed his shoes to save the soles for them to make that metallic, hollow sound. That spoke of careful economy on his part. He rapped on a door at the end, lifted the latch with a rattle and went in. Then came out. "You can go in," he said, and without waiting for them, walked back to a tall desk and took his place behind it.

Glancing at Livia, Dru swept forward. If not for the urgency of the situation, she would have burst into laughter. This was precious. She would write about it when she got home. No, she wouldn't. Changing her habits would mean more than the determination in her heart. She must stop thinking that way.

Or she'd end in exactly the same place doing the same thing.

"Mr. Wilkins." She did not offer her hand.

Mr. Wilkins took his time getting to his feet. He wore shabby, faded clothing but of a perfectly respectable nature. He glared at them over a pair of glasses and then took them off and put them aside before he scraped his hard chair back and rose. He had a stoop, most likely from constantly leaning over a desk. "Madam. Who do I have the honor of addressing?"

Dru brushed his question aside with a careless wave. Behind her, Livia sneezed, no doubt because of the strong perfume of lavender rising from the pastille burner over the fireplace. "I want to make you an offer for the new three-volume novel."

"It will be published on Monday. You may buy a copy then from any bookseller you care to name."

"How much would it cost to stop it being published on Monday?" Dru sighed with frustration. She hadn't meant to ask her question in that way. She wanted to make him an imperious offer and allow him to beat her up to the amount she had with her.

Wilkins's eyes narrowed. "More than you have, I'll be bound. That book will make my fortune."

"And hurt a great many other people. Believe me. You will not appreciate the repercussions of publishing it."

Wilkins was burlier than Dru had expected. Disturbingly so, if she were to admit it. Maybe she should have brought James, after all. But then her mother would hear of her transgression, and Dru could not bear her disappointment. He came out from behind his desk and took a step closer to her. Dru planted her heels firmly on the floor and stood her ground, but behind her Livia stumbled back.

A pity. She needed to show her resolve.

The publisher tilted his head to one side, like a great black bird, studying her. "How much? I will have people beating a path to my door for this book. Not only is it scandalous, it is well written. The story has merit, and it will keep people reading. I would like the author to come forward, so I might commission more work." He tilted his head to one side. "Are you a maid? Do you know who wrote it?"

Dru ignored his question. Near to angry tears, Dru persisted, forcing the mask of calm. "If you sell this one to me, I will make it worth your while."

"Young lady, I expect to make several hundred pounds from this book. Maybe more. And if the writer will not come forward..." Pausing, he swept her with a comprehensive gaze. "I'll have to make the most of it. That book is mine, fair and square. I paid good money for it, so I mean to get that investment back." A slow smile crept over his face. "And now I know who wrote it, I'll make even more." He glanced over her shoulder at Livia.

He knew. He'd guessed she was the author. Oh, God, what if he recognized her? Dru was not the most distinctive member of her family, but Livia, with her glowing complexion and silky red-gold hair, was far more memorable. The hair was pulled back, and Livia wore a relatively plain bergère hat over her locks, but that wasn't enough to disguise her. And Dru's twin sister was married to a prominent peer of the realm.

What had she done?

"I have a mind to continue the series," Mr. Wilkins remarked, a savage smile curling his thin lips. "I will employ someone else to write them. Grub Street is full of struggling writers. I am sure I can find someone to produce another novel in a week."

Horror rooted Dru to the spot, and Livia's gasp told her she was not alone in her sentiments. She firmed her chin, which was threatening to wobble. "How much do you want?" He was driving up the price. That was all. Nothing else.

"How much do you have?"

Unfortunately, she had jingled the coins in her pocket, so he must know she had money with her. She didn't like this man. She wouldn't trust him, either, but she needed that book taken off sale. Desperately. "I need the copies you've made and the original manuscript. And the printing blocks dismantled."

He raised both brows this time. "Thorough. But even if I wanted to, I could not stop production now."

"I think you can." Only Dru didn't say that. Livia did, and she accompanied her words with an ominous metallic click.

Dru spun around, but she took care not to block her sister's aim.

"Livia, put it away!"

Livia was a crack shot with a pistol. She'd practiced for hours when they were children, but Dru had never known her aim her weapon at a human being. "Give her what she wants," she said now, perfectly steadily.

"Ah, as I was saying, dear young lady, I cannot." He spread his hands in a gesture of helplessness. "Some books are at the shops, and I do not own those."

"Don't print any more." Perhaps if only a few existed, they would sink without trace. "How much for that? And the manuscript?"

"Mostly destroyed," he said. He glanced at Livia. "Is that enough?"

Dru took in the determination on Livia's face. She wouldn't have crossed her sister right now. "Yes." It would have to be. At least without the manuscript they couldn't publish any more.

"So we come to the price. Five hundred pounds."

Dru gasped. "That's extortion! One hundred."

"Four."

She got him down to two hundred, fortunate because that was all she had. Except she did not. She had to add the pearl necklace her grandmother had given her on the occasion of her come-out. They were worth more, but further haggling might lose her the arrangement. At least they were not family treasures.

Mr. Wilkins bit—bit!—a pearl or two before he agreed, but eventually he unlocked a drawer in his desk.

He crossed the room to where a safe stood in clear sight. Drawing out a key, he inserted it into the lock and then found another key for the smaller lock above. The door swung open, the hinges so well-oiled that it didn't make a sound. Mr. Wilkins drew out a plain brown parcel done up with blue tape. He handed it over to Dru, giving Livia a wary look. Dru took it. Even now her manners prevailed and she thanked him. It felt right, the pile of papers the proper size, but she would not risk it.

She unfastened the tape and unwrapped the parcel. Pulling out a handful at random, she recognized her writing and the part of the story it depicted. She did it twice more and then refastened it and shoved the unruly bundle under her arm. "It's the book," she said to her sister. She nodded to Mr. Wilkins. "Thank you, sir. Do I have to watch you dismantle the types? I will stay here if I think it necessary." Inwardly she quailed, because she could not stay here much longer. But she knew from Val the value of the bluff. In Val's card playing days, he was known as a devil at the tables, and he'd taught his sisters how.

Dru met Wilkins's eyes steadily. "Lead the way."

Mr. Wilkins glanced at Livia again. "There's no need."

"If there is, I will come back," Livia promised.

Outside the dank offices of Wilkins' Publishing, Dru breathed a heavy sigh of relief. "I never want to do that again. Do you think he will do as we say?"

"Without a doubt," Livia said firmly, but she didn't meet Dru's eyes when she said it.

"I had no idea you had a weapon. What would we have gained from shooting Mr. Wilkins?"

Livia's lips curved in a wicked smile. "I could have shot him in the arm, or hurt him."

"But then he'd have had you taken up for attempted murder. Andrew Grey might be good, but he can't work miracles every time one of us requests his services."

Livia laughed. "The money was probably enough. A shame about Grandmother's pearls, though."

"Yes." Dru gave the necklace one last lingering thought and firmly put it out of her mind.

Dru wasn't sure, either, but at least she had her book back. She'd dispose of it as soon as possible, even if it meant ordering a fire in her room. No, she had a better idea.

She set a brisk pace back to the bookseller, no longer caring if her skirts brushed against the wall or not. Forde would have to cope with the results. That was all. Striding through the shop, she found the proprietor waiting for them, a couple of heavy tomes on the counter.

"One of these would serve your purpose, I believe."

She glanced inside the first one. "I'll take both, please." She heaved the untidy parcel on top. "Wrap this with them, and we will take them with us."

Nobody could see the way her heart beat so hard it took her breath. She worked not to let it show. She had done it. She had her story back, and nobody would take it away from her again. She would destroy it herself, page by page, that very night.

James didn't groan when the bookseller loaded the large parcel wrapped neatly in brown paper into his arms, but he did sag a little. Dru heard his sigh of relief when she announced they would take a hackney.

"Oh, they're so dirty!" Livia exclaimed. "We could send James back to the house for the carriage."

"That would take an hour or more," Dru pointed out.

Livia lifted a shoulder. "Not if he runs. He can leave the books here."

Dru was about to object, but then she had a thought. "Very well. We can wait in the shop. With the parcel."

Livia nodded. The proprietor would give them some refreshment. True, they should really have a chaperone, but nobody would object. "We should have had two footmen."

"Yes," she said sweetly, and before Livia could argue out of her complaint, she led the way back into the shop.

Ten minutes later, Dru left with her parcel tucked under her arm. London Bridge must be twenty minutes' walk, but she was fit and healthy. She walked much farther than that in the country. She wanted this unfortunate event dealt with here and now.

Although the establishments on Cheapside were not the most fashionable, the Strenshalls knew them. Similarly, she passed through familiar landmarks on Lombard Street. She scurried past a shop with silverware on proud display, catching the sun when it glinted through the clouds, temporarily dazzling her. Then Mercer's Hall, grand and stately. The turn to Lombard Street signaled banks. Dru ducked her head, letting the broad brim of her hat shade her and praying all the way nobody would see her and recognize her. She wouldn't walk back that way. When she reached Fish Street Hill, she breathed a sigh of relief but kept her head down.

London Bridge loomed before her, with the grim walls of the Tower of London on her right. She crossed the busy thoroughfare with a few other people. One or two men sent her sideways glances, but she refused to look at them.

Halfway across the bridge, she found a passage dividing two rickety houses and slipped between them to lean over the parapet. A chunk of stone tumbled to the river as she leaned over, the splash barely visible in the busy waters. A ferryman looked up at her and shook his fist, but nobody else took any notice. Hastily, she drew back and took her little fruit knife from her pocket, slicing through the tape and the brown paper that covered her book.

Ferrymen plied their small boats below where she stood, going constantly from side to side. Pleasure vessels and the ones carrying cargo went with the tide and against it. The Thames must have been the busiest river in the country. It acted as thoroughfare, transportation, and amusement to the ever-growing populace. She would have to take care. She didn't want to send her book down as a gift to an unsuspecting river traveler. A stray breeze whipped against her cheek, nearly dislodging her hat. Automatically, Dru reached up to secure it and lost her grip on the parcel.

It tumbled into the water, leaving barely a splash. A few papers floated out and landed on the surface.

There went her youthful dreams, her revenge on people who had snubbed her, her desire to be beautiful, gracious, admired by all. It disappeared beneath the gray, murky depths. The water would cleanse it, make it unreadable, and then rot it down. It would become part of the mud that seeped out and provided a tomb for a multitude of crimes. People who fell in were rarely recovered or never came out alive. The river would drag them down as human sacrifices. The ancients worshiped it. Now, Dru gave thanks to the river, to God, and to anyone else who was listening for accepting her sacrifice.

She ignored the sadness coursing through her system and depressing her thoughts. She went back to the road, dodging the carts, carriages, and riders who constantly threatened to run her over, and smoothed the skirts of the gown she had probably ruined. Not that she cared, and after her talk with Forde, the maid had behaved much better. Dru should have spoken to her years before instead of putting up with the barely there tuts and humphs and the cold shoulder when she did something to upset her maid.

The reminder buoyed her spirits, and she went back to the end of the bridge with a spring in her step.

Goodbye the overlooked, reticent girl she had been. Dru was to become a duchess, and she determined to act like one.

Chapter 9

Despite her resolve never to write a word of fiction again, Dru still kept her journal. She wanted to leave something for the future. From there she found it easy to let her imagination fly, but after a flirtation with appalling poetry, she returned to her favorite medium. She would write improving stories and moral tales for children. That was how she would make amends.

But on the Monday after her fateful visit to the horrid man who had stolen her manuscript, Dru passed a bookshop to see her own creation displayed in the window. Fortunately, most people were also passing by. There did not seem to be a queue.

Her father had reported that he could not get a copy for his own perusal, and Dru let out a sigh of relief. That must mean Wilkins had done as he promised. A few copies remained in circulation, but that was all. They would pass unnoticed.

On the Tuesday, she was to attend the theater with her betrothed and his mother, who had arrived in town with her husband the day before. Then they would make their appearance at a ball. Her trousseau had mostly arrived. She'd had it packed and sent to the new house she was to occupy in less than two weeks. Everything was getting so close. Her reality was swooping down on her before she had time to assimilate it. Oliver was the center of it all.

She went down to the drawing room and met his mother and her husband, both charming people and delighted to see their son marry. Tactfully, they went down to the carriage first.

When she offered her hand, Oliver took it, but instead of bending over it, tugged her into his arms and kissed her senseless. She bathed in his regard. If this was not love, she didn't know what was. He spread his hands over her back, gripping tightly as if he didn't want to let her go.

She drew back with a shaky laugh. "I will not be fit to be seen."

"You are always fit to be seen, sweetheart."

Oliver didn't throw endearments around carelessly, as other men did. Dru cherished every one. He warmed her, made her feel wanted and safe. And entirely his. The force of his personality made up for her lack, the way people barely noticed she was in the room. She hadn't minded before now, but she would become strong. For him, and for what he represented.

He kissed her again, and she stretched up eagerly to return it. He groaned into her mouth and drew back, gently urging her away. "You undermine my resolve, Dru. I want you badly. Can we bring the wedding forward, do you think?"

"By running away?" Not that it mattered now. The release of the book had passed unnoticed, and she'd disposed of the manuscript. There would be no more books. But he'd offered it now, when it was too late.

He smiled. "Although the idea of a week spent with you fleeing to Gretna tempts me almost beyond reason, a little commonsense remains. Imagine how disappointed we would make our families. The ceremony will be modest, but the wedding breakfast could go on for some time."

Society considered the parading of tender emotion in public vulgar in the extreme. Men could weep and wail in Parliament, women could come to fisticuffs in the fashionable salons, but they must never show love or affection to their loved ones. Foolish, she called it. She would spend all evening ignoring the play and kissing Oliver, were it allowed.

He chuckled when she said so but stole another kiss. "As would I. Come, my poor mama and her husband will freeze to death, waiting in the carriage, and she is longing to speak with you. The night is unusually chilly for this time of year, so ensure you have a decent wrap."

She sent up for her light woolen shawl, and when they stood in the hall, she allowed him to help her arrange it. Forde stepped back, holding Dru's gloves. Oliver spared her a glance. "You will be moving with her ladyship?"

"Yes, your grace."

"I prefer a simple 'sir' from my servants, unless in company."

"Yes, sir."

He favored Forde with one of his blinding smiles. A pang of foolish jealousy shot through Dru, but she quelled it easily. Oliver would have no interest in Forde.

How did Forde feel about that? Did she have a sweetheart of her own?

Suitably arrayed in hat, shawl, and gloves, she went out to the pretty town carriage that his mother owned. Her ladyship welcomed her warmly. "I do approve of my son's choice, Drusilla. I have been speaking to him for this age to find a wife."

"Oh."

"And I have steadfastly told you that I would find a wife in due course," Oliver reminded her. "I trust you're happy I've now done so." A slight note of brusqueness marked his words. Obviously he and his mother had had this conversation before. Probably more than once.

Lady Bixby smiled. That was where Oliver had his smile from—the sweetness overlaid with a touch of wickedness that in him reduced her to a quivering jelly.

"I can almost feel glad that he waited," her ladyship continued. "You will make a perfect duchess. More than that, you will make a good wife."

Dru liked Oliver's mother. She had kept her youthful figure and presented an elegant appearance with a touch of frivolity. Her smiles came frequently and held a degree of sincerity, and she had just subtly offered to leave Oliver and Dru alone to enjoy their honeymoon by themselves.

Hastily, she turned her mind away from any thought of honeymoon. She would welcome their wedding night and what lay ahead joyfully. To be truthful, she couldn't wait.

"We always enjoy the season," she said primly. But she should have known better. Oliver noticed her pause. "You don't relish it as much as your brothers and sisters," he commented. "I've seen you hiding at the back of the room with the spinsters and companions."

"I like their company." She spoke the truth. Those women, forgotten or never noticed in the first place, had a quirky society of their own and their own way of looking at the exalted personages before them. "I will not abandon them, at least those I consider my friends."

"Good." Oliver smiled warmly. He was sitting opposite Dru and her mother, leaning back, occasionally jolted by a pit in the road.

Outside, the sky was slowly darkening. Soon they would not need lights until ten, but after that the nights would draw in. Dru was never sure which part of the year she preferred, but this year she would have someone to snuggle up against in the cold of winter.

"Is your business legal?" she asked hesitantly.

"No." He lost the smile, and Dru was sorry she'd asked him. "My brother is meeting with his physician and undergoing some new treatment. We are expecting his recovery to improve."

"He will be well?"

"He will never be completely well." Oliver leaned forward. "Indeed, I should speak to you about him. You will be a member of our family, and as a part of it, completely privy to our secrets."

The question rose to her lips. Why did they keep Lord Charles a secret? Why did nobody ever see him? She had no clue, and neither did anyone else.

"Not here," his mother said hastily. "Come to visit tomorrow. We'll tell you everything then." She covered Dru's hand with her own. "Truly, you have nothing to fear. Charles lives quietly because he wishes it, and we honor that. The speculations that go around make him even more determined to retain his privacy."

Yes, she could understand it. Sometimes she wished she could go into seclusion herself, but what chance did she have of that?

Lord Bixby, a distinguished man wearing sober but well-made clothes, nodded. "That would be best. I have met Charles once or twice, but even I am not allowed to visit without an invitation."

And Charles had been ill recently. Maybe that was why he preferred to remain in seclusion. Nerves prickled at her stomach, but she smiled. "I would love to. Thank you. May I bring someone?"

Oliver exchanged a glance with his mother. "I will chaperone you, my dear. I think it would be best to introduce just you. If Charles is up to it, of course."

Because Charles wanted complete privacy. Did he keep to one set of apartments and never go out? Doing that would drive her insane. If he wasn't insane already. Her stomach clenched in apprehension. Was that it? Did he present a danger? His servants were in reality his warders?

She forced pleasant compliance to her face. "I'm looking forward to meeting him." And the house. She had never visited, but with Oliver's mother in residence, she could now do so.

As she alighted from the carriage and accepted Oliver's arm, she glanced up at the façade of Drury Lane Theatre. Like the rest of London, the building was soot-blackened. It was a favorite haunt of the *haut monde*. Close to the theater stood King's coffeehouse, Weatherbys, and other establishments where actresses and their clients gathered after the performance. They would not be going to any of those places, since only the *demi-monde* and worse went there. Of course, Dru wanted to, having a natural curiosity, but she would be condemned forever if she ventured there.

They would attend the play and then skip the rest of the evening's entertainment and go to Lord and Lady Swithland's rout. As Dru turned to ensure her mother-in-law was being looked after, she caught sight of someone she vaguely knew. The man bowed, but she spotted speculation in the man's eyes before he turned away. Perhaps the woman approaching him was the cause. Most of her bosom was on display, and she had festooned her skin with black patches. "I wouldn't trust a whore with all those patches," she murmured, forgetting who she was with. "Who knows what blemishes she's covering?"

A hoot came from beside her. Her future husband was grinning. "I never knew my betrothed was so worldly-wise."

Heat rose to her cheeks, and she wanted to die. She hadn't meant to say anything like that aloud. "It's having older brothers," she mumbled. "We often heard things we weren't supposed to. Mama used to threaten us with a thrashing, but she never went ahead with her promise."

"I'm glad."

They climbed the steps while their footman rushed ahead to open the door for them.

"I thought you would say that she should have beaten us often."

"And ruin that perfect skin?" He watched her with a quizzical smile.

Now she was blushing even more, but he laughed again when she ducked her head to hide her embarrassment.

Although nobody had made any formal announcement, everybody knew about the betrothal. A few casual referrals to it, and the whole of London knew. All eyes turned to them as they entered the box, but nobody smiled, as she'd expected. Tilting her chin, Dru pretended she didn't care and ignored the jealous cats who wanted to spoil her happiness.

The actors came on stage and the performance began. As usual, the level of conversation dimmed just a little, and the actors had to declaim and bellow to make themselves heard. Only Garrick could control a crowd, and he was not present tonight. The huge chandelier blazed above. "This is another social gathering. That is all," Dru said.

Oliver, leaning with his arm draped across the back of her chair in a protective gesture, agreed. "Appearing here during the season truly tests an actor's resolve."

Had he ever gone to the green room after the performance? Actresses displayed their availability, and the conversation grew ribald. Dru had sometimes thought wistfully of the places she could never go. Her sister Claudia had inherited a brothel and ventured there, but Dru had never done anything so shocking. Perhaps she should have. She might not feel as wary as she did now.

"Our first appearance as a couple," Oliver murmured. "Perhaps they are overawed. If someone else does not snap up a Richmond girl, we're in danger of becoming the match of the season."

"Oh, dear." Dru didn't mind very much. She was used to being stared at. With the guest list to the wedding breakfast filled, her trousseau ready, and most of all, that damned book taken care of, she had nothing to fear.

A small part of her regretted losing the manuscript she'd spent so many years on, but she was determined to make the best start to her marriage. Her fondness for Oliver had blossomed the more she saw of him. He set her on fire. Every kiss and gentle caress made her want more. Once or twice he'd kissed the tops of her breasts, but that was all. Enough to give her a taste of what was to come. She anticipated her wedding night with eagerness. Infuriatingly, he wouldn't go beyond a certain point. But in less than two weeks, she would have it all. And so would he.

The people in the boxes opposite were staring, chattering behind their fans. Surely Dru's betrothal would not cause such disturbance? Now and then they would flick a glance at her, as if afraid to meet her eyes.

Dru began to feel uncomfortable. Oliver moved closer to her. Lady Bixby shifted in her seat and readjusted her skirts, smoothing over the fine white silk. Her fingers caressed the tiny rosebuds embroidered there. Dru was wearing her favorite green damask, but even that did not give her a comfortable place to retreat into. "If you feel ill at ease, let your appearance speak for you," her mother had told her once, and Dru took that advice now.

At the first interval, nobody came to see them. Once their engagement had become known, Dru and Oliver had received many more visits and congratulations, sincere or otherwise. None came tonight. People murmured and kept looking at them. What was wrong?

Fear crept up on Dru. It couldn't be possible. So few copies of her book were available that the hundreds of people in the audience could not have read them all.

Then someone called from the gods, the level of the audience so high it could cause nosebleeds. "Prince of Tirolly! Free the princess. Give her what she wants!"

Raucous laughter rocked the audience. Even the actors on stage joined in, seeing when they had lost the attention of the audience.

Except for Dru. Determinedly she turned her eyes to the stage.

That was worse. The actors improvised, using the names of her characters. They referred to Drusetta, the heroine—Dru tried very hard not to groan aloud—and the hero, one Desidero, the wronged prince. The audience hissed when they spoke of the Prince of Tirolly. They cheered when the hero of the play compared himself to Desidero.

Oh, God. They had read it. Yesterday she had thought she was free of the curse, that tossing the manuscript into the Thames had marked the end of her youthful foolishness, but no. Wilkins had published the book anyway and produced all the copies he wanted.

She would destroy him. She'd tell her brothers and they'd— But that wouldn't help her now.

Although Wilkins had said he'd known her, he could well have been lying. She could pretend she was as much a victim as anyone else, and someone as yet unknown had written the wretched thing. Why would anyone associate her with the author of this scurrilous tome? Knowing what came next in the story sent her anxiety rocketing. She had a vivid imagination. Using the secret cache of documents and prints she'd found, she'd gone further than anyone since John Cleland scandalized society with his account of the life of a woman of pleasure. She'd recklessly put the two brothers in a carriage, and at the end of the first volume, the vehicle had crashed. She admitted she had the idea from the story of Oliver and Charles, but then— With relief, she recalled her rewrites. She had taken the brother out, given the villain a nephew instead, taken away his scars. Carriage accidents were common. Nobody need associate her revised manuscript with the Prince.

They must not know. She wanted to leap up, run all the way home, and lock the door to her room. She wanted to go now. But that would be to admit culpability, to show her guilt.

Oliver had not missed her tension. "I will find out what this is about," he murmured, his breath hot in her ear. "And I will deal with it, if necessary. Do not concern yourself, Dru. Would you like to leave?"

If Dru had learned anything from her family, it was to stand her ground. Never retreat. "Of course not," she snapped. "And leave the battle to the victor?"

"Oh, I do like you," his mother said from behind them. "Smile. Act as if there is nothing wrong. We will deal with this later."

The play dragged on, each mention of the names from the book achieving cheer after cheer. If she were really unlucky, they'd carry on doing it. She would ask her father to suppress it. This could not happen. Tears pricked her eyes until she bit the inside of her cheek so hard that the salty taste of blood flooded her mouth.

They made it to the end of the play. Then they could leave. They were, after all, expected at a ball. Could she attend it? If she had to. This affair felt like a fight for her life. She couldn't remember anything about the action on stage, only the references to her book. Each time an actor shouted the name, she braced herself, clamped her teeth together in an effort to retain the smile she'd fixed on her face. The names became everything, until she couldn't hear anything else except the raucous laughter that followed it.

By the end of the play, she was trembling inside but holding herself rigidly enough that her reaction did not show. Oliver got to his feet and offered his arm. His nostrils were white and pinched, his eyes sparkling with fury. She'd not seen him so angry since the incident at the ball, when she'd spun a fantasy and he'd left her to it.

He must never know she was the cause of his anger. Keeping a secret from her husband for all of their married life did not appeal, but not marrying him was even worse.

Silently they left the theater and got in the waiting carriage. Oliver rapped on the front harder than necessary and tersely directed the driver to take them to Grosvenor Square.

"We will see if your parents have the news," he said, and growled low in his throat. But he had handed Dru and his mother into the vehicle with punctilious care. As the driver gave the office to the horses, Oliver thumped the side of the carriage with his closed fist. "This is intolerable. I will not allow this to go on. Does anyone know the reason for the debacle back there?"

Dru said nothing. If she denied it, she'd be lying. If she said yes, she'd have to expand on it, and she couldn't bear to do that. Not now, not ever.

"I believe it is the new book," Lady Bixby said. "I have a copy at home. I was told by a friend that it would be the latest literary sensation. I have not read it yet, and I will not now, but when I opened it I saw some of those names that the crowd was chanting tonight."

"A book?" Oliver gave a hollow laugh. "Why would it cause such a sensation?"

"It may have nothing to do with our situation," the duchess continued, her tone so calm that Dru recognized the same level of iron control she was exercising. "It may be a coincidence, or the writer decided to have some mischief with the names. If you plan to go to the Strenshalls, we will return to our home."

Her husband put his hand over hers in a quiet gesture of affection. She smiled at him. "Yes, my dear, although we will stand ready to support you if we are needed."

"Very well, Mama. A good idea, I think."

An ominous silence descended on the carriage, and they traveled the rest of the way without speaking.

Inside Dru's London home, lights blazed, and a pair of *torchères* flared either side of the front door. To the passerby, the house would look normal. They alighted and let the carriage continue on its way. Oliver plied the knocker with not a little enthusiasm.

A liveried footman opened the door. Dru nodded to James, and he spared her a polite bow. It would have to be the footman who accompanied Dru and Livia to the bookshop. Dru lowered her head, using the removal of her hat as an excuse not to meet anyone's eyes. "The marquess and marchioness are within," James said in reply to her murmured question. "They are alone."

"I see." Tight-lipped, Oliver offered his arm to her in the formal manner. They made their stately way upstairs to the drawing room, which was full of Strenshalls. As luck would have it, the clock struck the hour as they entered. The chime drowned out any effort at polite conversation. Since it went on for ten strokes, Dru had time to curtsy to her mother, who was in her ballroom finery, her wide skirts covered with elaborately embroidered and ruffled red silk. The color suited her mood. Everyone in the room was angry, Dru not the least of them.

How dare Wilkins take her necklace and her money and do this terrible thing? If she had a sword, she'd strike him down. She should have let Livia shoot him.

Livia stood when she entered and opened her mouth, but whatever she said was drowned by the clock.

The clock ended its racket as Oliver took his seat next to Dru on a sofa. There was not much room, but he draped her skirts over his lap, forcing her to press close to him. Dru regained the iron control she'd learned in her childhood, necessary for someone in the public eye so much.

The marchioness's chilly words broke the sudden silence. "We decided not to attend the ball. No doubt we would receive an interesting reception. You heard, I presume?"

"The theater was alive with it," Oliver said. "Does anyone know what this book contains?"

"Yes," Livia said eagerly. "I read it. It's a frivolous story." She bit her lip and glanced at her mother, who was sitting quietly, hands in her lap. "I know I am supposed to keep to improving books, but this was too much. Everyone was talking about it, and there were queues at the bookseller's. I only went in because of the crowds. But when I opened it, I could not put it down. It's very cleverly told. I'll wager Dru wishes she could write anything half so fine."

Her triumphant gaze met Dru's fulminating one, and she looked away hastily. Finally her sister had the opportunity to read the result of Dru's scribblings, something the twins had been demanding for years. "The book is a fantasy, set in a country that does not exist. Tirolly, the author called it. The Prince of Tirolly is the villain of the piece, and very well drawn." She shot a glance at Oliver. "That is, it is taken from life. The hero is clearly a depiction of the duke." Clasping her hands together, continued, but did not meet anyone's eye. "I'm sorry, but it is, right down to the scars on his chin and brow."

Oliver rolled his eyes. "Just the scars?"

"No, the way you can glaze over, and your preference for dressing plainly. Truly, it's impossible to mistake it." Livia stared at him, daring him to say something about her personal remarks.

Invisible cold fingers gripped Dru's throat.

She had eliminated that caricature, destroyed Oliver's resemblance and restored an earlier version. What had happened here? The question of who had got their hands on the manuscript became more urgent. Someone malicious, that was for sure. Someone who had constant access to the kitchen.

"The heroine, Drusetta, is Dru," Livia continued. "She's quiet, adoring, and a member of a large family. But they cast her out, and she lives simply in Tirolly. The prince sees her and falls in love with her. He abducts her and locks her in a dungeon, where she learns a terrible secret. The Prince is a usurper. He has locked up his brother, the real Prince of Tirolly, who has gone mad. But he sees Drusetta, falls madly in love with her, and comes to his senses. The prince's court is full of characters who are easily recognizable as people in society. In fact, someone who knows society very well must have written it."

Oliver groaned and covered his eyes with his hand. "Could it be any worse?"

"Have you made any enemies recently?" the marquess asked. "Someone who wanted to get revenge on you in some way?"

Oliver shook his head. Dropping his hand, he met Dru's father's direct gaze. "Not above the ordinary. I have a particularly annoying land dispute going on, but the man I am dealing with doesn't have the wit to do this. Or the devilry."

"The plot with the brother is unfortunate," Dru's mother said. She was at her most stately, the great lady, but outrage was written on every part of her body. She sat completely still, her pose queenly, but under her light coating of face paint, her features were white and her eyes narrowed. "I presume it is exaggerated."

"Probably," said Oliver.

"Are there any similarities?"

"I don't know." He turned to Livia. "What happens to the brother?" He sounded perfectly calm, but he was anything but.

Livia shifted uncomfortably. "The Prince usurps the throne. He says his brother is cared for, although he is kept in a dungeon and fed on bread and water. Before he locks him up, he tries to kill him by staging a number of accidents. He drops a boulder from the castle battlements, for instance, and puts a burr under his brother's horse's saddle. And at the end of the book there's a carriage accident, where both the brothers are involved."

Oliver's jaw tightened even more. "I see."

Dru met her sister's gaze. Livia was close to tears, her blue eyes glossy and reddened.

Downstairs the door slammed, and male voices drifted up to them. The troops had arrived. Val and Marcus and their wives and Darius and his partner. They'd be here in a minute. Dru couldn't stand it.

Their mother had not missed the brief exchange between her daughters. "Girls? What do you know about this?"

"What could we possibly know?" Livia shrugged. "Just what everyone else knows, that's all."

"Drusilla?" Her mother swung her head and met Dru's eyes.

Too late, Dru glanced down and composed herself.

"I'm waiting," her mother said softly.

Beside her, Oliver's body stiffened.

What could she say? If she lied, she would have to bear the burden for the rest of her life. What if somehow she was found out? She couldn't think it, mustn't think it. Who would know? She racked her brain to recall something that might identify her as the author.

The coldness froze her bones. She couldn't do it, couldn't confess what she'd done before her husband-to-be. "Nothing more."

Warmth flowed through her when Oliver moved back. "I'll send the carriage for you in the morning. Then we'll work out what to do together." Bending, he kissed her hand. "Don't worry. We'll get through this."

His care for her nearly killed Drusilla.

Chapter 10

Dru didn't sleep much that night. She wore a trench in her bed, rolling from side to side and dragging her sheets with her until her carefully made bed became a bird's nest. Her brothers had sworn retribution. They would find everything out if she wasn't careful. But what could she do to stop it? Nothing.

When Forde saw it, she gazed at it a moment too long before turning to the business of the day and dressing her mistress. Dru chose a blue gown with white snowdrops embroidered all around the hem. The petticoat was pure white. Innocence and purity prevailed. She even considered having her hair powdered, but she couldn't bear the fuss and the mess. Her heart would have been in her boots were she wearing any, but it had to make do with her pretty blue satin shoes.

"Your pearls would work to advantage with this gown, my lady." Forde moved to the jewelry box on top of the low dresser.

"No, I think not," she said hastily. "I will have a lace ruffle."

Forde turned back, her brows arched in surprise. "Very well, my lady." Without further argument, she tied a ruffle around Dru's neck.

A small spark of warmth hit Dru's chilled body. Talking straightly to her maid had reaped its reward. In the past Forde would have insisted, but she was definitely more amenable these days, if not outright downcast.

Now she had to talk straightly to her betrothed. After a night's exhausted sleep, she had come to a decision. She could not spend the rest of her life with him holding this dreadful secret inside her. The seed would fester and rot what they had. He insisted on honesty in all things, and if he found out from someone other than her, he would never forgive her for it. Whatever the consequences, she must tell him the truth.

Half an hour later she was handing her hat, cloak and gloves to the butler at the house of the Duke of Mountsorrel—the house she'd expected to spend the rest of the season in. Now, who knew? Livia had come with her, although she protested at the necessity.

Lady Bixby received them both and then asked Dru to fetch her something from the music room. "But take your time, my dear. I want to get to know your charming sister."

As she'd expected, Oliver met her alone, took her in his arms, and kissed her warmly. "Every day," he murmured, his mouth moving against hers, "Every day is one closer to our wedding day. You drive me beyond reason, Drusilla."

Flushing, she pulled away slightly. "Oliver, I have something to tell you." Then she froze. Looking at him, the stern face so openly fond, her loss struck her like a blow to the stomach. She would never see that expression again, or she would see it turned on to someone else. He could do nothing but reject her. Her future loomed before her—a dark, featureless void.

But still, she would tell the truth. She would.

"Let me talk to you first." He led her toward a comfortable-looking sofa, deeply upholstered. He took her hand. "I need to tell you what to expect when you meet my brother. You must, sweetheart. I want you to love him as I do, but I do not want what you find to come as a shock."

"I—"

He put his hand over hers. "You have nothing to fear."

"Yes, I do, Oliver, I really do." Desperate now, Dru abandoned her little speech and just came out with it. "It was me. I wrote that book."

Winter descended on the room despite the blue skies outside. "Explain." That was all he said. It was enough.

She shivered. "I…I'm sorry. There's no excuse, I know, but it was for my amusement only. I did not send it to the publisher. I swear."

"I trust it amused you." He had retreated several miles. His frosty tone echoed his status, and as she watched, the man inside retreated into the formidable figure of the Duke of Mountsorrel.

"Come with me. See what you have done." The man returned, fiercely furious. His eyes flashed fire and narrowed as he stared at her, as if she were less than the earth between his feet.

She dared not refuse. If she did, she would probably never see him again. Their broken engagement would happen at arms' length. She saw it in his eyes, in every line on his flushed face.

When she blindly reached for him, he grabbed her hand before she could regain her senses and snatch it back. He tugged her to his side and put his arm around her waist, as he had before. But not in this manner. Not with his hand spread over the small of her back urging her forward.

They left the drawing room and went up two flights of stairs to the floor below the attics. Here, the corridor was a little wider than she expected and the decoration as elegant as elsewhere in the house. But an air of hush prevailed here, stillness, as if time had stopped the clocks.

Apprehension gripped Dru's stomach, adding to the sense of doom she'd had since that morning and the distress pouring through her. She forced herself to breathe deeply, sucking air back into her lungs. A faint scent of lavender and something else she couldn't identify filled the air here. Something faintly metallic.

After tapping softly on the second door along, Oliver paused. "Upset him and I will see you in hell. Understand?"

Dru swallowed, nodded. Oliver flung open the door.

A man sat in a chair by the window. He was gazing at a newssheet, but as they entered he turned his head, a welcoming smile touching his mobile lips.

Dru caught her breath. This man was handsome. Where Oliver had a pleasant appearance, Charles had the kind of face that caused women to hold their breath. Despite his seclusion, he wore a perfectly curled white wig. His eyes were the blue of sapphires, his lips full, and his cheekbones high.

"And this is Drusilla." He did not get to his feet. His sapphire satin breeches covered legs she thought might be more spindly than normal, but they were presented immaculately, as were his coat and waistcoat. The waistcoat was in the latest style, embroidered with gold thread in a charming design of flowers and bees. He could go out into society now. Except that he never did. Nobody had seen Charles since his accident. And Dru had no idea why.

Dru made her curtsy. Deeply aware of Oliver watching her every move, she kept her gaze on the man before her.

"My brother, Lord Charles Fitzhugh," Oliver said softly. "Charles, you already know who this is."

Charles kept his eyes on her as she rose. In any other man she'd have called his stare insolent, too personal for her to enjoy. "You are lovely, my dear. I look forward to furthering our acquaintance."

He could not stand. Pity shaded her senses, but she knew better than to allow it to show. She guessed he would not welcome it. "Yes, sir. I would like that," she said, but she was not entirely sure she did. Or that she would be allowed to.

"Please take a seat." Graciously, he gestured to the sofa opposite his chair.

Dru obeyed, folding her hands in her lap.

This was the man she had wronged by writing her book? Why could he not have been twisted and ugly? Why did he have to be as handsome as sin? The similarities between Charles and her hero grew more glaringly apparent as she stared at him. The soulful eyes, the dark lashes, the air of total elegance—they were all there. Oliver was more brutish in build, powerful, his face rugged, his eyes gray rather than blue.

Why did they keep him locked away? She could hardly question Oliver now. Charles appeared perfectly normal. Except for one thing.

"I apologize for not getting up," he said. He gestured to a couple of instruments propped up close to his chair. Crutches, they were crutches. Fashioned from gleaming mahogany, well polished, with silk pads at the top to support his armpits, they were nevertheless sinister and ugly. "I can get up and sit down, shift myself from bed to chair and vice versa, but that is all."

"You should practice more." Oliver's voice flowed through the space between them, so softly melodic that Dru knew he was forcing it. Did he always talk to his brother in such a quiet, level tone, or was this put on for her? "Your physician says that you could regain the use of your legs with enough practice.

Charles's welcoming smile turned into a sneer, his patrician nostrils flaring. "He knows nothing. He is not subject to daily pain—" He broke off suddenly and switched his attention to Dru, giving her the blinding smile she'd seen when she'd come in. "I'm sorry, my dear. I must apologize. It is not usual for me to complain."

"Are you in much pain?" she found herself asking, as if he drew the question out of her.

The smile faded, leaving gravity almost angelic in its perfection. "Yes, but I bear it willingly when I consider the alternative. My physician and my attendants care for me most diligently. I have three, you know—Burnett, Friedlander, and Carter. Burnett has been with me for the longest time. He was my"—he threw an apologetic glance at Oliver—"*our* groom, but he chose to stay with me after the accident. I have had reason to be grateful to him these many years."

That had to make it twenty years, probably a few more. Charles had been fourteen at the time of the accident. "I see. He does everything for you?"

Charles shuddered delicately. "Everything. I fear my needs have become more elaborate of late. I seem to have developed a few distressing tendencies." The smile broadened again, in a way Dru was coming to understand. He used that beautiful smile to cover something, and from what he said, most likely the pain he suffered every day. Every hour.

Why? She knew better than to ask that, of course. Although horror thrummed through her, a panicked reminder of what she had done, she was no longer out of her mind with distress. Would Oliver throw her out of the house now he'd brought her to a realization of what she'd done? Most likely he would. She would bear it. Go to the country, perhaps, although retreat was not in her nature.

Oliver sat next to her, seething. She could feel it, and it scared her, even though she was not easily frightened.

Reaching for the table at his elbow, Charles picked up a book. He only lifted his left hand when he needed to support it, and the shape remained, curved in on itself, instead of flattening under the volume. A useless hand. "Have you read this?"

Slowly, she took her attention from his damaged limb and, as he carefully turned the title page toward her and read the name and the author. "*The History and Fortunes of the Prince of Tirolly*, by A Lady."

Oh, God. No, please. If the building collapsed now, and she died in the rubble, Dru would be happier. "No," she said, licking her dry lips.

Charles followed the small gesture with his gaze. He let the book fall into his lap. "I found it amusing, but whoever wrote it knows society through and through. I have not moved out of the house for years, and even I can recognize them. Especially the main characters." His laugh rippled through the room. "I find the story most diverting, although I would rather have the next two volumes now, not wait two weeks. The last volume is to be published in one month, before the end of the season. Is that not amusing?"

Dru didn't know what to say. Oliver remained grimly silent.

Charles did not appear to notice the ominous silence. "The hero, my dear, is very like me, and the villain is undoubtedly Oliver. Nobody could mistake you, dear brother. Such a shame your face bears more marks from our unfortunate accident rather than mine. Much better if I had remained wizened, a hideous reminder of our transgressions, and you were beautiful and unmarked." Bitterness tinged his last words, but his face remained perfectly smooth.

Oliver opened his mouth and drew a breath, but his brother had not yet finished.

"In this book I get to be the hero and rescue the heroine, but at the end of this volume, he is probably dead. Such a pity we cannot ask the author what are her intentions."

"Oh, but we can," Oliver murmured. "Don't hide your light under a bushel, Drusilla. I have to tell you, brother, that Drusilla claims she wrote the book currently taking society by storm."

Tears pricked Dru's eyes. A slow, hot trickle marked where one escaped and tracked its way down the side of her face. "I did not mean it to see daylight, ever. I locked it up. Only my sisters and I knew it existed, and nobody read it except me. I wrote it over many years, and I swear, I destroyed it."

"Since it has reached this form, I fail to see how you could have done so," Oliver said coldly.

"I did. I swear it." In her mind's eye she saw the parcel plummeting into the river.

"Then how did it reach the publisher? How is it here, for everyone—*everyone*—to read?"

He would not let her retreat from this. She would have to humiliate herself. Perhaps that was what he wanted, before he turned his back on her and destroyed her in society's eyes, too. She had no guarantees, would have to do what she thought was right. Not that taking that course had helped her much so far.

She would get through this. Today would be the worst, when all her dreams crumbled. Her siblings would be dragged in, and she'd have to tell her cousin Julius that this mess was because of what happened at the ball. Her fault. The least she could do was accept all blame.

Although she could not face Oliver without fear, she could face what she had done and tell him the truth. At last.

That was when she realized what must hurt him the most. She had lied to him. Or rather she had not been entirely honest with him. "I meant to tell you." She clasped her hands together until the knuckles turned white. "I did not know how."

"How about, 'I wrote that book, Oliver.' Or are you lying now?" His voice rose at the end, as if he wanted her to agree with him.

She could tell him she was lying, that she had made a bad joke, and he would forget it.

Except she could not. "I wrote that book, Oliver." Saying it drove her closer to breaking down, but she couldn't afford that luxury. She'd do it another time, when she didn't have to face people. "I wrote it as amusement and consigned it to the kitchen fire."

"Except that you did not. You gave it to a publisher instead. I trust, my lady, that you know how to make a bargain and you got a good price."

"I didn't get a penny." She should not have said that. It implied she had given it to Wilkins. "I didn't give it—"

He held up a hand imperiously. "Do not try to explain."

A sound she had not expected broke into the tension that crackled between them. A tinkling laugh from Charles. "Oh, dear, Oliver. Have you read it? It's an amusing bagatelle, no more. A short and sweet distraction. Show them you are upset, and you will play into their hands. They'll be avid for more."

Oliver turned to face his brother, his expression softening as he gazed at him. "What do you mean?"

"It's a frivolous story. With all due respect"—he nodded to her and then returned his attention to his brother—"this is no *Pamela*. It is no *Robinson Crusoe*. It will not last. A plethora of books have come out since those, and very few have held the public's attention for long. Wait for the newest sensation. Something that will take over from this one." He spread his good hand out. "Leave it alone. It will pass. We must, of course, stop the gossip, and there is a way." He met his brother's gaze.

Oliver raised his brows.

He changed the expansive gesture to one of mock obeisance to Dru. She flinched. "My dear, I enjoyed meeting you. I regret we will not meet again, but maybe we can write."

So that was what he meant. They were to separate. Although she had herself come to that conclusion, Dru's heart plummeted to the bottom of her silver-buckled shoes.

Oliver got to his feet. "I have not yet decided." Striding toward her, he held out his hand. "My lady."

As if leading her into a dance, except she had never seen his face this stony, never felt so cold in his presence. She took his hand and went with him to the door.

A strangled cry came from behind him, as if an animal had come into the room and bayed a warning. A choking, grinding sound, terrible in its mindless pain.

Oliver spun around, and Dru came to her feet, pushing her problems into the background.

Charles sat in his chair, his blue eyes wide saucers of agony. Foam seethed from his mouth, through his clamped teeth. His legs stretched out before him, and his back jerked up, as if he a demon puppet master controlled him with an invisible set of strings.

Oliver leaped across the room, scooped his brother up, and laid him on the floor. "Call his attendant," he snapped.

Dru didn't need to be told twice. As Oliver straddled Charles, spreading his legs and kneeling between them, holding his brother's jaw steady with one hand, she scooped up her skirts and raced to the door. She had no idea who to call for, but in the event she didn't have to scream "Help!" into the void.

A plainly dressed man stood outside, and when she ripped open the door, he pushed past her and raced inside. "Sir, sir!" he cried, his distress evident in every line on his anguished face.

"Close that door!" Oliver commanded.

Dru did as she was told and waited for more orders. She would do whatever was necessary. She had never seen a man have a fit before, and she never wanted to see it again. Terrified, she watched. Was she seeing the death of Oliver's brother? She stood, helplessly, as the two men restrained Lord Charles Fitzhugh, preventing him from inflicting damage on himself. Charles strained and pulled up, his back arching in an inhuman effort to fight his way out of his bonds. Oliver tore at his brother's neck, dragging his neckcloth free, tossing it carelessly aside.

Surging forward, she swept a small table out of the way to prevent the thrashing man from destroying it with his uncoordinated movements. His body jerked, his head went back, rapping hard against the floor. Dru winced for him. The poor man, to have to undergo such terrible torture. What could help him?

He jerked and convulsed endlessly, that handsome face set in a fierce grimace, marred with saliva and sweat. His elegant coat tore and twisted around him. Dru didn't realize she was crying until her vision blurred, and she had to swipe at her eyes to clear them. Her starched lace ruffle scraped her neck.

What could she do? Feeling angry and helpless, she watched the agony of the man and the struggles of the two holding him for what seemed like forever. A delicate chime tinkled at a higher level than Charles's wordless growls, catching her attention. The clock on the mantel was striking the hour, as if nothing unusual were happening.

Charles had fallen into his fit ten minutes ago. Ten measly minutes had reduced him to the snarling animal on the floor. Oliver and the attendant were holding fast. Eventually, with a whimper, Charles slumped back, boneless and unconscious.

Oliver got to his feet while the attendant arranged his master's arms and legs back into a semblance of normality.

* * * *

Oliver glanced back, surprised to find his betrothed still here. "You didn't flee in terror?" He hardened his heart against her, despite her bedraggled appearance and her expression of utter dread. Before her confession, he would have gone to her, treated her with all the tenderness in his heart. No more. "Open that door. We need to carry him into bed." He jerked his head toward the inner door.

"That was a bad one, sir," Burnett murmured. "It lasted five minutes longer than the last."

Oliver nodded. Guilt washed over him, as it always did when he saw Charles, especially when Charles demonstrated the more distressing parts of his illness. He'd have rather Dru left, but she had seen it now. When he'd told her to close the door, he'd wanted her to shut it on her way out. Had he not made himself clear? He would take care to remedy that.

Drusilla hurried across the room and opened the door to the bedroom. Bending, Oliver scooped his brother into his arms. Charles was no lightweight, despite his illness. His body was muscular for a man who spent his life in a chair. But Charles had always been a fighter. He would not be here if he had not fought everything that opposed him. He would most likely angry when he came to himself.

Burnett pulled the brocade coverlet on the bed out of the way, allowing Oliver to lay his brother gently on the soft blanket beneath.

As he straightened, Charles blinked. His eyes opened, fixed on Oliver, and he cracked a heartbreaking grin. "That was a good one. How long?"

"Ten minutes," Oliver said softly. Charles usually had a moment of clarity until his headache struck. "You're back now. Let me help you sit."

The sickly stink of laudanum filled the air as Burnett prepared Charles's usual tincture. As Oliver packed pillows behind him, his brother's attention went to where Dru stood by the window. She still looked like an angel.

Only now Oliver knew how little she resembled one. Her mischief-making had led to this, and Oliver was determined that she would pay. He kept Charles stress-free for just this reason, but somehow Charles had a copy of the book in his possession. How typical of him to laugh the business away, when he was a victim of Dru's meddling. Oliver would ensure she paid.

How could he let her walk away scot-free after this? No, he refused to do that. Time the spoiled brat learned to face the consequences of her actions. She came from a family of privilege. Let her have a taste of real life.

Deeply aware of the hypocrisy of what he was thinking, he knew he was right. That accident had jolted the happy family group into another place, forced to face realities none of them wanted.

Charles glared at Dru. Oliver knew exactly why, but he didn't choose to enlighten her. Not yet. With savage fury, he looked forward to what was to come. His agony he kept to himself, as always. As he watched, Charles's gaze softened.

"Welcome to the family," he said to her.

When Burnett brought the mixture over, Oliver helped Charles hold the glass as he gulped the noxious stuff down and then wiped his mouth for him.

Charles slumped back with a sigh. "I hate that tincture."

"We could try something else," Oliver said casually.

"Nothing else works." Already Charles's eyes were drooping. Exhaustion from his fit plus the drug would serve to put him to sleep very soon.

"Let's get you settled, my lord." Burnett had a clean nightshirt draped over his arm.

Drusilla stood as if frozen. Time to talk.

Oliver placed a gentle kiss on his brother's forehead and received a tired smile and a word of thanks. It broke his heart that his brother, in such pain, remembered to thank him. No doubt he would thank Burnett too before he subsided into the slumber that would last for the rest of the day.

With a bitter smile, he strode forward and took her by the elbow. "Come."

She stumbled as she turned, but he didn't stop to help her. Let her find her feet on her own. She would have to do that rather a lot in the days to come. He pulled her out of Oliver's apartment and along the corridor toward his own.

Inside, every item of furniture was strewn with feminine garments. Only then did Oliver recall that her maid was coming to arrange Drusilla's trousseau in the dressing room set aside for her. His mother wanted him to move downstairs to the ducal suite, but he refused the honor. He preferred to be close to Charles, in case his brother needed him. He would remedy that omission. The main suite would be in use soon.

The maid came into the room, something silky draped over her arm. Blushing fiercely, she dropped a deep curtsy and stood, waiting.

"You may go," Oliver said. What was the woman's name? Damned if he could remember.

"Forde," Drusilla added dully.

Forde shook her head. "Her ladyship—"

"Go, Forde," Drusilla repeated.

Oliver turned. Whatever the maid saw on his features made her scuttle back into the dressing room, the lappets of her linen cap fluttering behind her. Oliver waited until he heard the outer door close. "Does she eavesdrop?" he demanded.

Drusilla blinked. "I don't think so. She used to run to my mother, but I put a stop to that."

Oliver gave a grim smile. "Good. Because I doubt you wish anyone to overhear what I have to say to you."

All the blood drained from Drusilla's face, leaving her pale and wan. She clasped her hands before her in a gesture Oliver knew well now. She was trying to stop her trembling. Well might she tremble. "I'm so sorry."

"What do you think will happen now?" Oliver leashed his temper tightly. He'd lost it a long time ago. If he'd spoken to Drusilla then, he'd have blasted her out of the room, the house, and his life, but he had thought better of his decision. If she was to pay, he wanted to see her do it.

She had brought devastation to this house, to his brother, and even more to himself. How could he have imagined he could fall in love with her? Deceit never sat well on his broad shoulders, even less so now. "Go on," he urged. Let her decree her own fate.

"I imagine you want to…talk to me about your brother," she said. "Then you will send me away. In a few days we will say that we did not suit." Bleakness filled her eyes. Either she did not want to hide her distress or she could not.

"What else?"

"You and your family will not speak to mine again. I take all the blame, Oliver. I will inform my family of that. You will receive no repercussions. I swear it."

He curled his lip. "Do you think I care for that? Your family, the Shaws in particular, have danced along the line of respectability for years. Your brother married his steward's daughter, and your sister led her husband-to-be on a merry chase around London before he finally caught her and tamed her."

"She was not tamed," Drusilla burst out. "They are in love."

"I thank God the same cannot be said of us."

She winced as if he'd struck her, even though he stood full two paces away. He leaned against the heavy oak footboard of his bed. That bed where he had slept alone, dreaming of when he would share it with this woman before she'd danced her little game around him.

"I will leave London as soon as I can," she went on. "You may say what you will. I will not contradict you."

"Do you think such a course will fool anyone?"

A lone tear trickled down the side of her face. She'd scratched herself close to her eye, he noticed, though the bleeding had stopped. Blood streaked down from the mark, as if she'd wiped at it with no heed for the consequences. Just as she'd done when she sent that book to the publisher. Heedlessly, without thinking of the consequences. The cruel picture she'd drawn of him told Oliver what she truly thought of him. He would find a copy of that damned book and read it cover to cover.

Why not behave like her villain, the Prince of Tirolly? She had destroyed his faith in her, driven him to his knees in a few simple words.

"They will know," she admitted. "They will understand the book was written about us. But not who wrote it."

"You're satisfied with that? You won't trumpet the truth to the world? Claim your masterpiece?"

She shook her head. The tears flowed, but she made no attempt to dry them. Even now his instincts told him to hold her, to comfort her, but he could never allow himself to do that. Never again.

Tugging his handkerchief out of his pocket, he crossed the room and pressed the square of linen into her hand. She stared at it as if she did not know what to do with it.

"Tidy yourself," he said gruffly. "Sit. And listen."

She did as he bade her, mopping her face and holding the cloth to her eyes when she'd cleaned up the worst of the mess.

"Face me." He would not say what he wanted to the back of her head.

She turned around, swiveling on the stool where he had spent so much time himself. His valet had settled his wig on his head that morning. He'd lost it somewhere, probably in the tussle with his brother, but he couldn't bring himself to care. She had not appeared to notice the lack. Lifting her head, she met his eyes.

The sorrow in her gaze nearly overset Oliver, but he fought his tender feelings back. She did not deserve them. "Your plan is very pretty, but it will not serve. Drusilla, what did you think you would achieve, writing that nonsense? Do you hate me so much you would expose my brother's problems to the world? He lives apart because he cannot bear the idea of falling into a fit in the middle of society. Of losing control."

The remnants of shock remained in her eyes, her pupils still wide. "Nobody knows anything about him. Do you not think people might understand better if they knew?"

Fury rocked him, not least because she had suggested what he had to his brother so many times. But Charles remained obdurate, and Oliver refused to justify his brother's choices to this woman. "You are in no case to criticize what we choose to do." Turning around, he slammed his clenched fist against the wall, but the pain brought him little relief. He still despaired. He spun back to face her. Surrounded by scented, delicate silks, he felt like destroying them all. For that reason, and for that alone, he refused to do it. Destruction never helped anyone, a bitter lesson that had taken him years to learn.

"Charles is delicate. The injury he received to his head continues to plague him. He forgets things. He remains in terrible pain. And he has fits. The carriage fell on his legs, shattering the bones, and he has lost the use of them."

"Does he often fall…into fits?"

"They are unpredictable. Sometimes he can have one a week, sometimes he will go for a month or two. But I would not have him far from me. It is my fault he is as he is, and he is my burden to bear. Also yours, my dear." He purred the last word, but felt no fondness when he said it. Only pure white anger. "Oh, yes. You do not get to walk away from this, whistling a merry tune."

"I will not. I promise I will do everything I can to prevent the next two volumes coming out, if he has them. Already I—"

Two more volumes! What hell awaited them in those? What other calumnies would society drop on their heads? "You will do nothing of the kind!" he shouted. Somehow, he'd let his temper free, and it burned between them like a living flame. Closing his mouth with a snap, he watched her wipe fresh tears away, forcing his ire to subside. The sound of their heavy breathing hung over them. Eventually, Oliver felt safe to continue. He would not do her the honor of allowing her to see how much she had angered him.

"I must," she protested, not cowed by him.

But he refused to admire her for that. Nothing was admirable about this woman. She had fooled him completely, lied to him, and deceived him. He should have stayed away from her after that damned ball. Not come back for more. What kind of pathetic creature did that make him?

"I cannot let the books come out. He might not have them, but he says he does, so I must assume he made copies."

"I said you will not." Pleased that he sounded so deadly, so steady, Oliver went on, "You will obey me, Drusilla. As you will for the rest of our lives. I chose my duchess, and I intend to keep to my decision, however foolish that might have been. My brother, God help him, appears to like you. Your duties will include spending at least an hour a day with him. You will tend him." He took advantage of her stunned silence. Her jaw had dropped, and she stared at him as if he were mad.

"The gossips will speculate about Charles again. Until I can persuade him to appear in public, that will continue. You will tell everyone, including your family, that Charles is sane, as healthy as a man with his injuries can be, and happy. You will not go into any detail. The Emperors will help to spread those stories. If... *When* we marry, we will say the book was written by an anonymous person, probably a jealous rival of yours who wanted to become duchess. Do you understand, Drusilla?"

Mutely, she nodded. She looked as Charles did after a fit, bewildered and exhausted. But he wasn't about to strip her and put her to bed.

Unaccountably, his body responded to that fleeting thought. Excitement zinged along his veins, rousing him. How could he have that reaction to her, after what she had done? Why did he still want her?

Grimly, he plowed on, letting her know what he had decided. "We marry, Drusilla. You become my duchess. You act like a proper duchess, and you laugh at that foolish book. You care for my brother, and you tell your family exactly what I tell you to say. You will obey me, and I will watch you until I am satisfied that you will not make another mistake, not for the rest of your life."

"Yes." She wrung her hands, clasping and working them, before she shuddered. "Thank you."

"Thank you?" he echoed.

"You could have thrown me to the wolves."

He strode closer and took her by the shoulders, staring down into her eyes. "Our new life starts tomorrow, Drusilla. I have the special license, and we will marry without delay. Go home and prepare. I will see you with a man of the cloth at eleven sharp."

Chapter 11

Dru sat numbly before her dressing table, watching her maid turn her into the perfect bride. Somehow Oliver had persuaded everyone that he wanted her so badly he wasn't prepared to wait. Her mother had expressed dismay at first but then turned her formidable powers of organization to bringing the wedding forward.

She had done it. "Who would refuse to come to wish the bride and groom good health?" she had demanded at dinner that evening. "I have already sent out the amendments, telling the guests they should come tomorrow. The cooks are busy, and the servants are adding the leaves to the table as we speak."

They were eating their dinner in the informal atmosphere of the breakfast parlor. After escorting her home, Oliver had returned to his house to make his own preparations. He had shown every sign of the eager lover who wanted to snatch his bride away before somebody else could. Mention of the Prince of Tirolly had him waving the matter away carelessly.

"Let's give them something else to gossip about," he'd said, hitting exactly the right note to persuade the marchioness to his side.

"I will pin a rose to the side of your head, my lady," Forde said, bringing her back to the present. Her wedding day.

Dru nodded listlessly. What did it matter, when she'd shattered all her dreams? She had nobody but herself to blame. All this was her fault. Meeting the secret brother, the person she'd made myth for her own stupid amusement had led to the destruction of everything she had ever longed for. She had never wanted high status, wealth, any of those things. Just love, and she'd been on her way to getting it before she'd wrecked her prospects and her future.

Now she would have everything most women in society would kill for. She should be happy, even if she had lost her betrothed's regard. However, having experienced a small, tantalizing taste of what she could have and then thrown it away, she doubted she would ever be happy again.

When Forde had done, Dru went downstairs, where the carriage awaited to take her to church. She was marrying in a small, fashionable chapel, one of the gracious buildings erected after the Fire. She didn't have to go to church, but Lady Bixby had requested it.

She went through the ceremony like a sleepwalker. This wasn't really happening, it couldn't be. Two weeks early, to a man who hated her. This was a trial, a case she would lose and then be condemned to lifelong punishment.

At that point Dru had to stop herself. As she gave her responses, she lifted her gaze and met her nearly husband's cool stare. He affected her deeply, still, and nothing would change that. She might not ever persuade him she would never behave in that way again. Fury still lurked in the depths of Oliver's eyes. Clearly he remained angry with her.

The final "I do" from her echoed like the voice of doom around the chapel. The trouble was, she didn't know him. Not really. He dazzled her, enchanted her, but she had no way of knowing how long his temper lasted, what he would do to her. They had been on their best behavior while they were courting. Now, she had to learn all about the man she had married.

If she had known him before, as her brother Marcus had known his Viola, they would have something more solid to build on. The Shaws were known as a family who acted on impulse, let their passions ride over reason. Perhaps Dru would be the unlucky one, the person who took on too much and lost.

Fell in love with a man determined not to fall for her.

Thoughts and speculation skittered through her head, and she lost track, didn't follow the rest of the service. When her father made the "tsk" sound she knew meant he was growing bored, the vicar ended the sermon. They were done. They had already signed the register, and she had remembered her new title. Having spent her life with aristocrats, she didn't have to think about her new style.

If ever she needed a mask, it was now.

Three full hours later, Dru entered the house she was to call home on her husband's arm. He took her straight upstairs to his brother's apartments. If she had thought, she would have requested the visit, but she had barely spoken a word all day. Only social niceties.

"Well," Oliver said cheerfully as he opened the door. "Here is my new bride."

Charles had dressed for a wedding. His coat of blue brocade glimmered in the late afternoon sun, and the gold-embroidered waistcoat was positively blinding. Did he have cut diamonds for buttons? No, probably brilliants, but they flashed like fire when he turned to regard them.

The chair he sat in had wheels. Before, when she'd visited, he'd been in an ordinary chair, but this one was higher than normal and sturdier. Like a throne, since it had wide armrests. Rather intimidating.

His smile blinded her, too. She dropped a curtsy.

"Now that is unfair, when I cannot get up and bow," he said softly. "Please don't do it again. I would rather we met as friends. No ceremony. Besides, you are a duchess. You outrank me."

When she glanced at Oliver, she saw a flush on his cheeks. What had Charles said? Or perhaps the rigors of the day were affecting him, too. The constant smiling and conversations and pretending that she was very happy had taken their inevitable toll. Dru was exhausted. "I'll do whatever you wish, of course."

"Drusilla has been kind enough to offer to spend some time with you every day," Oliver said.

She needed to get to know this man. Perhaps Charles would be more forthcoming about the accident and their childhood. Oliver had told her very little, only the details of the accident itself. That meant she knew more than most other people, but that wasn't saying much.

"I'm looking forward to our time together," she murmured.

"Burnett will tell you my routine." Charles wrinkled his nose. "I believe he knows it better than I. However, we will contrive, will we not, Drusilla? Does your family not call you Dru? I believe I heard my brother refer to you like that."

"Yes. Please call me Dru if you wish to. We have such outlandish names, but we have done our best to make them more acceptable. My brother Marcus Aurelius says he has quite forgotten the second part of his name."

"I see. And your siblings are?"

His gentle questioning was as precisely efficient as any leader of society. Difficult to believe he had effectively been incarcerated for the whole of his adult life, even if it was by his own choice.

"Marcus Aurelius, Darius, Valentinian, Claudia, and Livia," she told him.

He raised a brow. "Some interesting choices there. The Roman Livia was not a particularly admirable character."

"My mother liked the name." Dru didn't like any criticism of her family. And although she had joined another group, she would always consider herself a Shaw. "When we read about her, we found she was strong, as powerful as her husband, and she did what was necessary to survive."

"Did you take your cue from her?"

Dru didn't see the connection, but Oliver's "Charles!" told her that *he* had. Oh, of course, Livia had poisoned and murdered to get what she wanted. How did that play into her situation now? How would publishing that book have furthered her cause? It had not, and it did not. Perhaps Charles thought she was married against her will. A wave of exhaustion swept over her. She had not slept properly and then had had to smile for hour after hour and tell people how happy she was.

She hurt, inside and out. She'd worn a new pair of stays, stiff and uncomfortable, and Forde had drawn them very tight. Every breath was an effort. Her hair felt pulled up, and of course she'd had to powder. She felt as if she had a hard, tight pad glued to the top of her head. Her beautiful blue gown draped and dragged. And the evening had only just begun. She had no idea what Oliver had planned for the rest of the day. The night— She shuddered. She didn't want to think about it. Thinking of what might have been only sent her into despair.

With the rigorous training she had received and the example her mother constantly set, Dru kept her head up and a polite smile on her face. Nobody looking at her would imagine the depths of agony she suffered, and if she had anything to do with it, nobody ever would.

"I take my cue from God and my parents," she answered now. "I try to do my best in all things."

"As you did when you wrote your book? Really, my dear, your reputation will echo down the centuries." Did she detect an edge of bitterness in Charles's voice? "As, unfortunately, will ours. You have made us immortal."

"I thought you said society would forget it."

Charles met her gaze. His was shuttered and hard, as hers must be. She worked to keep them that way.

"We must pray it does so. Perhaps we may make an effort to create a new scandal. Maybe Miss Chudleigh will oblige." Elizabeth Chudleigh, one of the late Queen's ladies in waiting, had scandalized society more than once. When she had appeared all but naked at a masquerade, she had set society about its ears.

"Perhaps she will. Or someone else will. I understand that the book is not a literary masterpiece."

Beside her, Oliver stirred. "I must read this, I suppose."

"Oh, you must take mine." Charles picked up the volume, once more using his bunched up nearly useless left hand to support it. Carefully, he held it out.

Oliver had no choice but to take it. "Thank you. I will obtain my own copy, unless Mama has already done so. I have a clever wife, I am told."

"No!" The bitterness in his voice hurt Dru more than any sly remark anyone had made today. "I am the stupidest woman alive. I carried it on far too long. I should have put it aside years ago." Tears stained her voice as her throat tightened, but she refused to let them fall.

"You will tell me, if you please, of all the adventures your family fall into. I am unlikely to meet them, but I have read much about them." Charles gave another of his sweet smiles, his flash of temper seemingly gone. "I long to hear about them from someone who knows all the secrets. For instance, is it true your brother-in-law discovered your sister in a whorehouse?"

"That is so much a distortion of the truth—" Dru began, but she could not continue. The Emperors were custodians of a fact that would shake the world, were it known. They had blocked every attempt to reveal it, and that was why Claudia had been in that whorehouse. But Dru could reveal some of it. "She had no idea what the house was, but she had inherited it in our great-aunt's will. She went to view it. That is all."

"Some people say your brother-in-law was an agent of the king. Maybe more."

If sitting in a room alone all day led to this avidity to discover every secret society had to offer, Dru wanted none of it. Charles bewildered Dru. The sudden changes in his mood confused her, but she would learn to cope. She had no choice, since Oliver had decreed she should spend more time with him. She did not believe in obeying her husband without question, but for now, she would bow her head and behave. She owed him that at the very least.

"I can tell you nothing about that."

"Can you not?" His tone turned wheedling. "We are family now, Drusilla. Surely you have no secrets from your family. I would like to hear of your brother, too. I stay here in this room, and others like it, wondering what is going on in the world."

Before she could stop herself she asked, "Why don't you go outside? People would welcome you. I am sure."

A stony silence fell. Belatedly, she remembered the fit she'd witnessed. How could he fall into one of those in company? True, she had seen appalling examples of grown men throwing tantrums and ignoring polite behavior, but she had never seen anything half as terrifying as what she'd witnessed in this room a short time ago. "I'm sorry." Heat rushed to her face. "I should not have said that."

"No, you should not have," Charles said.

To her surprise, Oliver joined in. "I have asked you to attend a few small, intimate gatherings. I know how much you enjoy music. I can take you to concerts. Perhaps a booth at Ranelagh?" Ranelagh Pleasure Gardens was famed for its music, along with a few other, less respectable things. "The booths are dim, and you can extinguish the lights completely if you wish."

Charles sighed. "I cannot take the risk. You know that, Oliver. You, of all people, to go against me!"

Dru glanced at Oliver. He nodded, a small sign of approval. Something in the region of her heart eased.

"We could look into the matter for you," she told Charles. "People would love to meet you. My parents can help."

She saw the shutters come down. Charles shook his head. "It is impossible. Please go now."

Oliver got to his feet. "We can look into it. We shall have to see." He sighed, his powerful chest rising, sending the cut-steel buttons on his waistcoat glittering. "But I know we cannot force you. You are tired, and you should rest. I will send Burnett into you."

Charles turned his head, refusing to look at them, rather like a child ignoring its nurse when refused a treat. Except he was doing the refusing. When Oliver offered his arm to Dru, she took it gladly. Was he thawing toward her? She had experienced his fierce temper before, but it had passed quickly. Her transgression was far more serious than anything she'd seen rile him before, though. Was his temper proportionate?

She felt bewildered, at sea. Lost, with nobody to talk to, nobody to share her fears with. She could not scuttle back to her mother at the first sign of trouble, but oh, how she wished she could! Her mother would remind her of her fault, but she would hold her while she did it. Oliver's coldness hurt her so badly. She had never been so alone in her life before.

He took her downstairs. She thought perhaps for a late supper, but he stopped and opened a set of double doors. "Your bedroom, ma'am."

Dru gaped. She had seen beautiful rooms before, but this space awed her. Probably because he'd just said this was hers. The canopied bed was upholstered in white hangings embroidered with flowers and vines. The headboard had a carving of the family coat of arms, overlaid and padded with the same white fabric, but not embroidered. Underfoot, rich Aubusson carpet cushioned her feet. Matching cabinets of Chinese lacquer, black and gold, stood either side of the room.

"It's lovely."

"I'm gratified that you think so. You have a dressing room, a powder room, and a private boudoir next door. Anything you wish for, you need only ask." He nodded at a silver-gilt hand bell standing on a *bonheur-du-jour.* "I have assigned you two footmen to run any errands you require."

Inside the magnificent space, Forde waited. She dropped a deep curtsy. "Your graces."

Was that right? Dru had no idea, which surprised her. She presumed Forde had done proper research, since her maid was always meticulous about protocol. "Forde," she said stupidly. Her maid had a perfectly clear idea of who she was. She didn't need anyone else to identify her.

"I will leave you, my dear," Oliver said. "I have a number of urgent matters to deal with."

"I thought—" What had she thought? That he would stay with her? That— Yes, she had one question. "Your other room—"

"Is still my room," he assured her. "This is yours, to do with as you will. If you dislike the decorations, please order them changed."

"How could I dislike anything so lovely?" Dropping his arm, she turned to face him. "But you won't be here?"

"That would not be proper. I will have a supper served for you in the boudoir." Thus leaving her alone.

He bowed his head, turned, and left the room, closing the doors quietly behind him. They sounded like the clang of the doors of hell to Dru.

* * * *

When a gentle tap came on the door of her pretty sitting room, Dru smiled and called out, "Come!" Had Oliver changed his mind and come to her?

But no. It was her mother-in-law. Arrayed in fetching pink and white, Lady Bixby entered. "I saw Oliver upstairs, so I knew you were alone. Do you mind if I come in?"

"Of course not." Dru made haste to get to her feet and make her curtsy. Her ladyship settled herself on the gold brocade sofa while Dru poured her a dish of tea. She took it over herself. "This has only just been served."

"Thank you, my dear. I wanted to drop in, because Lord Bixby and I are planning to return to the country tomorrow. We will leave early, so I'm unlikely to see you for a while, though I do want you to visit us. My dearest Bix isn't comfortable in town. I will stay, if you think you need me." She took a sip of her tea, looking at Dru over the gilded rim of the dish. She replaced it in the saucer without a sound.

Dru was overwhelmed. Nobody had shown her kindness until then. Her husband was cold as ice, her mother sorrowful, her father deeply troubled. Her brothers had laughed, called the book a fribble, but she hadn't allowed them to see her distress.

When the first tears trickled down her cheeks, her ladyship abandoned her tea and her sofa. She came across to hold Dru in her arms, rocking her as she wept, and talking to the top of her head.

"Hush, my dear. It will work itself out, you see. You wrote that book, did you not?"

Dru nodded, sobbing all the more. What was the point of denying it?

"Oh, dear, but society does not know."

"But Oliver, he is so...so angry!"

"That will pass too. He cares for you, Dru. He really does. He needs someone to help him with Charles, to share his burden. I pleaded with him to start his nursery because I thought having someone else to care for would be good for him. But the way he wrote to me and used terms so fondly. I had to meet you, dear."

"What happened?" She needed to know more than ever before. "I know so little." Only what everyone knew, and the snippets of what Oliver had told her. Enough for her to realize how guilty he felt about the carriage accident that had crippled his brother. Gulping down her tears, she blew her nose. But the tears still came.

Her mother-in-law held her in silence for a moment. "Charles and Oliver were driving their carriage in the parklands of our country home. They often did that. Being so close in age, they were always devoted to one another, and since I could have no more children, they knew they were the only ones. They went out that day in high spirits. I received a message an hour later." She stroked Dru's hair absently. "I raced out to where the servants were headed and discovered the carriage overturned, smashed and useless. They had found Charles lying under the wheels, barely alive. Oliver was conscious but frantic, out of his mind. Despite the servants holding him back, he got to his feet and staggered to Charles. He watched as they brought a door out from the house and carried him back on it." She sighed.

"No, I'm sorry. I didn't wish to bring the memories back. I'm so selfish!" Dru wailed into her capacious maternal bosom.

"I do not speak of it often, but you need to know. From the start, Oliver took all the blame. He would not leave Charles's bedside. We called a physician, who dressed Charles's legs, but at the time all our concerns were for his poor head. Part of his skull had been crushed in the fall, you see, and he was in a deep coma. Nobody thought he would live. We put the house into mourning and prepared the notices for his funeral.

"But ten days after the accident, he opened his eyes. We were overjoyed." Her voice warmed. "Especially Oliver and I."

"And your husband." She had mostly stopped crying now, but she remained in Lady Bixby's arms. She had needed comforting so much over the last few days.

She paused. "No, he was resigned and, well, frustrated. He was not a warm man. When we married, I was sixteen and he was forty, so we never had too much in common. But he was a well-set-up man, and he was kind."

Kind! What a terrible thing to say about your husband!

"At least at first, until it became obvious that the complications of Charles's birth meant I would have no more children. But I had done my duty, so he tolerated me."

"Oh, I'm so sorry."

"Hush," she murmured, stroking Dru's hair in a way that made her sigh as tension seeped away. "I have found love with Bix, and my first marriage gave me two fine sons. She moved, and reluctantly, Dru sat up. Lady Bixby held her shoulders and stared into her eyes. "I feel I don't know Charles well any more, but I think that's because he prefers to keep people at a distance. He is close with his servant. They are like brothers. Closer, since Burnett sees to all Charles's needs. They say that a person changes after such a severe knock on the head. Certainly it has given him the terrible fits. He changes his moods frequently, often in the course of an hour. He does not remember everything he says, at least that is what he claims. He keeps the household on its toes, despite insisting that he is only seen by his personal servants and his closest family. I have seen him once since I arrived in town, and only for a quarter of an hour. He has sent messages that he is not feeling well enough, or he is asleep, which might well be so. But I cannot deny I am a little hurt that he cannot spare time for me."

Dru gazed at this woman who had suffered so much. She deserved all the happiness she could find now. "I found Charles astonishingly well-informed. I do not understand why he refuses to enter society, at least in a small capacity, but he does. He is not the only person who cannot walk or who has fits."

Her ladyship nodded. "However, that is his choice, and we have to respect it."

Dru agreed. But she would try to help Charles. Considering all the trouble she'd brought to the family, she could do nothing else. "A wheel came off his carriage in Hyde Park. Oliver was very distressed, as if the fault lay with him, but the cause was a fault to the wheel. Nothing else."

"My oldest son takes the troubles of the world on his shoulders," she said, smiling now. "Come, my dear. Wash your face and drink your tea. You are a duchess, after all."

The twinkle in her eyes showed what she thought of that.

Chapter 12

Dru did not see Oliver for the rest of the day. Would he come to her tonight?

Dru always found having her hair brushed soothing, but today the maid had to wash the powder out first. The tugging and pulling irritated her already sensitive scalp, but she didn't complain. Well into martyr mode now, she suffered in silence.

Once Forde had stripped Dru and helped her wash, she'd arrayed her mistress in a sheer lawn night-rail that made Dru blush to think of anyone seeing her in it. Where had her maid found something like that? She couldn't remember ordering it. The fabric was as sheer as the gauze she used to veil her bosom, but this garment veiled nothing. However, Forde also had a new robe ready, one Dru *did* recall choosing. The green fabric added a touch of spice to the white and dark blue room. At least something had life to it.

She went and sat in solitary splendor in her sitting room, asking Forde to find her the newssheets, since she hadn't had time to read them.

"They'd taken them down to the kitchen, ma'am." The reversion to the simple "ma'am" had relieved Dru mightily. "Your grace" still didn't feel right.

That reminded Dru of the question she meant to ask her maid. "That day I asked you to take my papers to the kitchen. What happened?"

The corner of the maid's mouth twitched, and she busied herself tidying the pots of creams and powders on the dressing table. "I did what you said, ma'am. But they never let the kitchen fire go out, so they don't need much kindling. I put them in the stack of papers the housekeeper collected. In the winter, the maids take a few and use them to start fires upstairs. However, although we've had a lot of rain recently, the weather has not been cold enough for regular fires. Her ladyship gave orders that fires were only to be lit on request."

"So the papers could have remained in that pile for some time?" Why hadn't Dru made absolutely sure they were destroyed? Why hadn't she gone down and burned them herself?

The cook might not have been happy, and the maids shocked to see her downstairs, but what of that? And if she'd told her mother the reason for her unusual actions, the marchioness would have agreed. If Dru had told her in advance, her mother would have helped her, because she'd always told Dru to leave her scribblings alone.

There was no point repining now. She had done it, and that was that.

She sighed. Someone—anyone in the staff, anyone delivering goods to the kitchen—could have stolen the papers. Not Forde, who had the opportunity more than anyone, because she had nothing to gain and everything to lose from doing so. What Dru had bought from Wilkins was definitely her own work. And she should not have written it in the first place.

Oh, God, what a mess.

She would write a miserable wedding day for the Prince of Tirolly. No, of course she would not. But the picture floated into her mind anyway. Of her heroine standing miserably next to the Prince, and her hero rushing into the cathedral to rescue his loved one. So dramatic, she would love every word. But she would have to write it in her head now.

A plot twist shot into her mind. What if the Prince was the hero? What if he had been protecting Drusetta all along? Oh, she was a fool, even for thinking about it.

Resisting the temptation would prove hard, but she did it, rose as gracefully as she could, and followed her maid into the boudoir. A meal was laid out for her, the plates covered with silver domes. And only one place set. Despite her solitude, hunger rolled in her stomach, especially when she received the full power of the delectable scents awaiting her.

Refusing to repine, she dismissed Forde and helped herself to the delicious meal. Where was he? Had he eaten? Here she was, worrying like a real wife, when she wasn't even sure her husband would want anything to do with her.

Fear gripped her, but she refused to live that way. He must do what he thought was right, and she would do so too.

Lifting a lid, she found a lemon cream. Her favorite. Come to think of it, most of the dishes were her favorites. Had someone asked her maid? She wasn't even aware that Forde knew what she liked. Forde's job was to look after her jewels and clothes, nothing else. "She must have asked someone," she murmured, barely aware she was speaking aloud.

"She did not. I did."

With a gasp she turned around. Her husband stood there, leaning against the door, his arms folded. He wore a loose robe, fastened by a couple of elaborate fastenings at the neck that came to his thigh. Beneath, he still wore breeches and stockings.

"Thank you." She scraped her chair back.

He unfolded his arms and held up his hand. "May I join you?"

At her nod, he crossed the room, making a detour to collect a chair. He sat at the table, and found a spare plate. "I'll take some of that. I'm fond of that dish, too."

"Have you eaten?"

"I ate at the wedding breakfast. You did not." His lips quirked up in a smile. "Yes, I noticed." He took the plate she handed to him. "Thank you."

They ate in silence. While she wouldn't call it companionable, at least he'd come to her, and he cared enough to ensure she ate. Touched, hardly daring to speculate about what he'd done, she found herself almost afraid to speak, something that had never affected her before.

Replete, at least in food, she pushed her plate away. "Thank you."

"I can't have my wife starving to death." The quiet clink when he put his spoon on the plate echoed around the eerily silent room.

"I—"

"I—" He started to speak at the same time, but stopped, and gestured to her. "Go on."

Dru swallowed away her hesitancy. "I want to explain to you…"

"I don't want to hear it. Not tonight." He got to his feet. "This is our wedding night." He held out his hand to her.

She had no option but to take it.

"Madam, a request. I want to take this night as if nothing untoward had happened between us. We leave everything outside the bedroom door. If you allow me in, what we do there is not constrained by anything that goes on outside it."

"Oh." Yes, of course. If he did not join her tonight, the whole of society would know via the maids who cleaned the room, changed the sheets, and brought her hot water in the morning. That was how most of the juiciest gossip traveled. Through the domestic staff. He would spare her that, and to do so he needed to treat the bedroom as a place apart. Tomorrow he might hate her again, but at least she would have tonight.

She would make the most of it. With the insouciance of her sister Claudia, she went to him willingly. Who knew what would happen tomorrow?

Oliver took her hand and led her into the next room. Forde had turned the bed down, as she always did, but the sight of crisp, white sheets had never seemed so intimate before. She swallowed, nerves fluttering in her stomach and along her skin.

"Here we are only Oliver and Drusilla...Dru. Perhaps, if we start with that, we may find a way through. We cannot spend the whole of our married life at odds with one another." He touched her chin, tilting it up so he could see her eyes. "Although I doubt this will be the last time we are at odds with one another, perhaps next time we can make it something of a more trivial matter."

"I didn't mean to..." She clamped her mouth shut. She would say no more, not until she could explain herself properly.

He touched her lips with one finger. "Enough. We'll speak of it later and decide what's to be done. Perhaps tomorrow. Perhaps the day after. No more of it tonight."

She nodded, the sensitive skin of her mouth feeling the rasp of his finger. He took it away.

"I will take care of you tonight, Dru." For the first time she saw hesitation in the depths of his eyes. "I swear it."

Determination returned, together with a warmth she recognized and knew was only for her. She'd never seen that exact same expression when he'd looked at anyone else. That knowledge warmed her, gave her the courage to set her hands on his shoulders. The silk of his robe was smooth under her palms. He smelled good, of soap and a faint edge of lemon. Of course, he didn't wear his wig, and his dark hair was combed smoothly against his skull. Everything about him was perfect in her eyes, including the scars on his jaw and his brow.

He slid his arm around her waist, making no sudden movements, as if she were a small creature, a bird or a kitten he was afraid of scaring off. She loved that care. He was her husband. He could throw her on the bed, take her virginity, and leave her. He had the right, and nobody would gainsay him. She had thought the deed might happen that way and had privately steeled herself for it, but he had more consideration. His devotion to his brother and mother, his insistence on straight dealing told her that, and she should have remembered.

She recalled nothing, only that she wanted him.

When he bent his head to her, she went up on tiptoe to meet him. His kiss felt like always—familiar and welcome, as if she had done nothing between his last kiss and this one. When he drew her closer, she nestled into him and let him take her. Trusting him, as he'd taught her.

His hold on her tightened. She sighed into his mouth and received his tongue as a reward. She had no hesitation in sucking it gently, stroking it, and learning its contours. The act drove her to want him even more, to long to feel his mouth on her body. On her bare skin.

Oliver spread his hand over her back. She felt every finger beneath the thin layers of her clothing, each touch. She curled her hand around his neck, holding him close, claiming him as hers. He gave her that responsibility, allowing her to claim him in return. The privilege staggered her. This was real. This wasn't Dru, watching from the sidelines, but a woman claiming the man who was meant to belong to her.

The rightness of her actions settled into her, sinking deep. He lifted his mouth, his lips reddened, his eyes bright in the flickering candlelight. "Are you sure you've never done this before? You have the mouth of a temptress, Dru, and the body of one too, if I'm any judge."

"Are you?"

A wicked smile curved his mouth, his eyes lighting with humor. "I don't know. I cannot possibly explain to you, an innocent."

"Then tell me after I'm an innocent no more."

His hands went to the front fastenings of her gown. "I can't do that while you're trussed up like this. I want you naked, Drusilla."

If he'd tried to frighten her, he failed. She only wanted him to get on with it. Impatience drove her to fumble with the elaborate toggle at the top of his robe while he worked on hers.

He made short work of the silk tie, but she had to struggle to undo the two stiff fastenings. Dropping his hands, he let her do it, but as soon as she had, he spread her robe wide, holding it out so he could see her.

With tension rising in her throat, she let him see. She concentrated on his open robe, his neck free of the neckcloth that usually covered it. His tendons stood out, the shadows they cast exaggerated in their intensity. She stared so hard, until she thought she might burst from waiting. "Oliver?"

"Oh, yes, I'm sorry." He dropped the cloth and slid his arms around her waist from the inside. His hands, so warm, shocked her. His essential masculinity overwhelmed her, not least his size. She'd never felt so small, so helpless. Never loved it so much.

"You are beautiful, my wife," he murmured against her mouth. "I want you very much. But I will take care. If it kills me."

The last few growled words made her laugh aloud. His chest, hard and muscular, proved a delicious contrast with her own. She pressed her breasts against him, eager for more.

"You are not supposed to laugh." But he was smiling as he gazed down at her.

"Don't make me laugh, then. Kiss me instead."

"Willingly." He suited actions to words, but this time he didn't stop at her mouth. He nuzzled and kissed his way down her throat, to the hollow at the base where he would already know she was sensitive. After lingering there long enough to make her shiver, he continued, dropping soft kisses down the V made by the open neck of her night rail, until he met the cleavage between her breasts. He'd been there before, but tonight, the knowledge that he meant to go further made the touches more toe-curling than ever before. Clutching his head, feeling the short, silky strands between her fingers, Dru began to understand the power a woman could wield over a man. His soft sounds told her. She responded, murmuring his name.

Bending, he swept her into his arms. "Bed, I think."

Dru had no objection to that idea. Still tense, but with a growing anticipation that softened her body and gave her a longing she had yet to fully understand, she helped him rid her of the robe. It slid to the floor in a slithering whisper. She did not miss it. She crossed her arms over her body, ready to pull off the night rail, but then she remained, transfixed.

She'd seen a man without a shirt before. Having three brothers, she could hardly avoid it. She'd watched them swim in the river in summer, engage in boxing matches, any number of childhood activities, but she had never seen a chest like this. This was hers, to touch, to wonder at. To feel pressed against her. It had a light sprinkling of hair, a little more than her brothers'. It was broad and powerful, covered by defined slabs of muscle that moved fluidly as he dragged his shirt over his head and tossed it aside.

He met her avid gaze. "Ready for more?"

She nodded. His robe had already joined hers on the floor. His dark green pooled with her lighter blue, a pond of their own making, blending as no doubt they would very soon. The sight seemed prophetic. Or perhaps she was allowing her imagination to run riot again.

She watched as he unfastened the fall of his breeches and bent to loosen the buckles at his knee. He pulled his remaining clothes off with impatience, his arms bulging and flexing. Heedless of his wedding finery, he kicked the silk and worsted free and stood, entirely naked.

Dru caught her breath. Now that was new. His member was hard, the top shiny. As she stared, a bead of fluid leaked from the tip. She hadn't been aware that she licked her lips until he groaned.

"Dru, you test my resolve."

Her attention went to his face. She didn't understand what he meant, but she was, for once, content to wait. But not for long. "Oliver, I want you." She changed the words at the last second. He wasn't ready for that. Neither was she, not yet, although she held the truth close to her heart. She loved him. Her anguish today had only emphasized it.

"Are you wet for me?" His words, so intimate, shocked her to the core. Not least because he was right.

Lost for words, she only nodded. He smiled and at last climbed on the bed and came to her. Grasping her final garment, he tugged it up her body. Willingly she lifted her arms so he could pull it over her head. She didn't know what he did with it, because she kept her attention on him.

"Nothing between us," he murmured. "I want us as bare as the day we came into the world." He caught her hands, held her like that, gazing into her eyes. "Are you ready for that, Dru? For us to make a baby?"

"Isn't that why I'm here?"

He laughed, harsh and sudden, the sound gone as soon as it had arrived. "The world would have us think so. But there are other parts of making love. It should be enjoyable. Many couples contrive to do it without creating a baby too. Is that what you want?"

She gasped. She had never thought of that. "How?"

"There are ways. None are certain, but we can control the process."

"Why would you want to do that?"

She loved that he answered her questions promptly and without equivocation. "We could enjoy one another for a time. We are supposed to make heirs, but we don't have to do it at once."

Tonight was just about them, not anyone else. She didn't want to break the magic that lay between them. Only the truth would do now.

Inwardly she rejoiced. He wanted to spend time with her, to enjoy her. Perhaps this was the way back to his heart. "I want your children."

"Your decision matters to me." Twin creases appeared between his brows, but only briefly. Almost as if he did not want to admit what he'd just said, or he'd said it before the recognition had hit him. Dru knew what that felt like.

She said nothing but reached for him.

"Yes," he murmured as he took her in his arms. His words vibrated through her body, her nipples hardening even more than they were already.

"This is right. Don't ask for mercy, Dru, because you'll get none from me."
Those words could have been a threat in different circumstances. Now
she took them as a promise.

He touched his mouth to hers in a soft, feathery kiss, a brush of lips that
was almost not there at all. Then he passed on, reacquainted himself with
her throat and her cleavage. With a thrill, Dru knew he had no reason to
stop. His restraint since their increased freedom after their betrothal was
gone now, the reason for it completely evaporated.

He whispered her name against her nipple before he kissed around it
and then sucked it into his mouth. Dru pulled in a sharp breath, her gasp
echoing on the embroidered canopy above them and reflecting back at them.
Murmuring words of encouragement, Oliver treated her other nipple the
same way. He licked and sucked, at first gently, and then harder, until she
gripped his head, her hands curling like claws.

A laugh reverberated against her stomach as he moved farther down
her body. He licked the sensitive spot on the inside of her hip, telling her
how good she tasted. By then Dru could only moan. Another laugh and
then he slid down some more. "You're not... You can't..." she gasped,
shocked back into words.

"I am, and I can." Firmly, he urged her to part her legs wider.

How could she do that? At first she resisted, until he kissed her thighs,
and just inside them.

"If I don't do it tonight, I'll do it another time. I want to taste you, Dru,
to know every part of you, what you like, and how I can drive you insane."

"You do?" She licked her lips and gave in, let him open her legs and
gently push her feet so that she bent her legs at the knee. She felt completely
vulnerable, entering this new place. When his hot breath seared over her
sensitive skin, she shuddered, every inch of her alive with sensation.

Then he licked her. With a strangled cry, she arched off the bed,
her cheeks flaming at her inability to control her response. Planting his
hands on her thighs, he pushed her back down and continued with his
self-imposed task.

"No, no! You can't!"

Lifting his dark head, he met her eyes, his own twinkling with what
she considered misplaced mischief. "Do you really want me to stop?"

With that brief kiss, he'd given her sensations she had never experienced
before, not thought possible. When she'd imagined her wedding night—and
she had—she had thought of comfort, a quiet sharing. Not this—*this*—she
had no words for what was happening between them. What he was doing
to her. What was she supposed to do in return? She had no words, or at

least none that made any sense. She shook her head, nodded, and bit her lip. Her breasts rose between them, so private.

"You are pink all over," he murmured. Goodness, his lips were wet. With her. "Let me continue, Dru. Put yourself in my hands this once."

She swallowed and nodded.

He needed no more encouragement and bent back to his task. This time he licked and then tickled, rousing her to sensations she had no idea what to do with. Thrills coursed through her body, as if he'd set off a lightning storm inside her. Sparks fizzled along her veins, and flashes of intensity shot through them, making her press her open hands against the sheets to ground herself. He wasn't silent either. He made sounds of appreciation, as if he were enjoying a good meal, combined with moans and words that vibrated against her most sensitive flesh.

The striving became deliberate, and then—

He stopped, lifted up, and lay over her. She smelled what he'd been doing, and instead of repulsing her, it inflamed her. His hard, muscular body pressed against hers, his member falling between her upraised legs as if meant to be there.

Pushing his hand down, he took it in hand and guided it to her, notching it into her opening. Dru opened her mouth, cried out as he pushed. Pain split her delight, arcing through her but not completely dissipating the pleasure.

She panted as if she'd run a mile, her breasts heaving, her nipples grazing his chest each time she drew a breath. She met his gaze. His intent burned into her, waiting.

She was not the only person affected by this amazingly intimate act. She had not understood the meaning of the word "intimate" before. Never this close or this linked with someone.

"All right?" He sounded breathless.

"Yes." She must be, if she was still here and sentient. "Is that it?"

"You're not a virgin any more. But no, we have a long way to go."

She didn't know whether to be glad or sorry. But he was here, with her, and he had enjoyed her.

He began to move, withdrawing a little before pushing back in, steadily and slowly, until his passage eased. He increased the depth of his strokes, grinding against her, lifting a little, so he nudged the pearl of flesh he'd toyed with before. She'd known about its existence, but had avoided it, thinking it too sensitive. When she'd touched it she hadn't worked the magic he had but had shied away from contact, only ensuring its cleanliness when she bathed.

"I wanted you as open as I could make you," he said. "And as wet. You are a delight, Drusilla. You respond so keenly. Do not stop."

She knew what to do now. Those magical sensations had happened when she'd stopped thinking and let herself experience what was happening to her. Before tonight, her body had been something she took for granted, kept clean, and exercised, but otherwise thought little about. Now she responded as best she could, holding herself firmly to accept his strokes, staring up at him, watching his face. Occasionally his lips tensed, flexed, until she dared to slip her hand around his neck and pull him down.

She wanted his kiss. He obliged, opening his mouth against hers. This, at least, was familiar. She responded as always, kissing him deeply, but the unfamiliar but not unwelcome taste of herself on him gave more spice to the encounter.

The feeling swelled again, but this time subtly different—harder, somehow—deeper, as if he'd taken a shortcut to the heart of her being. Her body warmed to him, blossoming from where they joined. It spread out, filling her with unmistakable joy. Her body responded, as if it knew what to do even if she didn't. She convulsed around him, each hard contraction bringing an extra shot of pleasure to her overwhelmed system.

He gave one shout and went completely still, except for his member, which pulsed inside her. A flood of heat washed her anew, and then total exhaustion, the like of which she'd never known before.

Dru slept.

* * * *

Perhaps the most astonishing reaction Dru had to his lovemaking had been that total descent into sleep. Oliver had barely stopped coming before he felt her body go heavy and saw her eyes close.

Taking the greatest of care, he withdrew and rolled to one side. She accompanied him, although he hadn't drawn her. He could do nothing but hold her. Would she wake as quickly as she'd fallen asleep?

Her sweet and total response overwhelmed him. He had never known anything like it before. She gave him her emotions frankly, and after he'd told her not to hold back, had shown him how she felt. He had pleased her, that was for sure, but he had set out to do that. If they could get nothing else right, they should do their best to find satisfaction in the bedroom. But he had not planned for this. Their connection had shocked him—too intimate, too complete.

His plan was to go to her, take her as gently as possible, and then leave her to sleep. He was still angry with her, but he refused to humiliate her on their wedding night. If she sent him away, so be it. But she had not. She'd welcomed him.

He feared he would not get enough of his wife for some time. His plans were destroyed, flown away, and he had to think again. Except that he found thinking supremely difficult while he lay with her in his arms.

She curled her leg between his, as uninhibited now as she'd been reticent and apprehensive before he had brought her to bed. Trusting. That was what came of coming from a close, loving family, he supposed. After his father's death, his own family had drawn together, but they were so changed now. For three years before Oliver had become the Duke of Mountsorrel, they had worked to retain unity for the good of the title and the estate. But the joy had gone. It had left when the carriage had overturned and nearly killed Oliver and Charles. Perhaps, Oliver had sometimes thought guiltily, it would have been better if one of them had died.

She sighed, her breath sweeping over his chest, raising the hairs, and then spoke. "I didn't think it would be that way."

He gazed at her, drinking in the soft golden-brown hair that caressed his skin with silken beauty, the perfect soft flesh that had aroused him to desperate need. "What way?"

"So...so encompassing. I couldn't think of anything else while we were...doing it."

"Making love, Dru." He would allow that much. But her betrayal still rankled. She had not known what she was doing. He'd give her that. She could not, because Charles preferred to remain in seclusion. The fact that she'd come so close to describing them spoke of her imagination, not her spying skills.

"Yes." She settled closer to him, shifted position so her slick center moved against his thighs. His cock behaved in the inevitable way but more instantly than he was used to. It hardened to painful intensity.

He'd just taken her virginity, for God's sake. He couldn't pounce on her again like a rampant bull. He needed to calm down.

Deliberately, he invoked the vision that put everything else in his life into perspective. The sight of his brother lying under the smashed carriage after the horses had dragged it over him. That throb, the realization his brother was dead. Until Charles coughed, rolled over, and screamed.

That life-changing moment reminded Oliver of his purpose, of what he should hold important.

For the first time in his life the remembrance failed to work. His erection remained determinedly rampant and his desire for this woman charged through his system. "How do you feel?" he asked, in an attempt to regain touch with civilization.

"Wonderful."

Her drowsy, happy voice did nothing to quell his desire. "I'm glad to hear it. Would you object if we did it again?" She flinched, and he felt her pain as if it were his own. "Sometime."

"Oh."

God help him, she sounded disappointed.

"Was it... Did you..."

"You were adequate." He put on the voice of a bored dandy. If he'd had a lace-edged handkerchief to flourish, he couldn't have done it any better. But when he felt her sigh, and the way she stiffened against him, he relented. "You were wonderful, Dru. I want you like that all the time."

"Oh, yes. I didn't know what to do. I thought I should..." She gave a light chuckle.

"We'll have plenty of time to find out what you should and shouldn't. In the bedroom we are equals, Dru. We will explore one another. No secrets, ever."

After a hesitation, she nodded. "I'll do it."

"You seemed unaware. Reticent. As if you had never experienced such intimacy."

"That's what happens when you're sandwiched between two sets of twins. They shared a room, but I always had one of my own. Smaller than theirs, but solely mine. I read a lot." She swallowed. "And wrote."

Well, that helped his desire deflate. "What did you write?"

"A journal. Stories. I read *Pamela* and fell in love with the idea of telling other people's stories. Like writing a play, but more private."

And his damned cock was hardening again. With Dru moving so sensuously, something he suspected she didn't realize, he couldn't keep his hands off her for much longer. Clearly, he had work to do before he could trust himself with her sweetly feminine curves again.

Decisively, he moved, flung the sheets aside, and slid out of bed. Unconcerned by his state of nudity, he crossed to where he'd left his robe. Her sound of distress made him turn back to her.

Tears stood in her eyes, but her attention went to his groin. "I'm sorry. So sorry."

"About what?" Shrugging on his robe, he went back to her.

"I didn't mean to upset you, especially tonight. But you asked, and I wanted to tell you—"

He stopped her words with a kiss, the best way to demonstrate his feelings to her. "Shut up," he said tenderly against her lips. "It's not that. You saw me just now. I want you again, Dru."

"Yes, please. I wouldn't mind."

"Sweetheart, you're in no state to do anything further tonight." He kissed her. "If I were a brute, I'd take you again. Although both of us want it, we cannot. I took your virginity tonight. You are sore, much though I tried to ease the way. I want lovemaking to be a pleasurable activity, but if I stay, neither of us will get any sleep. You had a difficult day. Rest now." He touched her chin, stroked the soft vulnerable skin under it. "Do you understand?"

At least her tears had stopped. He had their marks on his chest. He would not forget that. She hadn't had to say she was sorry for him to know it. Their next steps had to be obfuscation, laughing at fools who thought they cared about some scurrilous tome. He had to ensure they were seen in public, and for that, she had to be able to walk.

She nodded. "I think so. Thank you. But I'd rather have you here."

Oliver closed his eyes. His wife had no sense of self-preservation, and if he stayed, she would not be safe from him. "I cannot. Should not."

"I want you to. I'm not too sore, truly."

With a groan, he shucked the robe and got back into bed, reaching for her. "Dru, you'll be the death of me."

Chapter 13

"I called for you last night." Seated in his usual wheeled chair, Charles looked as he did every morning—immaculately dressed, ready to receive visitors. But between the brothers a profound change had occurred. Oliver was a married man now.

Oliver raised a brow. "Charles, last night was my wedding night." He crossed his legs but uncrossed them when his chair rocked alarmingly. He had to move it to take the front leg off the rug that was sending it off-balance. He would order Burnett to have the thing removed or repaired.

"All night?"

Oliver laughed at his brother's wide-eyed incredulity. "Yes, all night." Twice, although his brother didn't need to know that. The second time had nearly killed him with joy. He'd taken as much time as he could, determined Dru would enjoy the experience. He flattered himself that she had.

Usually he shared everything with his brother. Painfully aware that Charles had ruled out any kind of intimacy for himself, Oliver had even shared details of evenings with one or another of his mistresses. But he knew he would never share anything about Dru.

So when Charles said, "So? Was it good?" Oliver knew what he meant. He was supposed to go with a blow-by-blow account, from first kiss to falling into an exhausted sleep. Much though he loved his brother, he would not do it. Every cell in his body rebelled against it. What he'd found with Dru was private, their own.

He'd never felt like that before, especially with Charles. He owed his brother. He put on a careless air, as if last night had been unremarkable. "Satisfactory. We are on the way to making an heir, which, after all, is the purpose of this exercise, is it not?"

"I suppose so." Charles's response was decidedly cool, his gaze chilly.

Normally Oliver would hurry to reassure him, but not on this point. "I will continue to use my bedroom, though." He would not spend all night with Dru. Last night was an excusable exception, though he would admit that he had enjoyed waking with her in his arms.

Charles nodded, and a touch of warmth returned. "Yes, of course. She has her place, does she not? I trust she is up to the position she is required to occupy?"

"Her father is a marquess, and she has been brought up to the dignity. I must presume so."

Charles shifted, and his hand drifted over the cover of the book on the table beside him, as if by accident. Oliver recognized the binding. He would know that book anywhere, since his wife had written it. Charles's gentle reminder served to bring Oliver back to reality. "She has made a serious error."

"Did you buy another copy?"

Charles had lent him the book yesterday. Oliver had not yet had a chance to read it, but he would remedy that today. He had previously wondered if he should concern himself with it, since it seemed set to become a nine days' wonder, but he supposed he should see what all the fuss was about.

"I didn't want to deprive you of yours, so I sent someone out for another. You could always ask the author to sign it."

Oliver snorted. "And leave another clue to people who want to discover the author? There's speculation already. But the affair will pass if the bonfire isn't fed."

Charles lifted his good shoulder in a half-shrug. "That is probable. It is a shame you did not wait until the affair had blown over, because if her identity is ever discovered, that drags our family into the mire."

"We are there already. Framing me as the villain of the piece." He grimaced, but without the venom of before. He had to learn to accept Dru's transgression if they were to exist together in any kind of harmony. They must get over this hurdle, but he was not yet prepared to let her completely into his life.

A tap on the door heralded the entrance of Burnett. Oliver disliked the way the manservant came in without waiting for a summons to enter. But this was Charles's room, so he must organize his servants the way he wished.

"Sir, you should try to eat something. I've had your favorite breakfast prepared."

Oliver's mild resentment dissipated. The man only had his brother's best interests at heart. "Indeed, I will leave you to your repast. Dru will join you soon, as you asked."

Although he would never admit it to anyone, least of all himself, relief washed through him before he sternly quelled it. Visiting his brother, having him close pleased him, he told himself firmly.

* * * *

Dru heard the "Enter!" with a degree of trepidation. Fixing her polite smile to her face, she went through to the pleasant room occupied by Oliver's brother. She felt better today. She and her husband had come to some kind of peace.

The sight of Charles stirred her. He resembled Oliver closely—at least, if Oliver were confined to a chair every day and one arm didn't work properly. But the eyes, they were the same shape and size. The mouth, so sensual, warm, living sculpted marble, and the face, strongly masculine with a firm jaw and the shadow of dark beard hair were enough the same to mark the men as brothers.

Charles was not Oliver, but close enough for her to feel pain at his predicament, so much that whenever she saw him, sympathy washed through her.

He gave her a sweet smile. "Do sit. We should not stand on ceremony, should we?"

"Of course not." Smoothing her skirts, she took her place in the chair set out for her. It tipped a little to one side as she sat, and she tightened her hold on the arms but then noticed the cause and relaxed. One of the legs was perched on the rug set to one side, and it put the chair slightly off-balance. She would have to favor the other side. That was all. "Are you feeling better now?"

His mouth flattened. "I am recovering well, although sometimes afraid I may never wake from the attack. What has Oliver told you of my injuries?"

She liked his frankness. Early afternoon sun streamed through the window, catching her eyes so she was forced to favor the wobbly side of the chair, after all. "That you were severely injured in the carriage accident. You are completely unable to walk, and you have...fits."

"Ah, yes, you saw that. You are not to be afraid. They come upon me without warning. That, you must be aware, is why I choose not to appear in public. I never know when they will happen, and I have no desire to become a laughingstock."

"Oh, you will not. Society speculates, but I have heard nothing of that nature."

"Did you ask?"

Shocked, she shook her head. "I take no pleasure in malicious gossip."

"Ah, but the other kind…" He leaned forward, taking his weight on his bad arm. "I do enjoy hearing the gossip. I would greatly appreciate you keeping me informed. Oliver can relay the talk in the clubs and coffee houses, but he has no entry into the feminine salons, and I'm afraid he doesn't always report it correctly." He waved vaguely to a pile of thumbed-through newssheets stacked neatly by the door, ready for the servants to remove.

That reminder of the foolish way she'd disposed of her book filled her with shame. But that was not Charles's fault, nor should she allow every little thing to remind her of her transgression. "You read all those?"

"Yes, indeed. They are from yesterday. I still have some to read, but I fear my eyes need to rest sometimes." He touched a gold and ivory magnifying glass. Its handle was dulled with use. "This helps. So does having books read to me."

That was such a blatant hint Dru couldn't help but smile. "So I am to read to you?"

"Would you mind?"

"I would enjoy it. What would you like me to read to you today?" She fumbled in her pocket for her glasses and perched them on her nose. Best that her brother-in-law knew her properly. She would not strain to read small print with these.

He arched his brows. "Very fetching." He lifted a book from the side table, supporting it underneath with his bad hand.

With a sinking heart, she recognized the tome. "This?"

"Indeed. How many people can say they have had a book read to them by the author herself?" He gave an easy smile, seemingly unaware of her discomfort. "Even that most people would not know if she did so. That is our secret, is it not?"

Numbly, she took the book and opened it, leafing through the prefaces and preambles. She had not written them, but publishers generally included dedications and devotions to sponsors. On the last page, she noticed a name, returning to study it. "An unknown person sponsored the printing of this book? It says a gentleman of great state and nobility is to be thanked." Had somebody paid more to have the book published? So Wilkins had taken her money and then accepted more from somebody else? The blackguard—she should have let Livia shoot him.

"Ah, they always say that." He dismissed the dedication with a careless wave. "The publisher probably put up the money himself."

"He seemed a poor man." She recalled the musty office and battered furniture.

Charles stilled, his eyes alert. "You met him?"

"I looked the office up on the map," she said, not precisely lying but not telling the whole truth. She didn't want to tell anyone of that miserable visit and its outcome. "The area he has his office in isn't known for its graciousness."

He tilted his head to one side. "I feel there is more to this story. But we will no doubt come to a point where we are good enough friends to trust one another with all our secrets."

She didn't like the way he said that. Why did it feel as if the exchanges would be one-sided? She was no doubt overly sensitive, since she was holding the source of her shame in her hands. Glancing down, she flicked over to the title page and then the first chapter.

"*The Prince of Tirolly*, Chapter One."

* * * *

"Why does Charles refuse so adamantly to go out?" she asked Oliver later.

They were sitting over dinner, only the two of them tonight, since her mother-in-law had bidden them a fond farewell and set out for the country. The servants had laid the table seating her to Oliver's left instead at the other end. She wondered if he had requested it, because she hadn't thought to do so. One course with six removed made an elegant though not too extravagant repast. She felt comfortable enough to ask him after the servants had taken the covers away and put a pretty dessert service in its place, leaving the newlyweds alone.

"He does go out," Oliver answered, selecting a succulent peach and finding a fruit knife to peel it with. "He takes the air sometimes, but he does it in an unmarked carriage and he doesn't go to the places society expects. He prefers to sit in the garden, when the weather permits it." He carefully discarded the first sliver of fuzzy skin.

"But not into society. That would quell some of the more outrageous rumors." Leaning back, Dru sipped her glass of Madeira wine. The sweetness trickled deliciously down her throat.

"What kind of rumors?" Oliver seemed intent on his self-imposed task, not looking at her.

"I do not care to repeat the more scurrilous ones. But some say he is terribly disfigured, or that his mind is completely gone. Neither is true."

"Underneath the fine clothes, he *is* terribly disfigured," Oliver remarked. He looked up as he quartered the peach and removed the stone.

His hands dripped with juice. What would it be like to lick the juice from his hands? Would he enjoy it? Uncertainty kept her still. That kind of behavior would not have crossed her mind before yesterday, before that night that had changed her perception of marriage forever.

Oliver continued, "His scars are terrible and his injuries worse. So much that I have not seen him unclothed for some time. He prefers to keep his body private. Only his caregivers see him."

"That's another thing. If the servants saw him and reported he was a fine man, not affected mentally, would that not be better?"

"In what way?" He placed the carefully sliced peach on her plate and picked up a napkin to wipe his fingers. "For them or for him?"

"For him. To pave the way. To show he is merely reclusive, not insane or deformed, or—" She bit her lip. "Of course I will do nothing."

He raked his cool gaze over her. "No, Dru, you will not. Do not talk to him about it. His mind is made up." He leaned back, picking up his glass of burgundy. "However, I agree with you on some points. I do want to change his mind. Perhaps a visit to the theater would amuse him, for instance. Then, if we refused entry to our box, he would not have to speak to anyone. But I will deal with the matter, if you please. You are too precipitate. You have met him only twice, whereas I have lived my whole life with him."

"Except for the first two," she pointed out, mentioning the age difference between the brothers. Picking up a slice of the fruit, she ate it slowly. She let the cool juice slither down her throat, the recollection of where it had been a moment before adding to her enjoyment.

"Of course," he agreed smoothly, but she saw something in his eyes—wariness, perhaps.

With a sigh, she acknowledged that he still didn't accept her. After what he saw as her betrayal, she would have to work hard to bring him around, if she ever could. That was why she hated keeping secrets from him, although Charles had bidden her to do exactly that.

He'd taken great enjoyment from her reading that day. Every word had been agony to her, but she had managed, by trying to pretend that the story had nothing to do with her. At least she had managed to read most of the first chapter without wavering.

As she had risen to leave, Charles had said, "Please don't tell Oliver we are doing this. If he knew, he would likely scold me severely. But I did enjoy the liveliness of the book, and it amuses me to have you read it. I don't want to have Oliver put a stop to it."

So she'd had no choice but to agree to keep their readings quiet.

The candlelight glimmered over the thin gold braid on Oliver's coat as he moved. "Allow me to know my brother better than you. I am aware you have a habit of behaving precipitately, but do not do it in this case."

That was an order if ever she'd heard one. And she had no choice but to obey. Sometimes people coming from outside a problem saw it more clearly. Perhaps this was the case, but she wouldn't push her view. Not when matters between her and the man she had married were so precarious. They had gone for this long with Charles living as a recluse, but she would not like to see the situation going on for too much longer. Charles was charming, personable and...bored. The books, the newssheets, and how did he bear living with the same three people around him? He saw no one else but Oliver, his mother, and now Dru herself. That could not be healthy for anyone.

"I like Charles," she told him now. "I'm sure he will do very well in society if he ever decides to enter it."

"I think so too," Oliver said unexpectedly. "But do nothing without telling me first." His glare reinforced his words.

Clearly he didn't trust her. But he wanted her. Even while he watched her, she saw warmth enter his eyes, and his mouth soften, ready for her kiss.

Was that what her mother meant when she'd talked about a woman having power over a man? And did she want that kind of power?

What would she do with it?

At five-and-twenty, Dru really ought to have known more about her female prowess, but she had never considered it. She would grow up, learn the skills she needed to run a great household, and make some man a good wife. She had dreams, of course, but she had never presumed they would come to pass in real life. Now she wasn't so sure.

As her husband got to his feet and walked around the table to her, she read his intent in his eyes and smiled, because she wanted it too.

He held out his hand. "Are you completely recovered from last night's ordeal?"

She would never admit she was still a little tender. "Yes, I am." She slipped her hand into his.

"Would you like another ordeal tonight?"

"Would you?"

His smile broadened. "I think I could endure it."

The clock chimed nine. Definitely time for bed.

* * * *

The newly married Lord and Lady Swithland were holding a rout, and Oliver and Dru chose it as their first appearance as a married couple. She was to be presented at court the following week, a stultifying event, so she wanted something more enjoyable before that. The rout would have boisterous dancing, heavy gaming, and lively gossip. Perfect.

Outside the house, not far from their own, Oliver moved closer to Dru. He was trying so hard to forget her error, and she appreciated that. But he kept his distance. Dru would behave like a great lady from now on. No faux-pas, no awkwardness. She was a duchess, and she'd better remember it. She outranked her mother, which was a staggering thought. But only by her title. In no other way.

But her gown, a masterpiece in dark blue satin with pink roses embroidered over the gown and skirt. She wore the diamonds that were part of the Mountsorrel treasure chest, a clear sign of her advent into married life. Would people fawn over her? She had seen that, had suffered it a little as an Emperor, but now? She had no idea. "How does a duchess behave?"

She hadn't been aware of saying that aloud until Oliver answered her. "Just as you do. Be yourself. You know how to do this."

"You've been a duke since you were—"

"Seventeen."

He sounded perfectly calm, but she knew him better now. Oliver felt very deeply. How much had he forced away when he had to enter Parliament as the new duke, or take his father's place in formal events?

She would take her cue from him. Oliver appeared perfectly affable, but with an air of "don't-get-too-close." She was experiencing some of that in private. Although he treated her well, he had never repeated the overwhelming passion of their first night together. He didn't spend all night in her bed, and they still had separate rooms on different floors. If she'd had the courage, she'd have gone to him, but the idea of his rejection terrified her. Not much terrified Dru. She faced the world head-on, but since she'd met Oliver, she'd become a mouse.

That would not happen tonight. Many members of her family would be there to support her. The fluttering in her stomach would settle in the first ten minutes. Dru had never told anyone, but she always felt apprehensive before a social event. Her position was assured, but not so the way people behaved toward her as a person. Before they realized who she was, she had been overlooked, patronized, and generally disregarded. Something she had never told her siblings, because they would go out of their way to get her revenge. She preferred to do that herself, with her pen.

And look where that had taken her.

She placed her hand on his velvet-clad arm at precisely the right angle as they entered. The footman bowed to them, and she gave him a gracious half-nod, just as her mother did. Only an ill-mannered person ignored the servants completely.

Oliver took her in the direction of her parents, who sat in a corner of the room. Her mother met Dru's eyes, a small frown furrowing her brow. The marchioness rarely showed emotion in public. What could be the matter? Dru's hand tightened on her husband's sleeve. Perhaps her mother's concern had nothing to do with her.

They had to speak to several people before they attained their goal. The first merely congratulated them on their marriage. The second, a friend of the Shaws, behaved coolly, as if she would prefer not to speak with them.

Bemused, Dru fixed the smile to her face and let Oliver lead her on. By now, his arm had stiffened, and by that she knew he was also wary. Had something happened? Perhaps someone important was dead. But nobody wore a black armband, and if it had been something like the King dying, this event would not be happening at all.

The next people were their hosts. Lord Swithland and his lovely dark-haired wife, who was intriguingly wearing a pair of gold spectacles with diamonds. His lordship, known for his rakish behavior before he married, gave his wife a fond smile. "You will have to give my dearest Penelope some lessons in writing a best-selling novel." His smile at Dru held no malice, no speculation, unlike those of the people standing around them. "She has her eyes on the sky for the most part, but your stories brought her back to earth, temporarily."

Lady Swithland batted her husband with her fan, but he caught it and gently pulled it out of her grip before opening it and fanning her. Dru would ordinarily have enjoyed the byplay, but the words transfixed her.

"I think you did a very clever thing," Lady Swithland said. "Who could you make into your villain who would not object? You asked him, of course."

"Naturally," Oliver said smoothly.

Dru could say nothing. Horror had struck her dumb. She had no idea if she still had that stupid smile on her face, but she wore it like a garment. It didn't belong to her any longer. "My wife is accomplished at many things, not least in telling a story."

Or a lie. That was what his tone indicated. "A mere amusement," he added.

"Yet you do have a brother, do you not?" his lordship said. He fixed with fascinated interest on to Dru's face, but he was talking to Oliver.

"Indeed. He prefers to live quietly."

"How does he see this?" her ladyship asked.

"He's very diverted," Dru said. At least she knew that was true. Only today Charles had laughed inordinately when the hero had declared his love for Drusetta. His ribald remarks followed suit. What else could she say? Society knew nothing about Charles. He could be a gibbering idiot, as far as they were concerned. And Oliver had asked her to say nothing. Ordered her, in fact.

"He is indeed," Oliver smoothly agreed. "As am I. I cannot wait for the next installment."

"You mean she has not told you?" Her ladyship's eyes rounded and her arched brows went up.

"Now do not tease, Penelope, my love." Her husband closed his wife's fan and returned it to her. "I daresay the duchess wants to keep some secrets in reserve. Ladies prefer to retain a certain mystery, do they not?"

"Not all of them. I don't, not anymore." She touched her spectacles and gave her husband a mischievous smile.

Dru hurt, seeing this couple so obviously in love, so happy with each other. They no doubt discussed everything together. Why, they would probably read the book together and laugh over it.

Even the next volume, and the one after that where— Dru had not imagined she could get any colder, but suddenly the warm late spring evening had icicles in it. Where the younger brother, the hero, had finally shot his older brother, the Prince of Tirolly, freeing himself and his loved one from a tyrant.

Oliver would never speak to her again.

Bowing to their hosts, Oliver made to move on. He had to drag Dru the first step, and then she put one foot before the other as if learning to walk for the first time. How could this have happened? Who had let the author of the piece be known?

The publisher. Wilkins would have done it. He'd said he recognized her, but Dru hadn't believed him. She still didn't, not completely. She'd seen the doubt in his rheumy eyes, and the challenge, as if she'd admit who she was.

No, someone else had told him.

How much would knowing she was the author add to the popularity of the book?

Her mother's eyes were hard and unforgiving. She accepted the greeting of her family, seeing that they had Livia with them. Her brother Darius stood behind the sofa. He shook his head slightly after she rose from her curtsy.

People were listening. She did not need words. She could hear her mother's recriminations without them. What hurt worst was the incredulity in her father's eyes, as if he blamed himself for her sins.

"You are well?" her mother said in the icy tone that indicated how little she cared.

"Very well, Mama."

"Even though you have had time to see your literary success come to fruition?"

Dru forced a smile, though she had no idea how she managed it. "That has happened all on its own, Mama."

"Deny it," her father said. "Of course you had nothing to do with this, did you?"

Ah, an answer. She would have to lie. She hadn't actually admitted her culpability to the Swithlands, had she? And in any case, her brother Val was particular friends with his lordship. He could ask him not to spread what they'd talked about.

She opened her mouth to agree with her father, but her husband forestalled her. "I think Dru was very clever. If the estate ever fails us, if the seven famines descend on my estates, I can rest easy. Dru can make enough from her scribblings to keep me in comfort." His smile promised retribution. Turning, he offered his arm. "Would you care to dance, my dear? I swear I will not abandon you this time."

Pain lanced through her. He had withdrawn completely.

Chapter 14

That ball took first prize for the worst Dru had ever attended. Her brother danced with her after Oliver had paraded her in front of society. Then forced her to acknowledge she had written *The Prince of Tirolly* by admitting it himself. He continued to act as if the whole thing were a great joke.

All those people she'd parodied, all the quirks she'd noticed and marked down, they were there. She made enemies that night. At least she did not receive the cut direct, though once they read the next two volumes she was sure they would do so. She went into detail about the Prince's court, every courtier a wickedly drawn portrait of someone in society. There was no way back from that. She had nightmares about her ostracism, when someone pretended not to see her or hear her. As if she'd suddenly become invisible. But she saw some people move away as if they had no desire to speak with her.

Her husband took her on to the floor for a country dance. That meant she had to change partners in the course of it. Everyone else laughed and chatted. Her partners gave her a tepid smile or made a polite enquiry about her health, some almost speaking through their teeth. She had no doubt they remained polite because of her family. Nobody wanted to cross the Emperors or, for that matter, the Shaws.

Oliver barely spoke to her. He smiled often, but he mirrored her own expression, the smile with nothing behind it. The only words he said to her in the whole of the dance were, "Keep smiling."

She did her best, although she was dying inside.

They stayed for far too long. An evening she had been looking forward to had turned to ashes, and she wanted to sink through the floor right into hell. At last, Oliver came over to where she sat with her mother and asked if she was ready to leave.

"I am a little tired," she said loudly, masking her mother's words.

"We will see what can be done. Wait at home for us."

Oliver turned an icy glare on to her. "You will do nothing, ma'am, if you please. This is not your concern."

The marchioness nodded, equally coolly.

Dru accompanied her husband to the carriage in stony silence. They had two more balls to attend that evening, but they needed no conversation to indicate they were going home.

Once inside the vehicle, when it had rounded the corner so nobody could see them, she let her head drop. "I'm sorry."

He didn't reply. As if he hadn't heard her, he crossed one leg over the other and leaned his elbow on the windowsill, staring out into the night.

So finally, Dru received the cut direct.

* * * *

Oliver strode up and down the carpet in Charles's room. His brother, calmer than he, watched him from his customary chair turned half toward the window. Oliver had interrupted him contemplating the garden, watching a man prune a tree. The tranquility had been complete until Oliver had stormed in, bringing his troubles with him. He could hardly wait to tell Charles and discuss the matter. His brother had a right to know.

"I cannot believe Dru did this." Oliver turned, facing Charles, whose compassionate gaze nearly undid him. "Everyone knows my wife has made a fool of me."

"And we cannot allow that, can we?" Charles said calmly. "Don't worry, brother. We will think of something. I told you not to marry in such a hurry."

Oliver shook his head in sorrow. "I cannot allow you to concern yourself with the business of the dukedom." Stopping at Charles's chair, he gently laid a hand over his brother's. "Don't try to hide it from me. I know you're weaker than you used to be."

Charles swallowed. "I had tried to hide it from you. But you could have waited to marry."

"I want an heir in place as quickly as I can." That meant taking Dru to bed again, something he didn't feel at all like doing at the moment. Her betrayal had cut deep. He didn't know if he could ever forgive her. "Tell me what Burnett saw again. I need to know."

Charles sighed. "Oh, dear. Very well. Burnett was on an errand for me." He touched the book at his elbow. "I had sent him to obtain a copy of this from the publisher. I could not wait to read it. He saw your wife and her sister enter the shop. They emerged twenty minutes later, and Dru was putting something in her pocket. A purse. They looked around them before sneaking down the alley by the side of the premises. I do not think they saw him." He shook his head, exasperated. "I believe your wife is an innocent. She had no idea of the trouble she would cause or that her identity would be revealed so shockingly. Can you not overlook her behavior? I'm positive she did not mean it maliciously."

"How can you say that when you are the main target of her insinuations?" Oliver paced again. He couldn't keep still. What could he do? What was there for him to do?

"You should not approach her when you're in this mood," Charles advised. "You will scare her into silence."

That was true enough.

His wife had gone to the publisher and pocketed the money. She did not need funds so badly, surely?

Oliver halted in his tracks, turning to face his brother.

"A gambling debt?" he said.

Eagerly he grasped at the straw. He would ask, try to find out if she played the tables. Ladies held salons where men rarely featured. They called them literary salons, but many were little more than clubs for gossip, tea, and gambling.

But to sell out a whole family to pay a debt? He followed his own reasoning. "People lose fortunes at the tables."

Charles pursed his lips, touching them with one long finger. "That could be so. Will you allow me to make a few enquiries? I think the questions are better coming from my people. You are too agitated to face her. She will not speak to you. Stay away for the next few days, dear brother. Let tempers cool."

If she was in debt, he could help her. Gambling amounted to a sickness in society these days. He'd seen men unable to stop, even when they'd lost everything they had. But after the way he'd made his feelings clear, she would not speak to him. She would not confide in him. Yes, much though he hated to admit it, Charles was right. "Very well. But do nothing without coming to me first."

Anger still rode him, but a touch of fear curled in his stomach. If he had married an inveterate gambler, he would have to force her to stop. He could never stop watching her.

* * * *

Two mornings later, Dru tapped on Charles's door. Reading her own book could not be worse than the cold shoulder she'd received from Oliver. She was close to begging him to talk to her. He spoke to her when he had to, but only to ask her to pass the butter or to remind her they had some social event to attend that evening. He never came to her at night. Dru didn't know a way to cope with this. After their close intimacy, how did anyone walk away from that? She might as well be an unwelcome guest for all the notice he took of her. This must be how discarded mistresses felt. Or couples who detested one another.

"Come!"

Obeying Charles's gentle command, she entered the room. His smile broke her, but she retained her calm demeanor and even managed to smile in return. The room was flooded with sunlight, and Charles wore spring green, the color of the grass in the garden. A bird sang outside the window. How could anything be wrong on a day like this? Except it was, of course. Everything was wrong.

She went to the table and picked up the book. It would hurt so much to read it. Punishment, perhaps. Taking her seat, she watched Burnett pour tea, part of their daily ritual.

"I wish you and Oliver would finish your stupid quarrel," Charles said, a touch of petulance coloring his soft voice.

"I wish it too," she answered, "but he is dreadfully hurt."

Charles shrugged in that one-shouldered way he had. "Angry, more like. He does that, you know. Always responds with anger. I swear, he needs to control that temper." He paused, glanced behind him, and motioned for Burnett to leave the room.

The door closed. Beneath the watercolor on the wall stood an odd object. A walking cane, its silver knob gleaming with polishing.

He followed her gaze. "Ah, yes. I keep it in case I might need it one day. I do not think I will."

The engraving on the top wasn't fresh. "It looks used."

"It belonged to my father." A reminiscent smile touched Charles's lips. "That is the main reason I keep it."

She could understand that. If her father—God forbid—died, she would want his spectacles as a keepsake, not the signet ring or something more valuable and less personal. "I see. Do you miss him?"

"Not particularly." He turned his attention back to her, his eyes chilly. "He always put the dukedom first and then his sons. He was a cold man."

She had heard different from his mother. Returning the day after the ball, her ladyship had wisely chosen not to comment directly on the breach between the newlyweds. Instead, she'd taken to reminiscing about her own marriage. "He was indulgent to a fault," she had said. "Always ready to listen to me and attend to my needs." Perhaps she'd said that to persuade Oliver to do the same. But he had not disagreed, instead clasping his mother's hand warmly, in a way that brought a lump to Dru's throat. Would she ever feel his touch again?

But a man in charge of an estate as wealthy and extensive as the Mountsorrel one might take his responsibilities seriously and try to make his sons do the same. However, the soft expression in Oliver's eyes was not only for his mother. Dru would have sworn he was sparing a thought for his father, too.

Forcing a bright smile, she picked up the book and found the leather marker she had set in it. "Shall we continue?"

"Yes, let's." They only had a few chapters to go before the end of the book. "I would dearly love to know what happens next."

Dru felt sick. "I no longer have the original manuscript, so I cannot read it to you until it is released."

"But you can tell me what happens. Or do you mean to make me wait?"

"Yes." Longer if she could, but Dru had run out of ideas. She could not face Wilkins again, and in any case, what good would it do?

"Poor Dru," Charles said so sympathetically she could not bear it any longer.

After whipping off her spectacles she fumbled in her pocket and found her handkerchief, pressing it to her eyes.

"Does this foolish fuss cause you so much distress?"

She nodded, unable to speak, fighting to regain control. Eventually she lifted her face to him. What she saw, the sympathy and kindness, nearly overset her all over again. He just didn't understand what it felt like to face the people so ready to condemn her. Seeing her happy ending turn to dust in her hands and to have nobody to blame but herself.

"Oliver will not speak to me about it. He is so angry. I don't think he will ever speak to me again in anything but a civil tone." She swallowed and blew her nose, not in the least gracefully.

"You caught many things truthfully. For instance, I have never been completely sure if the disaster that caused me to lose so much was an accident at all."

Shocked, Dru stared at him. "Someone would have been brought to justice."

"It depends on who plotted it and what control they had of the outcome." He met her gaze, his own bleak.

Their father? Why would he—

Dru's mind came to a complete stop. Oliver? He meant Oliver?

"That's madness."

Charles gave her one of his sympathetic smiles. "If it was, it was done on impulse. Oliver had always resented being the heir, you know, and teased me that I had all the benefits and none of the responsibilities. An edge of rivalry always existed between us. But I do not think it. Only, when I cannot sleep some nights, I am reminded of that moment just before. He turned to me…" He shook his head. "Forget what I said, Dru. A nightmare, no more. You see, you are not the only one with a vivid imagination!"

But Dru could not forget. That night, in her lonely bed, she recalled what Charles had said and went over his words. Could Oliver, in a moment of impulsive behavior, have caused the accident? Did he have it in him to do such a thing?

Her heart said no, but she had seen such behavior in him. He was impulsive. The way he'd stolen kisses from her, his sudden decision to propose marriage, and above all the swift marriage ceremony told of it. He could have done something—aimed for a fallen branch, pulled too hard on the reins—and caused much more than he'd planned. That would increase his guilt. That would explain why he flew off the handle so much, instead of choosing to discuss the matter frankly.

She could do nothing about what had happened in the past. But she could help herself in the future. If she could only prevent Wilkins from publishing that book! Would he have distributed it yet? No, it was too early. If he sent it out too soon, the booksellers could preempt the release. They had special customers they would oblige. He would not send them out until the end of the week, Friday or Saturday. Even Saturday night, to give the booksellers, who must close on the Sunday, even less opportunity to read the book and release the details ahead of the planned day.

Wilkins had taken out advertisements in all the newssheets, and they had posted bills all over town. Dru had seen them and longed to leap out of her carriage and tear them down.

"What did he say?"

Charles shook his head. "Nothing important. Only that he did not want the dukedom, and wouldn't it be fine if we could change places?" He trained his attention on her. "As I said, foolish. He has made an excellent duke. A little dour, but that is his privilege, is it not?" He smiled brightly.

Dru listened to him in horror. That didn't sound like Oliver at all. But how well did she really know him?

Did Charles know his comments pointed to Oliver perpetrating such an unthinkable act? As an accident, it was a tragedy. A deliberate incident would make it a crime. But Oliver wouldn't do that. Would he?

She wished she'd known him better before she married him. But she knew she loved him.

* * * *

Oliver sat in his study, tapping his pen against the paper before him. He had dedicated today to catching up with the business that had brought him to London in the first place. But he could not keep his mind on the job. He read everything before he signed it, however tedious he found it, but after perusing the same legal paragraph four times without understanding it any better, he gave up.

He leaned back, letting the worn leather enclose his body. The feeling had always soothed him. It failed now. Because of Dru. His wife, Drusilla, Duchess of Mountsorrel. She was his wife, and he had to find a way to cope with her, to give her what she needed.

After his initial fury had subsided, he received letters from people concerned about his wife's activities. People she had never heard of, but who had immense influence in society and the wider world of business and finance. They wanted reliable partners, and Oliver found himself crowded out of a few deals. None would make a great difference to his position and wealth, but they were indicators of what might come if he did not stop the rot.

He could divest himself of Dru. While divorce was out of the question, he could create a distance between them. Once they had produced the heir, they need not even live in the same house. But even thinking of that hurt him. Forgoing what he had so briefly found to return to the soulless world of bought women and kept mistresses hurt him in a place he thought he'd hardened—his heart.

In everything else he'd found Dru a delight, a charming companion and passionate lover. Standing with her had the inevitable risk. Some would call him henpecked. Others would judge that a man who could not control his wife or who considered such a flighty piece a suitable partner for him.

He heaved a sigh and tossed the pen on to the desk. He had become such a sadly predictable, serious person. The hint of devilry had gone, crushed by that carriage as surely as Charles's legs.

And he had other concerns, which he had shared with nobody. Those strange accidents that had forced him to bring the marriage forward because he was so worried about Dru. They still stood. Losing the wheel of the carriage and a stone in a horse's hoof—they had been done on purpose. The first could have meant to hurt either or both of them. The second was definitely aimed at Dru. To incapacitate her, to kill her...or to deter her from marrying him?

Oliver sat up, suddenly alert. He needed to talk to somebody. He checked his watch. Lord Strenshall would probably be at his club at this time of day. Oliver could catch him there. He might find Strenshall's oldest son, too. They needed to know of his suspicions. Then he would make his plans. The book would have to wait. The only person damaged by that was he, and he could take it.

Having made his decision, he strode into the hall and called for his coat, although he found it annoying to have to follow the dictates of society. The day was sunny, and he could easily walk to the club in his shirt-sleeves. Except they wouldn't let him enter in such a scandalous state of undress. At least his valet had the sense to bring a light coat, one of the fine wool ones with silk lining, together with his small sword. The coat's wine-red color seemed vaguely appropriate, considering where he was going.

He waved away the offer of a carriage, a hackney, or a sedan chair. He wasn't soft yet, and the walk would help him clear his head.

Through the West End, where the rich disported themselves and the poor darted among them, selling flowers at extortionate prices, snatching handkerchiefs, snuffboxes, and quizzing glasses. Not from him, though. He only had one of those items, and it was tucked into an inner pocket.

He barely stopped at the surprisingly small and cozy foyer of White's Club to scrawl his name in the book and toss his hat to the man behind the desk. Then, more reluctantly, he handed over his small sword.

The more imposing entrance held classical columns and a statue, together with a huge painting on the landing of the founders of the club and their distinguished members. Her father was in there somewhere. Probably lurking at the back.

He found his quarry in the main member's room. Father and his son Marcus, Lord Malton, sat at a small table, a decanter of burgundy between them, desultorily tossing a die. Discarded newssheets lay on a table next to them. The marquess had a paper in his hand, and as Oliver approached, he tossed it on to the discarded pile.

Oliver strode across the polished parquet floor, barely acknowledging the stares and murmurs as he passed. He caught the word "Tirolly" more than once.

He snapped a bow. "May I speak with you?"

Lord Malton hooked a foot in the rails of a nearby chair and dragged it over. "Do take a seat," he said civilly, raising a finger to get the attention of the waiter. "Do we need a private room?"

Oliver accepted the invitation and took the seat. "Perhaps we do. But the club isn't full, and if we keep our voices down, nobody will hear us."

"So you're not here to call us out?"

Oliver shook his head. "I need to know your family secrets. Who is trying to hurt Dru?"

Ten minutes later, in the private room the marquess had bespoken, Oliver outlined what had happened so far. "I believe the two incidents involving the carriage and the horse are connected. But the book?"

The marquess's mouth flattened. "Drusilla has scribbled and written stories, poems, and journals for years. None of them reached publication because she took care that they would not. I cannot believe she would risk it this time."

Marcus nodded. He leaned forward, his elbows firmly planted on the table between them. Oliver saw a man who faced his problems head-on, his blue eyes direct and uncompromising.

"Do you know how the book reached the publisher?"

Oliver shook his head. "Not exactly." Facing this man, he knew why not. He had backed off. Forbore from asking his wife in case she gave him the answer he was afraid of. That she had taken the book and sold it to Wilkins.

"She always kept her writing carefully locked up." Marcus lifted the decanter. The cut glass glittered in the beam of sunshine striking across the room as he poured two glasses of brandy.

Oliver retained his glass of burgundy.

"I am certain she never meant it to see the light of day," Marcus continued.

Oliver picked up his drink and took a reflective sip. The blinding revelation struck him as hard as a slap across the face. His concerns for his brother, insisting on tackling every problem on his own—what good had that done him? He needed help here. "So what's to be done?" he said.

"More to the point," the marquess said, "What are *we* going to do?"

Marcus sighed and leaned back, swallowing the contents of his glass in one gulp. "I foresee a long night ahead. Perhaps we should order dinner. And send for Darius and Andrew. Their particular expertise will be useful."

Chapter 15

Burnett appeared in Dru's room shortly after she'd finished the meager repast that was all she could manage. She pushed the plate away and glanced at Forde.

The maid stared at the intruder, but not with her usual air of superiority. Dru had never seen that expression on Forde's face before, but for all that, she knew it. Adoration. She'd seen it in her own eyes when she caught sight of herself in her dressing-table mirror after her husband had made love to her.

Forde was sweet on Burnett. Interesting.

Burnett bowed. "If you please, your grace, my master requests a moment of your time."

Nodding dismissal to Forde, Dru followed the man to Charles's room. Whatever could he want at this hour? Charles usually retired early. He'd never contacted her after nine at night, not even with a note. Halfway up the stairs, she turned around, a thought striking her hard. "Is he ill?"

"No more than usual, ma'am."

On scanning his face, she saw no perturbation. Burnett did not have the calm demeanor most servants cultivated. He cared deeply for his master, more than for Forde, she guessed. She would speak to her maid about her connection with the man in the morning. While she had no objection to servants enjoying their private time, she did prefer to know what went on in her own house.

She had given up all expectation of receiving her husband tonight. Or any night in the near future, come to that. Her silk robe swished against the stairs as she ascended, the hush in the house almost complete. Except for the city sounds outside, nothing stirred.

Charles's sitting room was empty, lit only by a couple of candles set in the wall sconces. They glimmered against the mirrors behind them, flickering as they reached the stubs. Burnett spoke, still keeping his voice low. "I have helped his lordship into bed, ma'am, after a small attack."

"A fit?" Alarm raised her voice. She clapped her hand to her mouth. The last thing Charles needed was her screaming all over the place.

"A minor one only, but it tired him. However, we have received news we thought you ought to know."

Dru raised her brows, surprised at the "we." "Bad news?" Was Charles more ill than she assumed?

"No, ma'am. Exceedingly good news, but since it concerns you, we thought you should know." He went ahead, pushing open the double doors leading to the bedroom and bowing her in.

Charles was lying in bed, propped up with a bank of pillows. Dru had only been in here once before, when Charles had his fit, and at that time she had taken little notice of her surroundings.

Charles lived in luxury. Although Dru occupied the ducal apartments, these rooms rivaled hers in sumptuousness. Perhaps more so. The room was ablaze with light, every double sconce occupied, each candelabrum filled and in use. The bed hangings had rich crimson braid on the edge of their cream purity. She recognized Chinese lacquer screens and a *pietra dura* cabinet with images of birds and flowers depicted in semiprecious stones. The room smelled of roses and smoke, the thin spiral from a Meissen figure on the mantelpiece showing her where the heady scent originated. A new Aubusson carpet cushioned her slippered feet as she crossed to where Charles was smiling at her. He did not wear his customary wig but a heavily embroidered silk cap, which matched the moss-green robe fastened around his body.

He appeared surprisingly strong. The formal clothes he habitually wore had their own padding and stiffening. Dru had assumed he got much of his shape from that and admired the tailoring, but he filled out the soft robe well. True, he didn't have Oliver's bulk and sheer power, but his limber athleticism surprised her. He must practice some kind of exercise. His father's walking stick leaned against the nightstand. Burnett had to move it to put a chair in place for Drusilla.

"Do I find you well?" Her anxiety was all for him.

"Indeed, as much as ever." His soft but firm voice came as a relief. She detected no trace of weakness there. "But I have received news this last hour. Good news, Dru. I have discovered where they are holding the copies of your book."

"You have?" Elation filled her. "Can we have them destroyed?"

Charles spread his hands. "We can apply to the courts, but today is Friday and they do not sit on Saturday or, of course, Sunday. Your book comes out on Monday. But the bookseller has yet to distribute them. This is the last night they will be in one place. Tomorrow the carters will arrive, and they will be all over the country."

Dru swallowed her bile. Her stomach churned. This time the response would be worse. How could she face people ever again?

She should start packing now. If she could rely on Oliver's support, they could perhaps fight through it, but he showed no sign of that. She clenched her fist, the cool silk of her robe crumpling in her hand.

Charles leaned forward, a gleam in his bright eyes. "I have thought of another way. If we act now, we can prevail."

"How did you find out?"

Charles tapped the side of his nose. "I have agencies of my own. Ably assisted by Burnett here."

She had almost forgotten the presence of the manservant. But she had to listen. Charles was doing his best to help her. "So where are they?"

"In a warehouse at the docks. Presumably Wilkins did not want to keep them close to his shop and offices. People would be watching him there. But at the docks, vehicles are unloading, loading, moving, all day. Another load would not be unusual."

"You're sure?"

Charles nodded. "Positive. We must move quickly, Dru, and quietly. We cannot afford to let these books into the public arena. Are you brave? Ready to act decisively?"

Dru nodded. "Anything." She did not exaggerate. She would do anything to regain Oliver's regard. Anything at all.

* * * *

An hour later, as dusk fell over the city, Dru and Burnett slipped out of the back gate of the house. Horses snorted and harrumphed in their mews, but the alley between the blocks was thankfully deserted. Dru had changed into the clothes Burnett had acquired for her from one of the many pawn shops dotted around the city. The coarse rust-colored petticoat and faded bottle-green caraco jacket transformed Dru into the kind of shabby but respectable woman nobody looked at twice. She'd bound her head in a plain linen cap, only a strip of her hair showing at the front. She topped it with a faded straw hat with a floppy brim. All the better to hide behind. Burnett was similarly plainly attired. Burnett went first and cleared his throat if anyone lurked in any of the rooms. Dru slid past a housemaid busy cleaning out the grate in a downstairs room, feeling like a thief. In a way, she was. Or worse. But she could see no other course. Charles had provided the wherewithal and the information.

They walked to the end of the square and caught a hackney. The leather upholstery was rotting, and it stank of mold, humanity, and piss. The boarded floor had holes in it, and there was, of course, no glass in the windows. Fortunately, the night was clement, with no rain.

The hackney dropped them at Charing Cross, and then they caught another. They didn't want anyone—Oliver—tracking them.

When they told the driver where they wanted to go, he gave them a good, hard stare. "You her pimp?" he demanded.

Burnett answered while Dru was still gaping. "No. We're going to meet her husband, if you must know."

"Humph. It'll cost you."

Dru gave the man sixpence on account and let him see the purse Charles had prepared. It held one gold coin, a little silver, and more coppers. She was a woman of substance, but not wealth. He'd thought of everything.

Inside, the hackney was a little better than the previous one in appearance. But it smelled of piss and fish. Dru had good reason to be glad of the unglazed windows. Night was falling now, and by the time they reached their destination, had fallen completely.

Dru stepped out of the carriage and drew a deep breath of air. She couldn't call it fresh, tainted as it was with fish, tar, and damp, but at least she could breathe more freely again. If she could have held her breath in that carriage, she would have kept it held all the way there.

A forest of masts bristled before them, their swaying uneven wobble adding a nightmare-like quality to the sky. She stood and stared. She'd never come this far along the river before, not even in the family pleasure barge. They generally used that on fete days and holidays or took ferries across the river. Here, where the Thames widened into the Pool of London, before sweeping into the sea, the tang of salt tinged the air and struck cold on her cheeks.

Someone bumped into her and swore, the language so inventive she didn't understand most of it.

Burnett pulled her aside. "We're going over here."

Strange not to hear her title, but they had agreed on that. If he spoke to her, Burnett would call her "Mrs. Smith" or "Jane." She was to call him "John."

Men and horses trundled carts, rolled barrels, carried impossible weights on their shoulders. Some had large hooks suspended from their belts to haul the cargo off the ships. Nobody paid them any notice. Dodging all the obstacles, including the large capstans that were set along the water's edge, Burnett took her to a row of warehouses. They appeared rickety, the wood partially rotten, but the owners had patched them with fresh wood and tarred it. More substantial warehouses stood farther off, brick built to reduce the risk of fire. Ever since the Great Fire, buildings in London could not be of wood, but where there was a law, there was a way of getting around it. A man walked by with a flaming torch. Lights glimmered from the ships, where watchmen passed the night, guarding the vessels. Other watchmen sat huddled in huts or waiting inside the warehouses. Dru and Burnett were headed for one of these.

Before they'd left, Dru made Burnett swear he would not cause permanent hurt to anyone. He agreed, but Charles had scowled. "You need the courage to face this," he warned her. "If you cannot, Burnett will go alone."

"No." She wanted to see the conclusion of this nightmare for herself, ensure the book would go no further. Her creation, the story she'd labored on for years, would be no more after tonight, and she could not be anything but glad. She wouldn't deny that fear clutched her stomach—the thought of being caught, hurt, failing in her mission terrified her—but she went forward.

At the edge of a pier, Burnett touched her. "Here," he said softly, and turned her to face him. His craggy features appeared even more weathered in the dim light. "Are you sure you want to do this? Do you truly wish to take this risk?"

She bit her lip. "I have to." She had thought and thought, and there was no other way. "You don't know what's in that book. It could finish me, and my husband, and…Charles. We can't allow it. Time is too short to do anything else. Nobody but us knows where the…things are stored."

The seemingly rickety warehouse was set back from others nearby. She was glad of that.

Burnett skillfully boxed the watch. Dru had heard of the practice, usually done as a joke by reckless young men with more hair than wit, but she had never seen it happen. A tiny light glimmered from the tall sentry box, where a watchman sat, guarding the property. Burnett came up from one side, and before the person inside could respond, had the box turned and rammed against the wall behind him. The man inside yelled and banged at the sides, but it held. Spotting a barrel nearby, she tipped it on to its side and rolled it over to where Burnett held the box secure and the man trapped. In the second when he moved aside, she pushed it into place, and with Burnett's help, tipped it on to its base. Something sloshed inside.

"He'll be fine there," Burnett assured her.

"He's too close to the warehouse. When we go, we'll push the barrel aside. He should be able to get out."

With a resigned sigh, the manservant nodded. "Very well. Let's get this job done."

Slipping a hand into her pocket, Dru gripped the handle of her pistol. She had two, one in each pocket. They were loaded, and yes, she'd assured Charles, she knew how to use them. Not that she was planning to do much more than shoot over the head of anyone trying to stop her, to give her the time she'd need to get away.

"Stay here. I'll make sure there's nobody to stop us."

Dru nodded. While Burnett was gone, she took a few deep breaths and tried to concentrate on the task ahead.

But she was glad they were there. These were ordinary weapons, not fancy dueling pistols, but they would do the job just as well, given the opportunity.

Burnett took ten minutes getting them inside. He returned from where he'd left her twiddling her thumbs, growing increasingly afraid and nervous. "This way."

"Did you find anyone?"

Burnett shook his head.

Inside, the smell of paper mingled with the acrid aroma of ink. That alone would have told Dru she was in the presence of books, usually her favorite items in the world, but not tonight. Forcing herself into the present, she gazed around the cramped space.

Crate after crate piled up, leaving only a small area to walk between. So many, Dru didn't know where to start counting them. And this was only the first edition. More printings could happen, but Charles had explained that once they got rid of the immediate threat, they would take legal action to prevent any more printings. But they had to get rid of these before they were distributed in the morning.

Crowbars leaned against the wall. Dru hefted one and dragged it to the nearest crate. Glancing at Burnett, she shoved the toothed end under the rim of the nearest wooden box, and with the man's help, levered off the top.

She stood back, as Burnett pulled out the first book. She opened it, finding the title page and the author, "A Lady," printed beneath. She touched it, ran her fingers over the words, mentally saying goodbye to this part of her life. Now the point had arrived, she felt sorry that her work should end this way. Foolish nonsense. But still, she turned the pages, skimmed the dedication, and found chapter one.

When she saw her own words in print, they looked different, as if somebody else had written them. She'd started this book right after the carriage accident, when the Prince was tussling with his injured brother. The characters belonged to her, even if she'd obtained the inspiration elsewhere.

"Jane?"

At first Dru didn't respond, but then shook her head and closed the book. She would keep that one. Charles had made her promise to retain one copy, so he could discover what happened next. She could do no other, after all he had done for her. She slipped the volume into her pocket, beside the pistol.

"Yes?"

"You get the materials ready. I will keep watch." He put a small cloth parcel before her. She knew what it contained. Dry frayed linen and the most important item—a tinder box. She had one too, but she wouldn't use it unless she had to.

Dru went about her task methodically, ensuring plenty of tinder was set by the crates. They should catch fire on their own after the conflagration had taken hold. Those books not destroyed by fire would suffer from smoke damage or water when the fire company finally arrived. Did the docks have its own insurance company stationed nearby? That would make sense, although not everything that made sense actually happened in this world.

At the end of the warehouse farthest from the door, she struck the flint against the iron, letting the spark fall on to the crumpled scrap of linen.

A door opened, voices sounded, and the rough ground beneath her shook with the impact of heavy feet. Terror rose to her throat.

Shouts came from the far end of the warehouse. Her tinder had taken, but if she hid here, she'd be trapped in fire. What to do?

Dru had no choice. She stepped forward, praying she could escape from this predicament.

The first voice she could distinguish was Burnett's. "There she is! I told you I saw somebody! Take her quick. Fire! Fire!"

Rough hands seized her, dragging her forward, and a lit torch was pushed perilously close to her face.

"Arson, is it?" someone growled at her. A sickening gob of spittle landed on her cheek, but she was pinned tight. "You know what we do to arsonists 'ere in the docks? We 'ang 'em."

Chapter 16

Oliver arrived home in the early hours of the morning, weary but satisfied with his efforts. By tomorrow, he would have the situation well in hand, and then he could turn his mind to saving his marriage and his wife. After sharing his suspicions with her father and brother, his mind had eased considerably. He could think clearly again, the fog of anger and confusion that had obfuscated his mind clearing fast. But he had spent time contacting and on occasion rousing from sleep the people he needed to set his plans in action.

He was too late to wake her now. She'd probably been asleep for hours. His brother would be in bed, too.

Although he was buzzing with triumph, he forced himself to get ready and go to bed. Tomorrow would probably prove tiring as well as exhilarating. Perhaps, he thought before he fell asleep, he'd talk to Dru about her moving back up here. She must be lonely in that big bed downstairs. He was certainly lonely here.

Something stirring in his room woke him from what had turned out a deep slumber. He rolled over, blearily opening his eyes. Dawn filtered in through a crack in the curtains. Was it his valet, making preparations for the day ahead? Robinson knew better than that. The servants were under strict instructions not to enter Oliver's room until he woke.

Irritably, he reached for the watch on his nightstand. "Who's there?"

"Me."

Oliver stilled. The last person he expected. "Charles? How did you get in here?"

With a rattle, his brother dragged the curtain back from one half of the window. Light flooded into the room, cold and gray. Charles leaning heavily on their father's cane, the sentimental memento he liked to keep by his side. Now Oliver knew why.

Confusion filled him, and then cautious delight. "Charles? You can walk?" Jerked into full wakefulness, Oliver pushed himself up. He stared at Charles. He hadn't realized how tall his brother had grown. The last time he'd seen him upright was before the accident, when he'd been sixteen.

"This is marvelous!" Questions bubbled up in his delighted mind. "Are you tired? Do you need to sit?"

"No." Charles gazed at Oliver, his gaze cold.

"How long have you been walking?"

"For a while." Charles watched him closely, emotionlessly. He looked as if he had shed a skin and left it behind. His smiles, his affability, his constant patience were nowhere in evidence. "Only Burnett knows. I told him I wanted to make sure I could do it properly before I revealed myself." Then he did smile, and Oliver wished he had not, because he'd never seen a chillier expression. "So consider this the time."

"Good God, man, this is wonderful! You've been practicing?"

"Of course, but I wanted to be able to walk without this thing." He wobbled the cane. "Unfortunately, I have had to bring my plans forward. Why did you marry that woman, Oliver?"

"Drusilla?" Oliver frowned. "I need to make an heir. You can't take on the burden of the dukedom."

Charles gave a crack of laughter. The small sound broke the air, but the atmosphere immediately closed around them again, like a blanket hiding secrets. "Can't I? You've made a tedious, plodding job of it. Now it's my turn to take over."

"What?" Thoroughly confused, Oliver flung back the covers, preparing to stand and find his robe. The day was chillier than he'd expected. Charles wore only a thin nightshirt, similar to his own. Had the exercise made him hot?

A sickening click stilled his movements. Charles lifted his hand, a pistol gleaming dully in the growing light. His movement betrayed another weapon tucked into the waistband of his breeches. "Don't move. You loved Drusilla, didn't you? And such problems she gave you, too. I had to stop you sharing her bed. When I discovered the existence of the book, she provided me with the perfect excuse." He stifled a yawn, his jaw tensing with the effort.

He was mad. He had to be. The long years of solitude had disturbed his mind. Oliver had to be very careful. He needed to secure that weapon, one of the dueling pistols that customarily sat in his dressing room. Those pistols had hair triggers.

Wait— Oliver never left them loaded. Could he risk crossing the room? If he was wrong, he would die. Charles couldn't possibly miss at this range.

"You know what I wanted?" Charles said, as if engaging in everyday conversation. His voice remained smooth and melodic. Sunlight illuminated the left side of his body, as if he were an angel. Charles still appeared perfect, at least from the front. From the side, as Oliver knew only too well, his skull was misshapen, flat and pitted. That was the reason Charles always wore a wig or an elaborate cap. Except for today.

Oliver kept his attention on the gun. "No, tell me."

"I wanted you to die without marrying. The succession would be nice and clean, then, and I could take my place as the duke. You took too many decisions without me. But no more." This time he bared his teeth in a ghastly grin. "You're going to kill yourself because of Dru's death. So sad, they will all say."

Dru's death? "Charles, what have you done?" Terror filled him, not for himself but for his wife, the woman he loved so very much. Charles was mad. Completely insane. What he said made sense, if a person did not know the truth. Even if someone knew, what he said made twisted logic. "Nobody will believe you."

He needed to get to Dru, to discover what Charles had done.

"Of course they will. I've thought it all through. Burnett should be back soon."

As if answering a cue, a shuffle came from the door. Oliver turned his head to see Burnett, similarly equipped with a pistol, the twin of the one Charles held.

Dear God. "What have you done with Drusilla?" Terror clutched at his stomach, twisting it into a knot. He forced himself into calmness, as much as he could manage. He had to think clearly.

"Burnett took her out to the docks. He should have disposed of her by now."

"Did you take care of the duchess?" Charles demanded.

"Yes, my lord."

"She's dead?"

Oliver flinched. If he got out of this, he'd kill them both. No question about that.

"No, my lord. She's taken care of."

Charles raised the pitch of his voice slightly. Enough to make Oliver take notice. "What do you mean? She's not dead?"

So there was a chance. Oliver kept a knife in the drawer in his nightstand. Mainly to trim wicks, open letters, and such, but if he could get to it, he might stand a chance. Unfortunately, with two guns trained on him, he would have much less opportunity of escaping with his life. One, and he might have taken what fate offered. If Burnett had not said Dru was not dead, he'd have been far more reckless. He watched and waited for the first opportunity to take Charles off guard. He was standing closer and was a better target. If he hurled himself at Charles's legs, he could take him down.

Could he do it? Yes, yes he could, if it meant saving Dru. Himself, he cared less about.

He prepared to spring, curling his feet back, preparing to go up on his knees, the better to propel himself off the bed. He could get there with one firm shove on the mattress, or near enough to reach his brother.

"Now, now," Burnett said, as if talking to a child. His tone was soothing, conciliatory. "Put the weapon down, my lord."

"Call me your grace," Charles said. He glanced at the manservant, frowning. "You're pointing the gun in the wrong direction."

"No, sir, no, I'm not. Put it down, please." He sounded patient, quiet. "We can get you back to your room and nobody the wiser. The maids'll be up soon."

"You knew he could walk?" Oliver said.

"Yes, sir, but he ordered me not to tell. I didn't know he was planning this. I swear. I followed his plans, but in the end I couldn't do it." Sorrow infused his voice. "I can't kill another human being. I did what I could to stop it from happening."

Oliver stared at Charles, who glared at his servant. It was like looking at a stranger. He didn't know this man at all.

Burnett motioned with his weapon. "Drop the gun, my lord."

Charles ignored him. "When I kill my brother, what will you do, Burnett?"

"I'll have to tell them. I'm sorry, my lord, but you can't go around killing people and get away with it."

Oliver breathed out very slowly, watching Charles carefully, waiting for his opportunity. Relief filled him. A witness would surely make Charles think twice.

"You do not want to be responsible for a person's death, my lord," Burnett said in the same level tone.

Charles's voice turned smooth. "You think not?" Moving his arm to one side, he fired. The explosion, coming so suddenly in the quiet room, deafened Oliver.

The thump meant Charles had reached his mark. Burnett was either dead or injured. But he had no time to turn and check. This was his chance, the only one he would get. He propelled himself off the bed, lunging head first to his target. He met hard flesh as he brought his brother down.

Charles's roar of anger echoed around the room, but Oliver ignored it, going for the pistol Charles had just drawn from his belt. Oliver put his knee on Charles's thigh and pressed, pinning him to the floor. A punch to the side of his head made Oliver grit his teeth and hold on, but his grip on Charles's arm weakened, and his brother wrenched himself free.

Ignoring his brother's shout, Oliver reached out, gripped Charles's shoulder and slid his hand down to the pistol.

The sound of thundering feet came from the hallway and into the room. Charles lifted his head and pushed up, sending Oliver off-balance.

Oliver sat, risking a shot, and swung his fist. He caught Charles under the chin, snapping his brother's head back and to one side.

Charles remained still, unconscious or dead.

Oliver grabbed the pistol from Charles's slack grip and sprang to his feet. He met his valet's clear gaze from where the man kneeled on the floor next to Burnett. Robinson shook his head. He didn't have to say any more. A footman stood by Oliver, staring down at Charles.

"Take my brother back to his room," Oliver said, his voice remarkably steady. "Guard him. He is dangerous, so secure him if you need to. Search him for anything he can use as a weapon, and do not allow him to leave his bed. He can walk."

The footman swore, a sign of his extreme agitation. "Sorry, so sorry, your grace."

Oliver waved his apology away. "I'm glad you came, Whatmough. Get him tucked into bed before he comes around, if you can. Secure his wrists loosely to the bedposts, and don't allow him anything, not even a drink of water." His mouth flattened. "However sweetly he begs for it."

They would have to call in the authorities. Oliver had no intention of tucking this event away, not allowing it to be made public. This matter must be dealt with properly, or Charles would use that, too. His eyes were wide open now. He should not have allowed his brother to interfere in his marriage. But he had loved Charles and felt deeply guilty about the accident. That guilt had crippled him as much as it had Charles, but in a different way.

What had Burnett said? He'd "taken care" of Dru, but she wasn't dead. Wasn't dead? What the hell did he mean by that?

The thought propelled him out of the room, now filling with servants, perturbed and confused. He raced downstairs and flung open the door to Dru's room.

The bed was empty.

Only one person would know where his wife was, now Burnett was dead. Charles would not be unconscious for long, Oliver determined.

Charles's rooms contained four servants, three of them who had never entered the suite before. "Where is he?" Oliver demanded. Someone held out his robe, and he shrugged into it, belatedly aware he still only wore his nightshirt. He strode into Charles's room. "Is he awake?"

One of Charles's other assistants, Atkinson, got to his feet as Oliver entered the room. "He is unconscious but resting peacefully, your grace."

"Wake him."

The man blinked at Oliver's insistent tone.

"He killed Burnett and would have killed me, had I not stopped him. Did nobody tell you?"

Atkinson shook his head. Charles had never seen the man bareheaded before. Without hat or wig, the man appeared completely different, a bruiser rather than a footman. His bald head gleamed in the light of two branches of candles. "They brought him here and said he was not to leave this room, sir. Is Mr. Burnett really dead?"

"I fear he is." Oliver crossed to the bed and gazed at his brother dispassionately. "All his displays of affection, all his pretenses, and I never noticed they were all meaningless. My brother has no soul, Atkinson."

"Yes, sir." Atkinson did not sound surprised.

"You knew?"

"I suspected, sir. When the family were not present, he did not care for anyone. He showed no emotion."

"Hmm." He used emotion to fool them. The accident had obviously removed more from Charles than the use of his legs.

He gave Charles an openhanded slap across his face. Not hard, although he longed to batter him into oblivion. Bitterness filled his heart, blending with regret that he had nearly thrown everything away.

Charles's eyes snapped open. He could have been awake all along. Not that Oliver cared.

"Where's my wife?"

Charles smiled. "Wouldn't you like to know?"

Oliver slapped him again, a little harder. "You will tell me."

The blow jerked Charles's head to one side, but other than that, he behaved as if Oliver had not touched him. "I should have been duke. You know that. I know it, too. It is my turn. My dukedom."

"You'd ruin it."

Charles shrugged. He was lying flat on his back, only his head supported by the pillows. He lifted his hand, signaling his servant. Oliver snapped his fingers at Atkinson, refusing to let him close.

"It is mine by right of succession. Then you married that slut. I managed to separate you, but not until the damage was done. Unless she's had her courses?" He raised his brows, expecting an answer.

Oliver didn't know. Nor did he care. He wanted Dru back, needed her. Nothing else would do. Nobody else would serve. "Did you interfere with the carriage and her horse?"

A sneer curled Charles's lips. "Burnett did. He was sweet on the maid, did you know? She stole the manuscript for him, and he brought it to me."

"Even that? You did even that?"

"It worked, didn't it? You hated her when that thing went into print. If we couldn't hurt her before she got to your bed, we'd do it after. Except he betrayed me. I thought better of Burnett."

He refused to say any more. His brother had planned to kill Dru to stop her bearing an heir to the dukedom. To him.

What had he done? "Where is she? What have you done with my wife?"

Chapter 17

Dru slumped to sit on the noxious narrow ledge in the Common Room in Newgate Gaol. She buried her head in her hands, the tears falling freely. She had not slept a wink all night. They'd brought her here and tossed her into the room, the jailer telling her she was lucky. "Wait until the judge puts on the black cap," he'd said. "Then you'll know what you're in for." He pinched her backside so hard she could feel a bruise forming there when she sat.

She'd invented a name. "Jane Robinson," she'd told a man wielding a quill over a big book.

"Arson," the constable had added. "In the docks. Caught in the act."

The jailer had peered at her over the rim of his spectacles. "Death," he'd said. "Fire at the docks. Mr. Fielding will love you." He looked past her. "Nobody else?"

The constable had shaken his head. "Another one with her, but he ran. We'll get him."

Dru kept her head down. The least she could do was to keep her name out of it. The constable and the men who'd handled her roughly on the way here had insisted she would hang. She had no doubt of it. Tried on Monday, hanged on Thursday, someone had said.

Would they ever discover what had happened to her? She'd even failed in her effort to destroy the books. They'd extinguished the fire, not a copy lost. Burnett had gone. Maybe he'd send somebody, but she doubted it. And in any case, how would they know her? She'd covered her tracks effectively. Who would think that Jane Robinson, wearing shabby clothes with barely a guinea to her name, was the Duchess of Mountsorrel?

They'd offered her food, which they wanted her to pay for, but she shook her head. She wouldn't starve in four days. It would only feel that way. She'd have to buy water, though. Or maybe she could die of thirst.

Anyway, she would die. Her book would be published, and the author would disappear, while a woman of no consequence called Jane Robinson would hang at Tyburn.

She shivered.

Nobody bothered her. The noise surprised her, but she ignored it. Men and women copulated in corners. They played with makeshift dice on the floor in the middle of the room, a space cleared of the noxious straw and filth to make a playing ground. Dawn had seeped through the high windows, but all night people had talked and sang and played dice. And fornicated. She huddled down, making as small a bundle of her body as she could, curling inside her shabby clothes. She lifted her knees and lowered her forehead to them. Despair coursed through her body.

Maybe if she pretended to be asleep they wouldn't bother her.

She should have known better, should have thought harder. Burnett had raised the alert, had told them she was responsible for the fire. He'd disappeared before they could question him. Perhaps he'd turn up for the trial on Monday. She doubted it. Enough men had seen her, tinderbox in hand, setting the rags alight. They would bear witness to her evil deed, and Dru did not intend to defend her act. What would be the point? More than that, what would she say? Short of giving her true identity, she could do nothing, and even if they knew who she was, that wouldn't help. She'd tried to set fire to a warehouse at the docks. She would not deny it.

Charles had known. She was sure of it now. He'd betrayed her. He was no more her friend than Burnett or anyone else.

What was the point?

A new sound reached her ears. Someone had opened the door, the jingle of keys indicating a jailer. Steps crossed the stone-flagged filth-strewn floor to where she stood. Dru lifted her head.

"This is the woman," the man said.

She blinked, struck dumb by the sight before her. Her husband was here? She opened her mouth and then closed it. She couldn't reveal herself.

"So it is," Oliver said calmly, his mouth a firm line. "Bring her."

The jailer grabbed her arm and hauled her to her feet. She stumbled but regained her footing.

"Not like that!" Oliver frowned at the man. "Treat her with respect."

The jailer spat at her feet. "She was caught in the act."

Oliver clinked coins, and gold changed hands. "She was trying to light a lamp. She is my employee, set to guard the warehouse."

"A printer rented that warehouse," the jailer said. "She has to go to court on Monday."

More gold changed hands, clinking as the jailer shoved it in his pocket. "She has done nothing. I am here to collect her."

"Proof?" the jailer asked.

"I've given the papers to the man outside. He has the details."

Around her, the prisoners had gone silent. Someone on the other side of the room yelled, "We're all innocent! Got enough for everybody, mister?"

Raucous laughter ensued. Oliver took no notice, but curved his arm around her waist. "Come with me...Jane." Laughter colored his tones.

How could he show amusement in this hellhole? Dru didn't know what to speak, what to feel. Confusion invaded her sleep-addled, stressed mind. "I did it," she said.

Oliver touched her lips with one cool finger. "Enough. We'll talk later."

For once, Dru subsided. When Oliver tried to lead her toward the door, she stumbled, her feet numb from sitting. With an exclamation rarely heard in the fashionable drawing rooms, Oliver swung her into his arms and strode out of the jail. Dru curled her arm around his neck, clinging on like a monkey. He'd come. How he'd discovered her, what had happened to alert him, she had no idea, but she could be nothing but glad.

She buried her face in his waistcoat as they hit the bright morning light. He climbed into a carriage, the vehicle rocking as he sat and arranged her across his lap. The carriage set off.

"How did you know I was there?" she mumbled into the soft woolen cloth.

"Charles told me." He sounded grim. He had every right to be, after what she'd done.

"He told you everything?"

Oliver grunted. "How he meant Burnett to murder you, how he wanted to kill me and make it look like suicide because he wanted to be duke? Yes. I'd have been sooner but I went to the docks first and then heard the story and found out where they'd taken you."

Shock gripped her hard as she lifted her head. Nausea roiled in her gut. "What?"

He gazed at her, his expression soft as he cupped her cheek. "He'd planned it all along."

The carriage jolted as it turned a corner, and he held her tighter. Or maybe he'd planned to do that anyway. "To k-kill us?"

"To kill you because you might be carrying my child. Burnett was to murder you in that warehouse. He didn't care whether the books burned or not. Just that you did. The reason for your presence there would be obvious. Burnett was to say he tried to deter you, that the fire was your idea. Dear God, Dru, I nearly lost you!" He fastened his lips to her, kissing her with no mercy.

Not that she wanted any. She tightened her grip on his neck, holding him close. This was all that mattered.

He pulled away, staring at her, drinking her in. "I will never forgive him for what he did."

"Burnett meant to kill me?" Disbelief swept through her at first, swiftly followed by acceptance. Yes, she had left herself open to attack. But Burnett?

"Burnett called the authorities, and they arrested you. At least Charles couldn't get to you if you were under lock and key. But he paid for his crime. Burnett is dead."

"What?"

The activities of early morning London went on outside as if nothing had happened. Nothing this portentous, anyway. Someone yelled "Chairs to mend!" as they rolled past, and another cry of "Vi'lets! Fresh vi'lets!" female and raucous, floated into the carriage through the open windows. The day was fine, sun already pouring its light down on the crowded streets.

And Lord Charles Fitzhugh had killed his faithful servant? "Why?"

"Because Burnett failed to carry out his orders. My brother is a murderer."

"Where is he now?"

"In his room, under guard. Dru, we're going to have to make this public."

They had reached the house. It looked as it always did, shiny black door that opened as Oliver stepped down from the carriage, still holding her. He carried her into the house, offering no explanation, shooting out a barrage of instructions, ending with,

"We will be in our room for the rest of the day. See that we are only disturbed if absolutely necessary."

Forde stood in the hall, wringing her hands.

"Not you," Oliver said. "You are not to attend the duchess."

Dru blinked up at him. "Not my maid?"

"She won't be your maid for much longer. She had an affair with Burnett. That's how they got hold of the manuscript. She says she only wanted to show him, but he wouldn't give it back." He strode up the stairs, taking them two at a time, and then the next flight, and straight through the double doors into her room.

The chamber looked different. Male garments were scattered around, as if someone had been putting them away. A hip bath stood before the fire, the water it contained steaming gently. As they entered, Forde's assistant came in, carrying a pile of soft towels.

"You may go," Oliver said. "I'll help the duchess myself."

The woman put the towels down and left the room without demur.

At last, Oliver gently lowered her to her feet. "Public?" she said, continuing the conversation.

"If we do not, Charles will find a way to use it against us. He will not come near you again. Why didn't you tell me he was making you read the book?"

"I…I don't know." She did, but she didn't want to say. Charles had asked her not to tell, but more than that, at the time Oliver was barely speaking to her.

His mouth twisted in a wry smile. "I do. I don't want that situation ever to happen again." He began to unfasten her jacket, pulling it off her and tossing it toward the door. "I love you, Dru. I should have told you before, I suppose…"

"What?" Her head spun.

"I love you," he repeated slowly. He stilled his hands at her waist, gazing down at her. "It took this event to bring me to my senses, but I've loved you all along. Since I saw you at that ball and left you on the dance floor. I couldn't cope with the way I was feeling."

"That was why I did that awful thing. Why I wrote you as the villain. But when you came back and took me driving, I changed the book. I did, Oliver."

"I deserved it." Tenderly, he released her and continued to undress her, letting the horrid, stained, stinking skirt fall to the floor.

She stepped out of it and he kicked it away. Unfastening her pockets from their string around her waist, he explored the contents. First the book she'd taken from the warehouse.

He kept that in his hand, staring at it. "The last copy," he said slowly. "We had better take care of it."

Right that moment the clock on the mantelpiece crashed out the hour. Before it could get to the chimes, without looking away from Dru, Oliver hurled the book at the clock.

The crash, a mixture of breaking glass, the sharp snap as a cherub broke off its base and the clang of bells and chimes deafened her.

"I never liked that clock," he said, satisfaction warming his eyes. "Good riddance to it. Why did your mother give it to you?"

"Because she hated it, but it's an expensive piece, so she didn't want to throw it away."

"Why did she keep it?"

"It had the loudest chime in the world, so it told visitors when it was time to go." Discussing the clock brought her back to earth. She was here, at home and she was safe.

"So she wished it on you." He grinned. "Well, it serves her right. I will buy you a delicate little French piece that barely tinkles the hour." His expression turned grave. "What I did at that ball was unforgivable, but I'm begging you to forgive me anyway."

She did that easily and told him so. "After all, if you had not, you might have danced with me once and forgotten me."

He gripped her hands tightly. "Never. Never in a million years, Dru." He recommended undressing her, removing her petticoat. "You said something about my brother, as I recall. At the time I was respecting his wishes and keeping any information about him secret. He wanted to surprise the public, jump out and announce he was the new duke, astound them with his brilliance." He heaved a deep sigh. "He fooled me as much as anyone else. There's something wrong with him, Dru."

"There must be." She had thought Charles strange, but not that strange. "He killed someone devoted to him. He was prepared to kill you."

"He feels nothing for anyone except himself. It's as if we don't exist once we leave his room." A frown furrowed his brow. "I don't understand completely, but I'm sure of that."

"We only exist for his amusement?"

"Something of that nature. Like actors on a stage." Quickly, he completed undressing her and lifted her into the bath. She sank gratefully into the hot water, as he fetched a water can from the door and poured it gently over her, rinsing off the dirt of Newgate. "You gave a false name."

"I didn't want to drag your name into it." She swallowed.

"It's our name, Dru, not just mine. Never do that again." He touched his lips to hers. "Sit up and I'll wash your hair."

"It must be filthy. That place is unspeakable."

"So are the people imprisoned there. Some of them, at any rate." He poured water over her hair. "You have lovely golden glints in this."

The scene would be mundane, beautifully so, if not for the events of the last few days. And he'd said he loved her. But he was washing her like a maid would, impersonally, though with care. However he did it, every touch made her want him more. Did he intend to tuck her into bed and leave her?

She couldn't bear that.

He stroked her shoulder, rinsing off suds. His hand trembled. "When I think of you alone in that place, I want to kill somebody. Myself, perhaps."

"No!" Water splashed as she turned around to face him. "Never say that! I thought I would hang, and you wouldn't know what happened to me. But that was better than disgracing you even more."

"You don't disgrace me at all. Not a bit."

"But the book…"

"What happened after put the book into perspective. But it won't come out. Not unless you want it to."

"How can you say that? There's a warehouse full of books at the docks."

"I bought the publisher," he said calmly.

She stared at him in silence, her heart hammering against her ribs. "How? I went there, and I paid him, but he took the money and published anyway." She wouldn't mention her pearls. They were her punishment for being so foolish.

"He is free to start another company, if he wishes, but not the one that published your book."

He got to his feet and found a towel, holding it out for her. She stepped into it, savoring the delicious sensation of having his arms fold around her. It appeared he felt the same.

"Mmm, that feels good. I need to get you dry before I go back on my good intentions. You need to rest."

She moved closer, nestling against him. "Not yet. I need you."

She had never said anything so bold before, but it felt good, especially when he smiled. "I was hoping you'd say that."

This time his kiss started gently, a press of his lips against hers. However, when she opened her mouth to him, he plunged inside and raised her temperature several degrees. She made a small sound at the back of her throat and received his answering groan. He spread his hands over her back, smoothing her skin as if petting a cat. She would have purred if she weren't busy tasting him.

When he broke away, they were both panting, their breaths heavy. The corner of his kiss-reddened lips curved in a knowing smile, and his gray eyes darkened with passion. "You are so lovely." He caught her damp hair in one hand, twisting the heavy fall and then using it to jerk her close. He gazed at her, looking his fill until he slid away.

The towel fell, and she was naked. This time his scrutiny was anything but impersonal. He scanned her from the top of her head to her toes and back again, lingering at her groin and then her breasts. "Mine," he murmured.

"Yes. Yours." As he was hers. Every moment that passed bound them more securely together, invisible but strong threads of belonging passing between them.

Oliver undressed. Not nearly as careful as he had been with her filthy garments, he stripped quickly, dropping his coat on the floor, soon joined by his waistcoat. He undid the fall of his breeches, and then the silver buckles at the knees, before kicking off his shoes and stripping the whole of his lower body in one decisive movement. His shirt followed, tugged over his head, shamelessly revealing his powerful hair-sprinkled chest and his arousal, proudly jutting out below.

Her mouth watered. Before she could outthink herself, she dropped to her knees and took him in her mouth. He groaned as she licked around the shiny cap, claiming it for her own, and then ventured deeper, sucking it in as far as she could. His low cry of "Have mercy!" merely drove her to increase her efforts.

He tasted like nothing else, all male, slightly salty, the soft flesh of his erection covering a muscle harder than any she had ever touched before. She wanted more. Everything. Between her legs, the tops of her thighs were red, her sex tingling, so she wanted to rub her legs together. But she could not. She had to endure the sensation without being able to do anything. She tortured herself deliciously.

She wanted this like she needed her next breath. If she didn't get it, she would die. The affirmation of life and every good thing.

Oliver cried out as he jerked inside her mouth. Seizing her under her arms, he hauled her up and fastened his lips to hers. "Witch!" he murmured when he pulled his mouth away. Cupping her breasts, he stroked his thumbs over her nipples, hardening them even more. "You are so responsive."

She laughed. "So are you."

"Bed," he said firmly, suiting actions to words, swinging her up and tossing her on to the mattress. He paused for a bare second before he joined her, and then he was on her, his erection pushing insistently between her legs.

"Cock," she said, liking the way the word sounded.

He rose above her, resting on his elbows. "So it is. Where did you learn that word?"

"I read a lot."

"Ha!" His sharply barked laugh had her joining him, her breasts quivering against his chest. "Then you'll have to show me what you know. But now, I need you. You have a talented mouth, my love. Carry on using it. Everything I am is yours. Everything I have is for you."

A little wild, but she loved the sentiment.

He didn't need to hold his erection to bring it to her. Dru knew what to do now. Lifting her knees, she opened her legs wide and found him, arching her back to let him in.

They found each other. He slid inside, no resistance now. "You're so wet," he moaned, reaching down to touch her, exploring and stimulating. "You feel so good, my love."

My love. She adored that. "Will you always call me your love?"

"Always," he promised. "But you have to say it as well." He slid right inside, his body deep in hers, contacting that magic spot she hadn't been aware of before their wedding night.

For the first time in her life, Dru felt complete. "I love you, Oliver. I'm yours."

He threaded his fingers between hers, linking their left hands before pressing it down on the pillow. "And I'm yours. Always, Dru."

Then he began to move.

His first stroke sent prickles up her spine, so she sucked in a breath and arched up, her head going back. With every stroke, he drove her up and up, climbing to their ultimate peak. He used his body to please her. Every time she opened her eyes he was watching her, marking her movements. She felt cherished and wanted. Excitement climbed to an impossible level. She clawed at his back with her right hand, clutching him, crying out, before closing her mouth with a snap.

"No, sweetheart. I want to hear your cries."

"But someone will hear!" Her instinctive response, used to holding herself back, was to silence any sounds, her reply instinctive.

"Who cares? The sounds of our loving are for us. For me. Do it for me, my love."

Her laugh turned into shouts of ecstasy as he brought her up and over. Her inner channel contracted hard. She would have pulled away had he not held her firmly and continued to work her, increasing his thrusts to pounding, pushing through any resistance to prolong her joy, keep her at that level.

How could he do that? Her sharp cries changed to whimpers, and then she called his name, "Oliver!" as it happened again.

Dru lost her breath but held on to her husband and kept her eyes open. She badly wanted to see him lose himself in her.

He did, letting go with a spectacular yell, the sound echoing around the large room. He throbbed inside her, giving her everything.

"I'm yours. Forever," she promised, as he fell into her arms.

* * * *

When Oliver opened his eyes, darkness had fallen outside. The bedroom looked out over the garden, but lights in the distance showed where other people were up and about. Moonlight poured into the room, adding silver-gilt highlights to his wife's hair.

As if sensing his wakefulness, she blinked awake and smiled up at him. He cupped the back of her head, meeting her eyes.

"I don't deserve you. I will spend the rest of my life proving that to you. You will always come first in my life, even before our children, if we are fortunate enough to have any."

"Isn't that why we married? You wanted an heir, you said." She traced a line down his chest with one finger. She would do her best to give him one.

He made a growling sound deep in his throat. "It doesn't matter now. I have cousins, competent men who could carry the title down. If we have children, I will consider myself blessed, though I hardly dare expect it."

"What about Charles?" She caught her lip between her teeth, as if afraid she had said too much.

He kissed her. "Say anything to me, my love. Anything. Charles will no longer feature in the succession. The only way he can avoid a trial and hanging is to admit he is insane. I believe he is. That will exclude him from the succession." He sighed when he thought of his brother, so talented. So evil. "So he has a choice. Either way, his transgression will become public. Everyone will know he killed his manservant. If the court allows, I'll send him to a house I own in Cumberland, well away from any others. He'll have people to look after him, but he will never leave the estate. This time I'll employ people who understand his kind."

"He doesn't seem ill." She frowned.

"But he is." Oliver knew that now, could think back clearly. "He was planning this for years." He had just asked her to tell him everything; she deserved the truth from him, too. "I have never told anyone this before. On the day of the accident, he was driving. I blamed myself. After all, I am older than he is, and I should have known better. Charles was never a good driver, but he made himself a worse one that day."

She gasped. "Are you saying he deliberately caused the accident?"

Oliver nodded, meeting her appalled gaze. "He admitted it when I questioned him. He wanted to kill me even then."

When he stopped, she put her hand flat on his chest. "I took the blame, because I felt guilty. I should not have allowed him to drive. Looking back, he used me frequently by invoking that emotion. He specialized in it. He played on my guilt for years and then created more reasons for me to feel badly for him."

"Why did he refuse to allow anyone to see him?"

He knew that, too. "Because then he controlled the story. You write stories, Dru. You must understand that."

When she flushed and her eyes brightened, he kissed her softly. "Hush, love. If you want to write, if it amuses you, we will publish. After all, I own a publishing company now. Your father and brother helped me locate the publisher and his legal counsel, so I got the job done quickly and cleanly."

"No!" she said, revulsion in her voice and her tight mouth. "I won't ever do it again. Although," she went on, her voice getting softer, "I did think of rewriting the third part of the story and making the Prince of Tirolly the hero after all." She clapped her hand over her mouth, her eyes rounding.

He caught her hand in his, sucking each finger in turn into his mouth, tickling them with his tongue. "If it amuses you, my love, I will become the husband of the greatest novelist in history. You must do it. I insist."

Their laughter mingled, a portent of their joined future. They would never be apart again.

Meet the Author

Lynne Connolly was born in Leicester, England, and lived in her family's cobbler's shop with her parents and sister. She loves all periods of history, but her favorites are the Tudor and Georgian eras. She loves doing research and creating a credible story with people who lived in past ages. In addition to her Emperors of London series and The Shaws series, she writes several historical, contemporary and paranormal romance series. Visit her on the web at lynneconnolly.com, read her blog at lynneconnolly.blogspot.co.uk, find her on Facebook, and follow her on Twitter @lynneconnolly.

Fearless

See where The Shaws began . . .

Scandal is his chosen path—until this infamous Shaw surrenders to love . . .

When Lady Charlotte Engles receives an offer of marriage from an eligible suitor, she's finally ready to let go of her long-held hope that her engagement to Lord Valentinian Shaw will result in marriage. For despite the betrothal their families made between them, Val shows no interest in leaving his reckless life behind in favor of one with Charlotte. But when her plea to end their arrangement ends in a heated embrace, suddenly Val seems reluctant to let her go . . .

The last thing Val wants is a wife, despite how desirous his lovely bride-to-be has become. But when he discovers sweet Charlotte is planning to marry a dastardly man, he feels duty bound to keep her safe, even if that means making good on his marriage pledge. Then Charlotte is taken hostage by her dangerous suitor and suddenly Val is ready to risk everything for the woman who has won his heart . . .

Chapter 1

Charlotte spared her betrothed a glance but took care not to linger. People might notice her looking. Val was talking animatedly to a group of friends, standing at the rear of the garden. As if he felt her regard, he turned his attention to her and returned her look, the corner of his mouth tilting so slightly she wasn't sure she'd seen it.

Then he returned his attention to his friends.

Of course he did, because that was what he always did. Indeed, why should he not? They might be affianced, but their attachment was not a romantic one. At least, it was not supposed to be.

Lord Valentinian Shaw and Lady Charlotte Engles had entered into an arranged marriage, brokered by their parents. What was so unusual about that?

Only the secret Charlotte held closely to her heart. Fortunately she had practiced at hiding her emotions, so only she knew the truth.

Charlotte gave the lady chatting to her a broad smile, not at all sure what she was talking about. Lady Duckworth had the proud reputation of boring for England, as Val had said once, but she meant well. Fortunately, all she required was an audience. Responses were optional.

She shuffled her toe in the gravel but kept the smile in place, listening to Lady Duckworth's conversation long enough to agree with her proposition that all satirical poets should be forced to debate their absurd propositions. Then she returned to her private thoughts.

She should be grateful for the brilliant match her father had contrived. People kept telling her, therefore it must be true. When Val had asked her to marry him, he'd done it formally, with a kiss on the back of her hand when she duly accepted. The betrothal was perfectly conventional. Nobody had asked for Charlotte's opinion. If they had, she might have begged for him. She had fallen deeply in love with her betrothed.

Her guilty secret accompanied her everywhere. She had agreed to the proposal as a way of getting away from her home, a way her father had agreed upon, but once she'd met Val, her opinions had changed. She wanted Lord Valentinian Shaw so badly, she'd even become his respectable companion while he roistered and scandalized society. She had continued with the arrangement as a way of providing a new home for herself and her sister, but after an inordinately long betrothal, she was forced to think again. She had to get away from her father's house and provide a place for herself and her younger sister.

A masculine voice broke into her thoughts. "Lady Charlotte."

She tilted her head, which would have meant she was staring directly into the sun, but someone was shielding her from it. The sun blazed on either side of him, leaving the man in darkness, as if he were a visitor from the heavens.

After bowing over Lady Duckworth's hand, the man begged her to grant him the favor of allowing him a few moments of her company.

Charming, elegant and smooth, Lord Kellett had shown her flattering attention of late, but Charlotte found him less daunting, more approachable than her future husband. He listened to her conversation, he sought her company at balls, and if she had not been spoken for, she would have given him even more attention. However, he had never stepped over the rules of propriety. He behaved to her like a friend, as he was doing now.

Having seen Lady Duckworth to another group of people she could bore, Lord Kellett offered his arm. Charlotte took it with a smile.

"You should smile more often," he said. "It suits you." He led her on a gentle stroll across the width of the terrace and then down the stairs at the end. The stone staircase led to the main part of the garden.

Rosebushes massed in pleasing abundance, trained well away from the paths. The fragrance surrounded them, perhaps a little too sweet for Charlotte's taste, but the effect was heavenly. "Whoever the gardener is, he deserves a medal for pruning the bushes so carefully."

"Hmm?"

Lord Kellett didn't sound interested, but Charlotte plowed on. "Sometimes negotiating a rose garden is more like fighting through a thicket."

He frowned, but gave her no response.

Charlotte sighed. "Never mind."

"You have a droll sense of humor, my lady," he said then, and laughed.

She hadn't meant her comment humorously. The gardener really had considered the width of ladies' hoops and taken the full skirts of a gentleman's coat into consideration too. The thorns did not discommode her wide skirts at all.

"Thank you." She consoled herself with the knowledge that he meant well.

They moved along the path that led to the next part of the garden, still well in view of the house. Her aunt, who acted as her chaperone, was somewhere indoors, so Charlotte had relative freedom. One would have thought that at her age her father would have allowed her more discretion, but they did not. Not many people had a father like hers, though. They should thank heaven every day for that.

Charlotte could relax and allow his lordship to take her for a little perambulation around the lovely gardens attached to this equally gracious London house.

The house belonged to her betrothed's family, and if she married him, she would live here, or Val might even lease an establishment of their own. The Shaws were a large family, sprawling, noisy and somewhat uncontrolled—all things her father detested. But he had agreed to the betrothal, because few people ever denied the Shaws anything.

Frankly, the family of the Marquess of Strenshall, and the extended family known in society as the Emperors of London, unnerved Charlotte, but she could hide behind her proper mask and smile and nod. She was perfectly aware that people thought she was dull, but she had little choice. So she smiled and nodded, just like always as Lord Kellett asked her about her favorite pieces of music, and the uncomfortably warm spring weather.

Charlotte was tempted to tip her head back and hold her face up to the sun. However, that would dislodge her hat and draw attention to her. She refrained, as she always did, from succumbing to temptation.

"I find the Italian operas somewhat too dramatic for my taste," she confessed.

"Indeed, ma'am? I must introduce you to the great Sodrendo. His tone is divine."

"A good countertenor is a marvelous thing." Not that Sodrendo was a great countertenor. He sounded as if he was imitating the pure tone of the greats. The passion for the high-toned male voice had led to much mutilation of young boys and a few men who had remained intact but could sing in the higher range. For Sodrendo's sake, Charlotte prayed he hadn't sacrificed his manhood for an inferior voice. However, she wouldn't dream of saying that out loud.

"Indeed, sir. I will ask Lord Valentinian to escort me and my chaperone one night."

"Now that," he said softly, "is what I would particularly like to talk to you about."

With a swift left turn, he rounded a hedge and kept going, taking her to a small building at the end of the path. Nobody could see them if they entered. Greatly daring, Charlotte allowed Lord Kellett to take her between the twisted columns into the cool space within.

He escorted her to one of the hard wooden benches lining the white-painted walls, and she sat, her smile fixed in place. He sat next to her, as close as he could get, gazing at her.

He glanced down and then back up at her face. A small crease marked his smooth forehead. "Lady Charlotte, I find you charming and a delightful companion."

If she didn't know better, she'd think he was making a declaration. However, he could not intend that. "Thank you, sir. I confess, it is delightfully cool in here. How clever of you to find it." She laid her fan on the seat next to her and folded her hands in her lap. "The garden is beautiful from this aspect."

He barely spared the vista a glance. "I prefer the view from where I am sitting."

"Sir—" She got no further.

"Madam, my lady…Charlotte. I have done my best to quell my feelings for you. But I can bear no more."

He paused, seemingly at a loss for words, catching his bottom lip between his teeth. Although his words made her uncomfortable, Charlotte stayed to listen. "Lord Kellett…" She laid a gentle hand over his, which proved a mistake, because he captured it in both of his.

"Hervey, please call me Hervey, at least in private."

She should not, but she'd do it to pacify him. "Hervey, then. You are aware I am betrothed?"

"Yes, and I am also aware that I am transgressing, not only with you, but with the hospitality of Lord Strenshall and his family."

She nodded. Being in their house, he most certainly was.

"I cannot hold my emotions back any longer. Lady Charlotte, why do you allow Lord Valentinian to treat you so?"

Now it was her turn to frown. What on earth did he mean? "He treats me with respect."

"I would not say so!" He spoke with such passion that she moved back. However, he did not let go of her hands. "He treats you with a great deal of carelessness. He is happy merely to have you in his sights, although he makes no move to further his connection with you."

"We like one another well enough, but we prefer not to live in one another's pocket." Wistfulness infused her. She would like to know what that felt like, to have a man devoted to her, one who could not wait to marry her. Val had enjoyed a number of mistresses. She had no idea if he had one now. The thought did not sit well with her, but she would have to endure many such once they married.

Her mother had tolerated many before her death, but her father kept his women carefully closeted. There was never any scandal. He never used a society lady and he paid off his mistresses with enough of an annuity to keep their mouths shut. Charlotte only knew because she'd heard her brother talking about it with a friend. "My father has to pay for his pleasures because of his proclivities," George had said with a sigh. George sent abroad for that transgression, to tour Europe with his tutor. Not that it proved any punishment, because he was soon setting Versailles on its ear.

"You have been betrothed for an age," Hervey gently pointed out.

As if she needed reminding.

"Two years," she said, setting her jaw. In all that time Val had treated her more like one of his sisters than his betrothed, and he had never broached the subject of setting a date for their wedding.

"Will Lord Valentinian not come to the mark? Because if he will not, there are plenty of people who will."

Was he speaking to her as a friend? He was caressing her palm with his thumb, which she found distracting. She wasn't at all sure she liked it. His gesture made her want to scratch her hand. "I haven't noticed a preponderance of men flocking to my door."

"You only need one. May I be frank, Charlotte?"

She allowed the use of her first name. Intrigued, she nodded.

"My dear, I have become very fond of you. More than fond, if truth be told."

"We have only been acquainted for three months."

"I only needed an hour." His fervent voice echoed around the hushed space, bouncing off the roof and back to her. "I have tried to remain silent, but I can do so no longer. I adore you, Charlotte, and I would love nothing more than to offer you my hand and protection in marriage."

Shocked, she stared at him. Was he truly saying this? She'd had no idea he felt so strongly toward her. His blue eyes were wide and his mouth partially open, even though he had stopped speaking, revealing the gleam of sharp, white teeth. "I can say nothing, you know that." What else could she say? The experience of having a man wildly in love with her had never come her way before, and she floundered, not knowing how to respond.

She found his fervency somewhat alarming, but all the same it fascinated her. "How can you possibly know you want me?" She bit her lip, wetting the suddenly dry, delicate skin.

"I know, dearest Charlotte. Believe me, I know. Is there any way our love can be fulfilled, or are we doomed to watch each other from afar?" He lifted her hand to his lips and kissed it, letting his tongue dip between her knuckles with a flicker she wasn't sure of until she saw the flash of pink that went with his gesture. He had tasted her.

Charlotte knew her duty. "We cannot, sir. I have always been obedient, never gone against what my father wished..." Indeed, how could she? Unlike her sister, who she had not seen in over a year, the sister she was forbidden to talk about. A tinge of sorrow touched her when she recalled Sarah, her laughing face and the daring ways that had eventually led to her downfall.

"You are a good and obedient daughter," he said in an approving tone. "I have spoken to your father, told him how irresistible I find you."

Charlotte quailed. "Did he not forbid you?"

"Not precisely. He reminded me of your contract to Lord Shaw, but he gave me permission to speak to you. However, he said the choice must be yours. You must speak to him yourself."

Her father was actually amenable to this change?

"Will you not ask your father on our behalf? Surely he does not wish to see his daughter dwindle into an old maid while her betrothed gads about with not a care to his responsibilities?"

Should he be talking about Val like that in front of her? But he had cause. However, honor demanded that she remind him of the proprieties.

A bee buzzed by her nose, circling her, probably after the roses in her hat. It was doomed to disappointment, since they were made of silk. "Sir, Lord Valentinian and I are considering our wedding date." They weren't, but it didn't hurt to say so.

With his free hand, he made a grand dismissive gesture worthy of an actor. "Pah! Lord Valentinian is deferring his wedding for all he is worth. If I thought there was true feeling between you, that you were devoted to each other, I would never dare speak, but that is not the case, is it, dearest Charlotte? I can make you happy. I swear I can. I will devote my life to you and consider it well lost!"

His fervency spoke volumes. Had he really lost his heart to her? Did she dare to believe that she, dowdy, quiet Charlotte, had engendered passion in a man?

More importantly, his estate assured Charlotte that he was no fortune hunter. The fervency of his declaration and the suddenness with which he made it could have made her suspicious. Society took her for granted, gave proper due to her status as the daughter of a duke, but nobody took much notice of her.

Or did he want a wife with status? Lord Kellett was a peer in his own right and possessed of considerable wealth. So no, he would not need her standing in society or her fortune, which, for a duke's daughter, was relatively modest.

He had brought her here for a private conversation, but he could easily have chosen this place to compromise her and force her decision. If she'd thought he'd have any degree of success, she would never have accompanied him to this secluded spot.

Charlotte was no naive society miss with feathers for brains. Moreover, if he sought to compromise her, this was not the house for it. The Shaws had their own scandals, most of which society forgave, because the Emperors were society's darlings. She stared at Hervey, a million different thoughts sparking in her head.

Had he really lost his heart to her? That would make a refreshing change. She'd waited a year to see if Val would see her as more than a convenient excuse. When they had become betrothed he'd been frank, asking her to allow him some freedom before pressing him for a wedding date. He'd proceeded to use her as a useful way of dissuading the more importunate matchmakers who clustered around the Shaw family every season.

Charlotte had allowed it. In the back of her mind, she'd waited for him to fall in love with her, or at least show her some affection, but he still treated her with the same careless but polite indifference he used with everyone else he knew.

Hervey was handsome and passionate. She was sure she could come to love him in time. He would be hers, devoted to her. Moreover, she did not feel the same despairing love for him. She liked him well enough, in a way that could, she imagined, easily turn to love as time passed.

Yes, she would do it, on one condition. "Would you offer my sister a home?"

He gave her a quizzical look but nodded after a moment. "I would be honored to do so, should she be in need of one."

That was the answer she needed. Resolution took her. She could not continue as she was, with her sister and herself under their father's thumb and with no prospect of actual marriage to Val. She had to move on with her life. If possible, she would take this man.

Ever since he had appeared in London at the start of the season, Hervey had paid her particular attention, so his regard, while premature, was not totally unexpected.

He clasped her hands, tightening his hold. "Please, my dearest one, give me an answer. If not now, tell me when you will be free. If you tell me to leave, I will never mention this again!"

"You had better not," a voice drawled from the doorway.

www.ingramcontent.com/pod-product-compliance
Lightning Source LLC
Chambersburg PA
CBHW031421250626
47155CB00004B/1570